Thomas Nast, David Ross Locke

Ekkoes from Kentucky

bein a perfect record uv the ups, downs, and experiences uv the dimocrisy ez seen

by a naturalized Kentuckian

Thomas Nast, David Ross Locke

Ekkoes from Kentucky
bein a perfect record uv the ups, downs, and experiences uv the dimocrisy ez seen by a naturalized Kentuckian

ISBN/EAN: 9783337382469

Printed in Europe, USA, Canada, Australia, Japan

Cover: Foto ©Andreas Hilbeck / pixelio.de

More available books at **www.hansebooks.com**

EKKOES FROM KENTUCKY

BY

PETROLEUM V. NASBY [PSEUD]

P. M. AT CONFEDRIT X ROADS (WICH IS IN THE STATE UV KEN-
TUCKY), AND PERFESSER UV BIBLIKLE POLITY IN THE
SOUTHERN MILITARY AND CLASSIKLE INSTITOOT.

BEIN

A PERFECT RECORD UV THE UPS, DOWNS, AND EX-
PERIENCES UV THE DIMOCRISY EZ SEEN BY
A NATURALIZED KENTUCKIAN.

Illustrated by Thomas Nast.

BOSTON
LEE AND SHEPARD PUBLISHERS
10 MILK STREET NEXT OLD SOUTH MEETING-HOUSE
1888

Entered, according to Act of Congress, in the year 1867, by

LEE AND SHEPARD,

In the Clerk's Office of the District Court of the District of Massachusetts.

DEDICASHUN.

Ez no one who is worldly-wise worships the settin sun,
but alluz the risin orb,

THIS BOOK is NOT dedikated to Androo Johnson,
whose sands uv life is neerly run out,
And who cannot remove me from my Post Offis, owin to
the restrainin power uv the Tenur uv Offis act,

BUT RUTHER TO

GEO. E. PENDLETON,
of Ohio;

GENERAL GEO. B. McCLELLAN,
When last heerd uv, in Dresden, Germany;

HORASHO SEYMORE,
uv Noo York; or

FRANKLIN PEERSE,
uv Noo Hampsheer:

One uv wich is certin of succeedin the individjooel fust
named upon this page, and uv hevin, therefore,
the disposin uv patronage, in case
we succeed in 1868,

THESE PAGES ARE INSCRIBED,

With sentimence uv profound respeck,

BY THE AUTHOR.

P. O.
Stamp.

P. O. CONFEDERIT X ROADS
(wich is in the Stait uv Kentucky),
Dec. 1, 1867.

CONTENTS.

PREFIS,

OR

INTERDUCTRY CHAPTER.

SKOLARS, and men wich wuzn't skolars, hev deprekated the manufakter uv so many books. Whether they were justified or not in their strikters, it doesn't become me to say. Probably they wood say to me, ef I should consult em (wich I shel not), "Don't publish this book ; there's reely no okkashun for it !" There isn't? Did the capchus adviser see the state uv my pants? Did he observe the wreckt condishun of my boots? Is he aware that I am in arrears for board? Not publish my book ! Kin I so far forget my dooty to humanity? Nary. Its publikashen will at least do ONE suffrin man good, and that's more than half uv the writers kin say. What recks it that that one is ME? Wat posterity will say I don't know; neither do I care. I ain't labrin for posterity; neither did my father, else I hed bin better off. Posterity may assign me a niche in the temple uv massive intellex, or may not; it's all one to the subscriber. I woodn't give a ten-cent postal currency for wat the next generashen will do for me. It's this generashen I'm goin for. So much for Buckinham!

When I last communed with my readers, Democrisy wuz about the most bustid institooshen in this country. Dimocrisy hed undertook to carry the President, and it broke down under the load. Then the President undertook to carry the Dimocrisy, and he broke down under that load. Both were sootable to be carried, but neither hed the strength to carry the tother. And so, doorin the winter, spring, and summer they lay, both at the bottom uv the ditch uv despondency, lookin helplessly at each other, but neither able to help his fellow-suffrer. They wood hev embraced, but they hedn't strength enuff to roll together.

The Fall elections revived us. The Ablishnists uv Maine didn't vote, wich give our people in Californy strength; the carryin uv that State discouraged em in Ohio and Pennsylvany, wich, follered up, give us the overwhelmin triumph in Noo York. That give us life; that infused vigger into us. It operatid like a invigorator — a stiff wun — does onto the bowels uv a Kentuckian whose flask is out, and who hezn't bin neer a bar-room for thirty-six hours. It wuz strengthenin.

These confliks may be considered the skirmishin percedin the main battle. We hev druv in their outposts; shel we be ez successful when we storm their works? Upon the anser to that conundrum depends much. Ef we do, then shel the Post Offis wich I now hold be mine four years longer; then shel I still enjoy the conjenial society uv them wich long assosiashen with hez made deer; then for four years will my sustenance be ashoored. That will do me. I probably wont eggsist longer. Within that time my venerable biler, now weakened in spots, will hev bustid, and I shel hev gone to join Elder Gavitt, wherever he may be.

We kin conker, however, and we must. We hev the Ablishnists onto the hip. They endorst the nigger in 1863 and 4, and the people stood it becoz they needed him. It didn't become the city, wich hed filled its quota with nigger troops, to go back on the Ethiopian. Neither did it look well for the Ablishnist, who praised em for ther devoshun at Petersburg, etcetra, to deny that they wuz a man and a brother. BUT NOW THE NIGGER AIN'T NEEDED. Grim war hez smoothed his wrinkled front, and we are ca-prin gayly in my lady's chamber to the lasciv-ious soundins uv the loot. Now, the servis the nigger rendered us fades out uv our remem-brance, wich it does faster than his color did in strikly Democratic States under the old arrange-ment. They don't want him any more; and, glory! he's the same d—d nigger he alluz wuz. So duz the wholesome prejudis agin color swal-low up gratitood! So does the pride uv race smother wat the thin-skind uv the Radikels call justis!

It is onto this string we must harp. The Democrisy hev alluz conkered when they went

calmly on — secoor in the beleef that all mankind wuz either ninnies or raskels. They ain't
fur out uv the way. The nigger is now onfit
for citizenship — let it be our dooty to see that
he continues onfit. Shood he rise to an intel-
lektooal level with us, we are out uv an argument agin. The law agin schoolin uv em
must be enforced; the laws regulatin their labor must be made ez stringent ez ever; for ef
they are allowed to go unregulated, the Ablishnists will say to-wunst that sich ain't nessary.
We must keep a worritin, and pokin, and
punchin this lion, that his roarin may show the
necessity uv our bein kep in power to restrain
him.

I bleeve in commencin early. Let outrages
by niggers be commenst to-wunst. Let niggers be found dead uv starvashen ez soon ez
possible. Let the shuddrin uv Democratic
damsels over the horrors uv bein forst to con-
tract matermonyel alliances with niggers be got
up immejitly, and let ther shudders be strong.
Let the heresy uv the Noo York World, that
niggers don't stink, be refooted by a body uv

Dimekratic ethnologists, who shel assert that they do, and make oath to it; and, in short, let all the old machinery, wich served us so well in days gone by, be set in moshen agin, and all will be well with us.

Then shel we conker. Then shel we regain that wich we lost in 1860, and in the haven uv success, feedin fat onto the manna uv public patronage, enjoy for a time the felicity of livin under Dimekratic laws, made by Dimekrats, and executed by Dimekrats.

So mote it be.

PETROLEUM V. NASBY

(Wich is Postmaster).

P. O., CONFEDERIT X ROADS
(wich is in the State uv Kentucky).

EKKOES FROM KENTUCKY.

***

L

The Amnesty Proposition. — The Inhabitants of the Cross Roads made the Victims of a Cruel and Heartless Hoax.

CONFEDRIT X ROADS
(wich is in the Stait uv Kentucky).
December 3, 1866.

I NEVER wuz so elevated, nor never so cast down, in my life, ez last nite, and the entire Corners wuz ditto. The circumstances uv the case wuz ez follows : Me and a party uv friends wuz a playin draw poker with a Noo York commershel travler, I believe they call em, a feller with a mustash and side whiskers, wich comes South a talkin secesh and a sellin goods. He made some inquiries about the standin uv the deelers at the Corners, and wuz, arter sed inquiries, eggstreemly anxious to sell em goods, for cash. They wanted em on ninety

(13)

days' time, and on this they split. He agreed with em in principle — he drank to Jeff Davis, and damned Linkin flooently — but on the cash question he wuz inflexible and unmovable. To while away the rosy hours, a knot of choice sperits, him inclooded, gathered in the Post Orifis, to enjoy a game uv draw poker. There wuz me and Square Gavitt, and Deekin Pogram, and Elder Slathers, and the Noo York drummer. We played till past the witchin hour of 12 M., when graveyards yawn and gosts troop forth — when the Noo Yorker suckumd. His innocent, unseasoned bowels hedn't bin eddicated up to the standard uv Kentucky whiskey, wich, new ez we drink it, is pizen to foreigners. The Deekin and Elder grabbed the stakes wich wuz onto the table, and rifled his pockets on the suspishen that he wuz a Ablishinist, and rolled him out, and while in the very act, Pollock, the Illinoy storekeeper, cum rushin in, askin us ef we'd heerd the news.

We ansered yoonanimusly that we hedn't.

" I'm jist in from Looisville," sed he ; " I jist rode over from the stashen. Looisville is in a blaze uv glory ! "

" Wat," sez I, " hez Sumner killed Thad Stevens and immejitly committed sooicide ? "

" Nary," sez he, " but Johnson and Congress hev come together on the basis uv yooniversal Amnesty, wich wuz proclaimed yesterday, to be follered by yooniversal suffrage ez soon ez the South kin conveniently do it. They hev met and embraced on Horris Greely's plan."

Deekin Pogram bust into a hysterical laff, and in his joy handed me the proceeds uv his explorashen uv the pockets uv the Noo Yorker, and like a blessed old lunatic broke for the meetin-house. In a moment or two the bell pealed forth its joyous notes, and in a minit more the half-dressed villagers wuz seen emergin from their respective domiciles in all stiles uv attire. A few minits sufficed to make them understand wat wuz the occasion uv the uproar, and a more enthoosiastic population never woke the ekkoes. Afore five minutes hed rolled off into eternity, ther wuz a bonfire blazin on the North side uv the square, the sed bonfire bein a nigger skoolhouse wich the Freedmen's Commishn hed erected, and wich our enthoosiastic citizens hed in their delirium uv joy set fire to. It was emblematic. The smoke ez it rolled to the South methawt assoomed the shape uv a olive branch — the cry uv the nigger children wich coolent escape, symbolized their desertid condishn, and the smell uv em ez they roasted wuz like unto incense, grateful to our nostrils.

A informal meetin wuz to wunst organized by the lite of the burnin skool-house, to wich Deekin Pogram addressed hisself. He remarked that this wuz a solemn occasion, so solemn indeed that he felt inadekate to express the feelins wich filled him. His mouth wuzn't big enough to give vent to his sole, though ef he didn't he'd bust. "Wat are we met for to-nite, my friends?" sed he; "wat calls us together? Wherefore these sounds uv joy — wherefore this fire, and wherefore is Bascom sellin likker at half price? Becoz we are rehabilitated — that's wat we are. Becoz the North hez gone into the olive branch bizness agin, and we hev wunst more our rites. We are amnestied. We kin vote — we kin go to Congress — we are agin citizins uv the great Republic."

Pollock, the Illinoy storekeeper, riz and begged permishn to say a word. He protested agin these doins. He understood, akkordin to Horris Greely's plan, that yooniversal suffrage wuz to follow yooniversal amnesty — why then this makin John Rodgerses uv the niggers? Wuz the South a goin tc act in good faith?

Deekin Pogram replied : The South never yit

broke plighted faith save when she cood make suthin by so doin. At this present junkter uv affairs he presoomed the South wood extend, not precisely universal suffrage to the niggers, but the way wood be opened to em. Sich a mass uv ignorance cood never be trusted with the ballot without preparashen, and to prepare em wood be a over-turnin the Kentucky theory, that the nigger is a beast, and the Northern Demokratic idea that the nigger wuz cust by Noer and doomed forever to be a slave.

"The gentleman from Illinoy will to-wunst perceive the fix we are in. They ain't fit for the ballot now, and ef we make em so, it overturns our theory, wich we can't do. Still we propose to be just to em. We shel give sich uv em the ballot ez are suffishently intellijent, and we shel not put the standard too high nuther. We shel give every wun uv em the ballot who is able to reed the Greek testament flooently and pass a credible examinashen in Lattin, embroidery, French, German, English Grammar and double-entry book-keepin. The path to the polls, yoo see, is open to em. Uv course we can't be expectid to tolerate skool-houses for em, coz that wood raise em above their normal condishen. Also, ther must be proper regulashens controllin em, for, my deer sir,

they are mere infants, and ther totterin steps on the
road to freedom needs directing. Society is a com-
promise in wich every one resigns ez much uv his
persnel liberty ez the good uv the hull may demand.
We count ourselves the hull, and the resinin uv persnel liberty must come from them. That nigger,"
sed he, pintin to wun wich the joyous citizens wuz
stringin up to Bascom's sign-post, " that nigger is a
resinin his persnel freedom for the good of the hull.
No doubt in his heart he murmurs, and ef the cord
wich is chokin him cood be loosened, he wood re-
pine. It is rough on him ; but the sooperiority uv
the Caucashn race must be — My God ! it's one
uv my niggers ! Stop ! Bascom, stop !" ejackilated
the Deekin, but it wuz too late. The nigger wuz
already black in the face and hed ceased to kick,
and the Deekin, heavin a sigh, perceeded.

" We shel scroopulously regard their rites. They
shel hev the rite to buy land, and be in all respecks
like us, ez soon ez they kin be trusted. Till then
they will hev to be restrained. There must be
laws prohibitin em from receivin more than $4 50
per month, that they may not become bloated aristocrats and pampered sons uv luxury — the proper
development of the country, and likewise the payment of the Confedrit debt, requires manuel labor,

wich we wuz never edjucated to do, and therefore
the good of the whole requires that they shel resigne
their persnel liberty so fur ez to be confined to the
plantashuns, onto which they hev engaged to laber,
that they may relijusly do it, which is cleerly nessary, for yoo see ef I hire a nigger in Janooary, I
must not be exposed to the chances uv his quittin
me in July. But wat more kin they want? They
are free to ez great a extent ez the good of sosiety
will permit. We shel give em qualified suffrage,
fixin, uv course, wich is just, the qualifications ourselves, and bein valyooable members of society, hereafter we shel care fur em, so long ez they are healthy — Good Lord, why will them cusses persist in
hangin up able-bodied niggers when there's so many
old ones around, good for nuthin but to celebrate
with?" and to save another wun uv his former servants, the Deekin closed abruptly.

It is onnecessary to recount the further doins uv
the nite. There wuz a skool-house and church, recently erected, burnd, with some skore or sich a
matter uv young niggers in em, which wuz too young
to be uv any yoose, save one girl, wich wuz neerly
white and almost fifteen, wich ought to hev bin res-
kood, and five, ef I counted correctly, able-bodied
men and wimin wuz hung. Bascom sold out his

stock entirely, and by 3 A. M. the entire inhab-
itance uv the Corners wuz a layin around the square,
in festoons.

There wuz a bitter awakenin to this scene uv fes-
tivity. At a little after 7, while the Deekin, the
Elder, and myself, wuz in Bascom's tryin to get an
assuager — and the best we cood do wuz to pour a
quart uv water into a barrel wich hed bin emptied,
and roll it around and thus flavor it — Captain
McPelter, late uv Morgan's cavalry, cum in from
Looisville. Eagerly we asked him the confirmation
uv the tidins, when he informed us that it wuz a
hoax — that no such thing hed been done, nor wuz
Congris in any sich a noshen. Pollock dropped in,
and when I reproached him with his dooplicity, he
ansered that it wuz a hoax, but he hoped we'd
excoose him. He hed a cravin desire to see whether
ef Amnesty and Suffrage shood be adopted, how
fur we'd go in the latter direction. He wuz satisfied, and honestly hoped we'd forgive him the pleasant jest. He'd made the Corners lively one nite,
any how. I wuz too profoundly disgusted to reply
to the wretch.

PETROLEUM V. NASBY, P. M.
(Wich is Postmaster).

II.

Mr. Nasby and the Circle of Friends of which he is the Mentor, Ornament and Guide, feeling the need of an Institution of Learning for the Youth of Kentucky, project a College.

CONFEDRIT X ROADS
(wich is in the Stait uv Kentucky),
December 9, 1866.

SQUARE Gavitt, Deekin Pogram, Capt. Mc-Pelter and myself wuz in the Post Offis last nite, wich, next to Bascom's, hez got to be the cheef resort uv the leading intellex uv the Corners, a talkin over matters and things, when the Deekin happened to menshun that next week his second son, Elijer, who hez intelleck into him, was a goin to start for Michigan to enter a college.

"Wat!" sed I, "do yoo perpose to send that noble yooth, Elijer Pogram, to a Ablishn State, to enter a Ablishn college, to suck his knollege from a Ablishn mother? Good Heavens! Frailty, thy name is woman.

[I hedn't any ijee that this last remark wuz ap-propos, but it sounds well, and I hev notist that it don't make much difference wat the cotashun is so ez yoo end a remark with a cotoshun.]

The Deekin remarked that it wuz painful; but the fact wuz, Elijer must hev a edjucashen. He didn't bleeve in edjucashen, generally speekin. The common people wuz better off without it, ez edju-cashen hed a tendency to unsettle their minds. He hed seen the evil effex uv it in niggers and poor whites. So soon ez a nigger masters the spellin book and gits into noosepapers, he becomes dissatis-fied with his condishn, and hankers after a better cabin and more wages. He to-wunst begins to in-sist onto ownin land hisself, and givin his children educashen, and, ez a nigger, for our purposes, aint worth a soo markee. Jes so with the poor whites. He knowd one melloncolly instance. A poor cuss up toards Garrittstown, named Ramsey, learnt to read afore the war, and then commenst deterioratin. For two years he refoozed to vote the Dimocratic ticket, then he blossomed out into a Ablishnist and tried to make the others uv his class discontented by tellin uv em that Slavery wuz wat kept them down, and finally, after pashense ceased to be a virchoo, and we tarred and fethered him one nite for a incendiary, he went to Injiany. That cuss cum back here, doorin the late onpleasantniss, kernel of a rigiment, wich he campt on my farm and subsisted em off it.

" Sum educashen is, however, nessary. I design Elijer for Congris, and he must hev it. He's a true Pogram, and nothin will strike in wich kin hurt him."

" Why not," sez I, " that the Southern yooth may be properly trained, start a College uv our own? Why, Deekin, run risks uv hevin the minds uv our young men tainted with heresy?"

The entire company wuz struck with the idea, and it wuz earnestly canvassed, and finally decided upon; and I wuz deppytized to start it, wich I immejitly did. The name by wich the new college is to be known is " The Southern Classikle, Theo-logikle and Military Institoot uv Confedrit X Roads (wich is in the Stait uv Kentucky)."

The college grounds is to comprise one hundred akers taken from corners uv the farms uv Deekin Pogram, Elder Slathers and Capt. McPelter, wich ground they sell the college, seein it's for that pur-pose, for $300 per aker.

The faculty will be, ef we kin sekoor em, com-posed uv these trooly great minds :—

Genril Forrest, late C. S. A., Professor uv Moral Philosophy.

Kernell Mosby, late C. S. A., Professor uv Rhetoric and Belles Lettres.

Capt. McGee, late C. S. A., Professor uv Natural Sciences.

Genril Magruder, late C. S. A., Professor uv watever is understood by them ez is posted in college matters, ez Classics, wich I shel look up ez soon ez I hev time.

This is a killin two birds with one stun. We not only pervide educashen, wich is safe for our young men, but we pervide comfortable places for the heroes uv the late onpleasantniss.

In addition to these, Deekin Pogram, Square Gavitt and myself, each pledged ourselves to endow a Professorship in the Theologikle Department, to be known by our names, and we to hev the appintin uv the Professors.

The Pogram Chair uv Biblikle Theology will be offered to Rev. Henry Clay Dean, uv Iowa, provided he will stipulate to wash his feet wunst per quarter and change his shirt at least twice per annum.

The Gavitt Chair uv Biblikle Literatoor will be offered to Rev. C. Chauncey Burr, uv Noo York; and,

The Nasby Chair uv Biblikle Politicks will be filled by Rev. Petroleum Vesoovius Nasby, whose eminent fitniss for the place is undispooted.

In the Scientific and Classikle Departments the text-books will be keerfully revised, and everything uv a Northern or levelin tendency will be scroopulously expergated. In the Theologikle Department speshl attenshun will be given to the highly nessary work uv preparin the stoodents for comin out strong on the holinis uv Slavery, and to this end the three years' course will be devotid thus : —

1st year — To the cuss uv Noer.

2d year — To provin that the Afrikin nigger wuz reely the descendants uv Ham.

3d year — Considerin the various texts wich go to show that Afrikin slavery is not only permitted by the skripters, but especially enjoined.

I shell myself lectur, from time to time, on Ham, Hager and Onesimus, that the bearins uv these individooals upon our system may be fully understood, and also on sich subjects ez the inflooense uv stimulatin flooids upon the human system, the cat-o'-nine-tails ez a evangelizer, and sich other topics ez may from time to time sejest themselves.

The young men confided to our care will receive not only a solid collegiate educashun, ez it is understood at the North, but careful attention will be paid to the accomplishments so nessary to the troo Southern gentleman. They will be taught draw poker, pitchin dollars (real Spanish dollars will be provided for the purpose), spittin at a mark, revolver and bowie knife practice, tournament ridin at rings (real injy rubber rings will be provided — this'll be extra), and cat-o'-nine-tails. The morals uv the stoodents will be scroopulously looked after. No card-playin will be allowed afore servis on Sunday, and none watever with the servants. They will be taught to respeck themselves.

Uv course, there will hev to be a large outlay uv money, wich it stands to reason can't be outlayed till it's inlayed.

We, therefore, formed an Executive Committe, whose dooty it wuz made to solissit funds for this purpose, and to inaugerate a series uv Gift Enterprises, and sich, wich is ez follows : —

Deekin Pogram,	President.
Elder Slathers,	Vice-President.
Capt. McPelter,	Corresponding Secretary.
Myself,	Financial Secretary and Treasurer.

The high standin uv the Board, particklerly the Treasurer, wich hez the handlin uv the funds, is a suffishent guarantee that all money subscribed will be faithfully applied. It wuz resolved, in order that the Board may present that respectable appearance wich their posishen demands, that the first funds reseeved should be applied to the purchis uv each uv em a new soot uv clothes, a step, I am confident, the friends uv southern educashen will approve uv and heartily endorse.

I hev hopes in the course uv a week to report progress. Every subscriber uv $2.50 and upwards, will hev a Honorary Professorship named after him, or will be made a Honorary Member uv the Board uv Directors, ez he chooses. We regret that we wuz too late to git Admiral Semmes to fill one uv the chairs ; but we pledge our friends to sekoor his fust lootenant, or sekkond, at farthest. We hev high hopes uv a libral support from the Dimocrisy north. They cannot but realize the dangers uv sendin their sons to sich institooshens uv learnin north ez must turn em out Ablishnists, or chill, at least, the ardoor uv their Dimocrisy.

It is to be hoped that contributions for the buildin uv the institooshen and its proper endowment will

be commenst immejitly, ez there is a morgage on
Deekin Pogram's farm, and I am in pressin need
uv a substanshel soot uv winter clothes.

Petroleum V. Nasby, P. M.

(Wich is Postmaster).

III.

Mr. Nasby tries to weep at the Tomb of a Friend, and witnesses a Sisterly Fight. — The Disadvantages of the Patriarchal System.

POST OFFIS, CONFEDRIT X ROADS
(Wich is in the Stait uv Kentucky),
December 15, 1866.

I HEERD, nearly two months ago, that my old friend, John Guttle, uv Mobeel, hed departed this life and gone to that other and better world where the wicked cease from troublin and the weery are at rest, and wuz profoundly shocked. John Guttle wuz my friend, and I much feer his like I ne'er shall look upon agin. He wuz a Democrat uv the old skool, one uv the few links wich remaned to connect the present generation with the past. Well do I remember the gellorious old man! How often hev I set in the square room in his country residence, and drunk wiskey and water with him till we neither on us could see a hole thro a forty-foot ladder; how many times hez he flogged niggers for my amoozment, to show me the proper way uv managin uv em; and how many times hez he lent me small sums uv money, varyin from five to thirty-one dollars, akkordin to the state uv mellernis he wuz in when I approached him on the delikit sub-jik! Alas! poor John Guttle. Let not the skoffer say that I regret his death becoz his sons will be apt to try and collect the notes the old man departed holds uv mine! No, no! they know me too well to waste any time on that. I mourn becoz I loved him, and becoz uv the misfortunes which druv him to a prematoor grave. A. Linkin is responsible for this dark shadder onto my pathway. John Guttle hed three hundred niggers on his plantashens and in his house in town — these wuz wrencht from him by the Proclamashen, and turned out from his pater-nal care to starve, which the most uv em are indus-trously doin at about $3 per day. He hed em uv all hues — there wuz the full-blooded Black, the disgustin Mulatter, the pleasant Quadroon, the beau-tiful Octoroon, and them which hed so nearly lost the cuss of Ham ez to be hardly distinguishable from the pure Caucashun; and it wuz noticeable that the nearly white niggers on the Guttleses plan-tatin wuz all beautiful. The Guttleses theirselves wuz perfeck specimens uv manly beauty, and it probably hed its effeck upon the blacks. The nigger is a imitative animal.

It wuz this robbin uv him uv his property — this overturnin uv the normal condishn uv things — which killed John Guttle. He never held up his head after the Proclamashen, but faded away like a frostid flower!

I wus in Mobeel last week on biznis connected with our college (it wuz solisitin funds to endow my Professorship), and I felt that I cood not leave the sity without droppin a dozen teers or sich onto his grave. I felt, ez he hed contribbitted at various times so much to moisten my clay, that it would be ungentlemanly not to do suthin toward moistenin hizzen. And in pursuance uv my resolve, I wended my way sadly to the cemetry, and, findin the tomb, struck an attitood uv dispair, and leanin pensively onto the moniment, strove, to the best uv my ability, to weep, but it wuz a futile endeavor. My eyes woodent give down. I strove to recall his virchoos, but sich is the weaknis uv human nacher that whenever his form rose in my memory, my mind involuntarily wandered to his wiskey, and my mouth would water to sich an extent ez to monopolize all the moisture in my system. I cood hev spit onto his grave, but weep I could not. Alas for poor humanity!

When I wuz a standin there tryin to weep, and makin a bad fist uv it, I notist three beautiful young ladies approachin, with baskits ov hot-house flowers a hangin onto their arms. I recognized em to-wunst. They wuz John Guttle's daughters, and they wuz a comin to strew flowers onto the grave uv their paternal ancestor on their father's side. It wuz a techin site; and feelin that I wuz a introoder, not bein a blood relashun, and only connected with the deceest by notes uv hand, I withdrew a short distants. Skasely had they got to the tomb, when from the other side approached three more ravishin-ly beautiful young ladies, with baskits uv hot-house flowers onto their arms. The last ones resembled in a strikin manner the fust ones, ceptin they wuz a shade darker, and their hare waved bootiful, where-as the hare uv the fust wuz perfeckly strate.

The two parties faced each other on opposite sides uv the toom, and party Number One glared fiercely at party Number Two.

"Lize! Flora! Jane!" sed the oldest uv party Number One, "wat are yoo doin here?"

"Sisters," sed the eldest uv party Number Two, "we're here dischargin a fillyel dooty. Beneeth these sod lies the remains uv our father, and we are goin to strew these flowers onto his toom. Jine us in the strew."

"Father?" shreeked the three uv party Number One. "Yoor all niggers and wuz servants unto—"

"Our half-sisters," sed the spokesman uv party Number Two; "but Linkin removed the cuss uv Ham, and we're now free, and hev ez much rite to strew the grave uv our common parient, which wuz John Guttle, ez yoo. O! our sisters, our father wuz a good man — let us bedew his grave with our teers and—"

"Wat impudence!" shreeked party Number One, all in korious.

"Impudence yoorself!" retorted party Number Two, getting red in the face. "We are John Guttleses daughters percisely ez much ez yoo, and the only advantage yoo hev over us is in the article of mothers. Yoo three hev wun, which wuz John Guttleses wife, while we three hev three — one apiece eggsackly — which wuz John Guttleses servants; but we can't, nevertheless, stifle our emoshuns. I shel command myself, and thus perceed to perform a act uv fillyel dooty."

And she histed out the flowers and commenced to strew.

The tother wuns wuz a gettin hot. The oldest wun cood stand this impudence no longer, and droppin her basket, went for her, follered by her sisters. It wuz a sperited conflict, and lasted perhaps four minits, or until I parted em, when they gathered themselves together, and departed — one party went one way, and tother, tother.

Fillyel love hed done more in the strewin biznis than it sot out to do. The six lovin daughters uv the deceest John hed not only strewed flowers onto his grave, but hair, and collars, and buzzum pins, and shreds uv silk, and water-falls, and cotton, and false teeth, and pieces uv almost everything which goes to make up the sum total uv female attire.

Ez I gazed at the wreck and saw their tattered forms vanish in the dim distance, I cood not help admittin that when it come to strewin the graves uv deceest ancestors, there wuz sum disadvantages attendin the patriarkle system.

Petroleum V. Nasby, P. M.,

(Wich is Postmaster), and likewise Professor uv Biblikle Politicks in the Southern Classikle & Military Institoot.

IV.

Mr. Nasby in North Carolina. — The Abrogation of General Sickles' Order. — The aid he rendered Colonel Podgers.

Post Offis, Confedrit X Roads
(Wich is in the Stait uv Kentucky),
December 31, 1866.

FOR two weeks past I hev bin in North Carolina, and hev hed an oppertoonity uv bein uv service to my friends and the good cause.

I wuz there collectin funds fur the new College at this pint, to wich I am devoted heart and sole, and wuz a makin my home at Kernel Abslum Podgers, who resides just back of Rawly, and whose table and cellar, permit me to say, are unsurpassed in the South. Kernel Podgers is a gentleman uv the old skool, who lives in luxurious elegance onto a plantashn uv 1500 akers, and who hez troo piety into him, and alluz wears a shirt-frill. Afore the war he owned 200 niggers, and his sole runnin out after em, he hez managed, sence the war, to collect the most uv em and get em together on the old place. He hez bin busily engaged in subdooin uv em and bringing em back to ther normal condishun; but alas! ther wuz difficulties in the way. The men niggers, with an obstinacy wich I can't account for, refused to work for $4 per month, and the wimen, hevin ben mostly. married to ther husbands by the chaplin uv a regiment wich wuz stashened here doorin the war, refused to resoom their old relations, and things looked serious. Most men would hev yielded to circumstances and give up, but Kernel Podgers wuz not uv that stripe. He owed a dooty to these misguided beins wich he felt he must rulfil; and besides, he is desirous of buildin a new house next summer and sendin two daughters (by his wife) to a seminary next season, and he felt that he must bring em to their senses. He sed that he stood in the relation uv a father, figgeratively speekin, to all uv em, and literally to many uv em; and wuz he agoin to let em go on a flyin out ov their normal speer? Not any.

The fust day I wuz there, a crisis occurred. John Podgers, his son, insisted upon takin away the wife uv a mulatto, and the nigger, forgettin his posishen, wuz impudent. John struck him, and the degraded wretch waded in and whaled him unmerciful. This, uv course, cood not be endoored. The Podgers' blood riz, and that nigger wuz seized and catted till he died. Ef I remember right, he expired while undergoin discipline. It may be he lived till mornin; but it matters not, ceptin that I like to be accurate.

It wuz a solem and impressive scene. The Kernel had the Ethiopian's wife present doorin the infliction uv the punishment, and to show her that he did not perceed without authority, before commencin he read to her from Scripter the chapters treatin uv Ham and Hager, and the passage commencin " servance, obey your masters," and then walloped him with more vigger than I spozed wuz left in a man so old. He pinted to the nigger on the ground, after he wuz cut down, and tellin her that he hoped it wood be a lesson to her, bade her go to her quarters. But the perverse creecher didn't. She ran away and complained to the officer at the neerest post, who instid uv sendin uv her back under guard, with his compliments to Kernel Podgers, actilly forwarded her complaint to Gen. Sickles, who forthwith struck a blow at the foundashens uv the fabric uv Southern sosiety,

and ordered the arrest uv the Kernel, who wuz to-
wunst placed in doorance vile.

There wuz eggscitement in the visinity. I never
saw sich a fermentashen. Men run to and fro with
blancht cheeks, and askt, " Wat next? Is our rites
to be taken from us? Is Johnson a holler mock-
ery ?" And they made up a purse, and begged
me to go to Androo, and stand between em and
destruckshen. I run up to Washinton, and hed an
interview with his Eggslency, the President. He
knowd Kernel Podgers,— in his younger days he
hed made his coats,— and ez I tetched upon the
old man immured in a dismal dungeon, he wept.
But A. Johnson hez decision uv character. Wipin
his eyes, he isshood a order for the revokashen uv
Sickleses absurd order that niggers shoodent be
whipt, and a speshl order commandin the offiser
who hed the Kernel in custody, to turn him over
to the Civil Courts, to be tried in accordance with
the laws of North Karliny.

Armed with these documents, I flew back, and
the nite I arrived I hed the satisfackshen uv takin
the Kernel out uv Jail, and takin him afore a Justis
uv the Peace, where he gave bail to appear afore
the Common Pleas to answer a charge uv man-

slaughter, prefered by the widder uv the dead nigger.

A day or two after, the case wuz heard, I appearin for the Kernel. I held that the case be dismissed for the followin reason : —

1. The charge uv manslaughter wuz absurd, for the reason that in the minds uv the Southern people there hez alluz bin the gravest doubts ez to whether the nigger is actilly a man. I held that the length uv his heel, the thickness uv his skull, the length uv his arm, all showd that he wuz uv a distink species. Ef this is the case, ez a matter uv course the Kernel goes free.

2. The Kernel can't be held, allowin the nigger to be a man. The laws uv the State uv North Karliny permit the whippin uv niggers, but they don't prescribe the quantity uv whippin wich may be inflicted. It's a matter wich is left entirely to the discreshen of the whipper. It's a matter with wich the whippee hez nothin to do; neither hez the State. Ef the Kernel hed shot the nigger he wood be liable, for shootin ain't permitted; but ez whippin is, and ez the quantity ain't prescribed, uv course it intends the matter to be left solely to the discreshen uv the party who hez the power to whip. Nothin kin be clearer than that. Shel Kernel Pod-

gers be punisht becoz a nigger hedn't powers uv endoorence? Forbid it heven!

Here I rested the case. I showed to the satisfackshen uv the Court that the law was not only just but humane, and that any sich absurdity ez punishin the Kernel for carryin out its pervisions wood be strikin a blow at the framework uv society.

The Court coincided with me, and to-wunst discharged the Kernel, amid the acclamashuns uv the crowd. The event wuz sellebratid that afternoon by whippin every nigger within a cirkle uv ten miles. The exercise did our people good. It wuz soothin.

In the mean time John Podgers hed gone afore a Justice uv the Peace and made complaint uv Susan (that is the name uv the female wich wuz the cause uv the diffikilty) ez a vagrant, and she wuz so declared by the Justis and put up and sold. Under the circumstances no one wood bid agin John, and she was struck off to him at $50, wich the Justis under the pecoolyer circumstances uv the case refoosed to take. I saw John a marchin uv her home, and felt happy.

The Kernel's gratitood wuz boundlis.

"Wat kin I do for yoo?" sed he, wringin my hand in a fever uv joy.

"Nothin," sed I, "nothin! Virchoo is its own reward. But our College is languishin for want uv means — let yoor gratitood take that shape."

He subscribed and paid $200, wich constoots him a perpetooal Honorary Perfesser, and $100 to make his wife a perpetooal Honorary Perfesser. I borrowd uv him $50 to take me home, ez I coodent uv coorse yoose College funds, and departed $350 better. I left regretfully. Now that this portion uv the South is gettin her rites, it is trooly a deliteful place too live, and I shood like to end my days here. But my post offis, and that college! — I kin never leave em, never. To that college I hev dedikated the few remainin years uv my life, and I'll never desert it so long ez there's a dollar to be raised for it out uv anybody.

Petroleum V. Nasby, P. M.,

(Wich is Postmaster) and likewise Professor uv Biblikle Politicks in the Southern Classikle & Military Institoot.

V.

*Mr. Nasby renders an Account of his Steward-
ship. — Laying of the Corner Stone of the College Edifice. — An Awkward Denouement.*

POST OFFIS, CONFEDRIT X ROADS
(Wich is in the Stait uv Kentucky),
Janooary 2, 1866.

ON my return from my trip to North Karliny ther
wuz an immejit and irrepressible desire on the
part uv the Trustees uv the Institoot, to hev a statement from me uv the results of the trip. Much hed
bin expectid from the vencher, and the expectashuns
uv the Trustees wuz riz to a pitch from wich I felt
it wuz crooil to hurl em. Therefore I dodged em,
until finally, bein badgered, I thort I wood end it.
Hevin prepared the dockyments, I named the Post
Offis ez the place, and the mornin uv the 1st instant
ez the time to make an exhibit uv the receets and
expenditoors uv the trip. Deekin Pogram, Colonel
McPelter, and Elder Slathers were promptly on
hand, and so wuz I, with the statement, wich I red
to em ez follows : —

PETROLEUM V. NASBY, Professor uv Biblikle Politicks, in account with the Southern Classikle and Military Institoot Fund:

DR.

To cash uv Kernel Abslum Podgers, for self . . . $200 00
To cash uv Kernel Abslum Podgers, for wife . . 100 00
To cash uv Square Davis, proceeds uv the sale uv one nigger boy Jim, convicted uv steelin a red herrin, generously donated 50 00
To cash uv Major Galbreth, bein all he hed left after gettin a pardon from the President through Mrs. Cobb 1 00
To cash uv John Kessick, who encourages the Institoot, intendin to come here to start a grocery, ez soon ez it gits fairly a goin 10 00
To cash uv divers and sundry persons 20 00

Grand totle $381 00

CR.

By ralerode fare, the conductors unanimously refoosin to ded hed me either in my clericle, offishel or benevolent character $30 00
By refreshments, and meal after refreshments . . 90
By more refreshments 15
By bottle uv refreshments to use on cars 1 50
By refreshments at station 15
By refreshments at various places 60 00
By board at Rawley 60 00
By refreshments at Rawley, wich comes high, bein 25 cts. strate 70 00
By livery hire in that vicinity 90 00
By refreshments for self and driver, includin broken axels and sich 25 00
By meals for self and driver 3 00
By fare back home, wich cost more owin to my comin a round about way 50 00

Grand totle . . . . - $390 70
Leavin a balance in my favor of $9 30.

The brethren wuz somewat disappointed at the resu.t, and Bascom intimated that he bleeved it wuz a d—d swindle; but I withered him with a glance. I showed Deekin Pogram that it wuz not only reglar, but that it hed the stamp uv the Post Offis onto it, wich silenced all cavil. I asshoored em that that little balance needn't trouble em — I did not intend to make an assessment onto em, but that I cood wait until the treasury wuz in funds.

"But," sed Bascom, "when in thunder will the treasury ever be in funds, ef all the expedishuns result like this one?"

I explained to the obtoose man that it wuz all rite; that in most uv sich enterprises the expenses eat up the collekshuns, but that it wuz seed sown. "We must," sez I, "raise the wind from the North, aud to do it, let us show that suthin hez bin dun."

"Wat kin we do?" sed Bascom.

"Lay the corner stun uv the Institoot?" sez I. "On the square forninst us is the corner stun uv the nigger church we burnt a month or so ago, ready to our hand. Let us organize a percession and do it to-day, that we may publish to the world that the work is commenced, that our friends may shell out libreller than they hev."

The idea wuz considered good, and forthwith it

wuz actid upon. The stone wuz conveyed to the feeld onto wich the Institoot is to be built, and a cavity wuz hollered out into it.

At 4 P. M. (wich is in the afternoon) a percession wuz formed, headed by the Trustees, and we marched out to the feeld. Into the cavity in the stun wuz deposited, with approprit ceremonies, the followin articles : —

A copy uv the Constooshen uv the Confedrit States uv America.

A copy uv the message uv Androo Johnson vetoin the Freedmen's Buro Bill.

A copy uv the 22d uv Febrooary speech.

Portrates uv the Trustees.

A copy uv the veto uv the Civil Rites Bill.

A pair uv handcuffs.

Portrates uv President Johnson and Secretary Seward.

A nigger whip.

A $5 greenback contribbited for the purpose by Elder Pennibacker.

A pint bottle uv wisky, seeled, contribbited by Bascom.

Then the stun wuz placed in posishen; a nigger wuz tied to it and flogged, his blood bedoozlin it, and after a few feelin remarks by myself, in wich

I stated that this wuz a grate day for the Corners, and that posterity wood bless us for the work we hed that day done, the crowd dispersed, the Trustees goin back to my offis to draw up a statement uv the ceremonies, and an appele to the northern Dimocrisy for aid.

The nigger wich we whipt at the corner stun wuz shot in a dispoot by Capt. McPelter, wich circumstances greatly annoyed Deekin Pogram, ez it wus a nigger wich wuz formerly hizzen. He remonstrated with the Captain angrily, and ashoord him that ez soon ez the Soopreme Court hed declared the Amendment abolishin slavery unconstooshnel, he shood sue him for his value. With this triflin excepshun, the affair passed off ez pleasantly ez cood be wished. I remonstrated with both uv em for quarrelin, on sich a occasion, over so small a matter ez the shootin uv a nigger, and they finally settled it without hard feelins. How sweet is peace and friendliness atween man and man! How blessid is the offis uv a peace maker! The captain acknowledged he wuz wrong, and stood the drinks for the crowd.

That nite about 9 P. M., I wuz a sittin in my offis a musin onto the evence uv the day, and wonderin whether the Dimocrisy wood give down, it okkured to me that there wuz a pint bottle uv first-class corn wisky, and $5 in currency agoin to waste in that stun.

"Wat'll posterity ever know uv us?" thot I to myself.. "Ef posterity does ever overturn that stun, won't she git jest ez good an idea uv who we wuz from the other articles? Ef posterity ever reads the speeches uv His Eggslency, and the messages wich we hev placed there, won't the wisky be inferred? Ef it ain't, posterity is a consumate ass;" and thus musin, I wended my way thitherward, determined to reskoo these two articles from oblivion any how.

It wuz pitch dark, but I knew the way. Creepin cautiously up to the stun, I reached out ; and horror ! Ther wuz another hand onto it! Strikin a match quickly, there stood reveeled afore me the forms uv Deekin Pogram, Bascom, and Elder Slathers, to whom the same thot hed occurred wich moved me. But my presence uv mind did not forsake me. Strikin another match, I assoomed a look uv virchus indignashen, wich they all saw afore it went out, and reproacht em fur ther worldly-mindednis. How cood they expect the Institoot to prosper when those into whose hands its interests wuz confided, proves re- creant to the extent uv steeling the sacred memen- toes wich were to-day enclosed. "Go home," sed

I; " I forgive you this time, and will not expose yoo ez yoo deserve.   I spected yoo all, from the way yoo eyed the bottle and the greenback, and hastened hither to protect em.   Go!"

And they went; after wich I tipped over the stun and sekoored the prize.

The next mornin they all reproached me with hevin stolen the articles, in privit, wich satisfied me that all uv em hed gone back for the plunder after they thot I'd gone; but they didn't make no fuss about it.   They are all good men; but alas! sich is the depravity uv human nacher that they'll bear watchin.

I await with anxiety the result uv our appeal to the Northern Democrisy.   Ef they fail us ez shamefully ez they did durin the war, it is all up with us.

PETROLEUM V. NASBY, P. M.

(Wich is Postmaster), and likewise Professor uv
Biblikle Politicks in the Southern Classikle &
Military Institoot.

VI.

Mr. Nasby essays a Sermon but is interrupted by a Nigger, who is aided and abetted by the Perverse Joe Bigler.

Post Offis, Confedrit X Roads
(wich is in the Stait uv Kentucky),
Janovary 10, 1867.

I WUZ rekested a week ago to preech a discourse from the text wich the noble and high-minded Guvner Bramlette used with sich crushin force in his last annual message, to wit: "Kin the Leopard change his spots or the Ethiopian his skin?" and alluz feelin anxious to do wat I kin for the cause, I did it last nite or rather essayed to do it.

And here let me remark, that there ain't a more devoted people in Kentucky than them lambs ez compose my flock. It wuz a tetchin site, and one wich filled my sole with joy, to see em pour out uv the groceries at the first tootin uv the horn, and to see Pennebacker, wich owns the Distillery, stop pin work to come, but the most cheerin and encouragin sign to me wuz to see Deekin Pogram, who was playin seven-up for the drinks with Elder Slathers, at Bascom's, lay down his hand when he hed high low and jack in it, and hed only three to go. "Elder," sed he, his voice tremblin at the sacrifice he wuz a makin, and a tear steelin down his cheek, "Elder, them's the horn. Let us to our dooties. 'Ligion must take the front seat uv temp'ral matters," and sighin ez he cast a partin glance at his hand, he strode out resolootly to the sanktooary.

I opened by readin the follerin from Guvner Bramlette's message.

" ' The nigger is the inferior uv the white — he lacks the power to rise. Ontil the Leopard kin change his spots, or the Ethiopian his skin, all efforts to repeal or nullify God's laws will be unavailin.

" My bretherin, these words is words uv wisdom, and fur em let us be thankful. The skin uv the Ethiopian wuz inflicted onto him for the express purpose uv distingishin him from his bretherin, whose servants he wuz condemned to be, for all time, ez a punishment for the sin uv Cain or the improodence uv Ham, wich Democratic divines heven't settled on. With the black skin he wuz

given all the other marks uv inferiority. He wuz
cust with long arms, immense hands, flat nose, and
bowed legs, and that ther mite be no mistake in
the matter, he wuz given wool instead uv hair.
Halleloogy!

"Ah, my brethern, wat a blessid thing for us. is
this Ethiopian! Wat a consolation it must be to
yoo all to know that ther is a race below yoo, and
how blessid the refleckshun that they can't change
ther skin, and by that means git above yoo! That's
the comfort we draw from the skripters. Wat a
horror it wood be for Deekin Pogram, who is
snorin so peacefly,

'Dreamin, sweetly dreamin the happy hours away,'

ef when the Soopreme Court decides the Ablishn
amendment unconstooshnl, and he gits his niggers
back agin; ef ther shood be a new dispensashun,
and niggers shood be permitted to change ther
skins! Wat sekoority wood we hev for our property? Some mornin he'd wake up and find em
all white persons, wich it wood be unconstooshnel
to wollop.

"My brethern, ther hez bin many efforts to
change the skin uv the Ethiopian, or rather ther
hez bin many who wanted to. The Boston Ab-

lishnists hev tried it, but wat hez bin the result? Ain't they niggers yit, and ain't they still the degraded wretches they alluz wuz? I paws for a reply."

I made this latter remark becoz, and only becoz, it sounded well, not that I hed any idee that anybody wood reply. Imagine my surprise at seein a gray-headed nigger, wich hed bin, doorin and after the fratrisidle struggle, employed in the Freedman's Burow, rise, and remark that he hed a word to say onto that pint. There wuz a storm uv indignashun, and the impudent nigger, who wuz so sassy ez to presoom to speek in a white meetin, wood hev bin sacrificed on the spot, hed not Joe Bigler, who wuz half drunk, drawd a ugly-lookin navy revolver, and remarkin that he knowd that nigger, that he hed more sense than the hull bilin uv us, and he shood hev his say.

" Ef," sed this recklis Joe, " ef he beats yoo, Perfesser, trooth is trooth; lets hev it. Ef he don't, why, it's all the better for yoo. Ef yoor Websterian intelleck kivers the ground, all rite; ef his ponderous intellek gets the best on't, jist ez rite. ' Out uv the mouths uv babes and sucklins.' Elder, I go my bottom dollar on this sucklin. Speek up, venerable: there won't none uv em tech yoo;" and he cockt his revolver.

"Beggin pardon," sed the nigger, "I agree with yoo, Perfesser, that the Ethiopian can't change his skin hisself, but does the Scripter say that it can't be changed for him?"

"Anser the venrable babe," sed Joe Bigler, pintin his revolver at me.

"I can't say that it does," sez I.

"Very good," retorted the nigger, "hezn't there a change bin a goin on in Kaintuck from the beginnin? My mother wuz ez black ez a crow — I'm considble lighter — my wife's a half lighter than I am — my gal's childern is a half lighter than their mother, and I want to know wat Guvner Bramlette's got to say to that. The white man ain't got no cuss onto him, hez he?"

"Speek up Perfesser — the sucklin wants yoo to be prompt," sed Joe Bigler.

I answered that "he hed not — that it wuz piled onto Ham or Cain and their desendants, and nobody else."

"Very well, then," sed the nigger, chucklin all over, "ez I am only half Ham or Cain (wich, you hevn't decided), then uv coarse there's only half a cuss onto me, only a quarter onto my wife, only an eighth onto my daughters, only a sixteenth onto my daughters' childern, and there's lots uv niggers in this yer visinity wat hezn't got the thirty-sekkund or the sixty-fouth part uv it hangin to em. Guvnet Bramlette also sed suthin bout niggers bein degraded coz twuz their nacher, didn't he, and that edducashen woodent do for em?"

"Perfesser," sed the tormentin Bigler, wich hed just whisky enuff into him to be ugly, "I must remind yoo that the partikeler babe and sucklin, out uv whose mouth yoor bein immensely condemned, expex prompt ansers, or rather I, his guardian and pertecter do."

I ansered that sich wuz the tenor uv the Guvner's remarks.

"Ef that's troo, why don't the mulattoes come up faster? Ef it's the nateral stoopidity uv the nigger, the white man ain't effected by it, and the mulatto only half. I are 'quainted with the heft uv the people afore me, and I'll bet my last year's wages, wich Deekin Pogram ain't paid yit, that half uv em can't read any mor'n I kin. 'Pears to me I'd like to hev Guvner Bramlette take the load off us for a year two and see whether we'd rise or not. We moutn't and then agin we mout. But I ruther think its a leetle too much to put a millstone on top uv a man and then kick him for not gettin up."

"Bully!" sed Joe Bigler. "Go on! go on!"

"It ain't just square playin to make all sorts uv laws agin our risin, to flog us for hevin spellin-books, to make it a penitentiary offence to learn to read, and to burn our skool houses, and then because we ain't just ready to enter college, to insist on't that we are naterally incapable. And above all, ain't it presoomin a little to charge it onto the Lord? Ain't yoo mistakin your own work for hizzen? 'Praps ef Guvner Bramlette's father hed bin flogg'd for wantin to learn to read, and Guvner Bramlette's mother hed bin brought up ez a feeld hand, and the same strategy hed bin practised on Guvner Bramlette's grandfather, and great grandfather, and great, great grandfather, and great, great, great grandfather, and his great—"

"Hold on, venerable," sed Joe Bigler, "don't enumerate. Jest say his ancestors, back to the identicle time they wuz slaves to them Normans, wich held his projenitors jist ez closely ez yoo've bin held, and it'll be suffishent. But go on."

"I plead guilty to the big hands, flat nose, and bowd legs. Possibly the first nigger hed em — possibly not. Ef Guvner Bramlette's father, and his grand-fa— wich is to say ancestors, hed bin kept at the hoe, his hands wood hev bin ez big ez mine; ef they'd borne burdens forever his legs

wood be bowed, and ef ther noses hed bin perpetooally smasht hizzen wood be flatter than it is."

"Hev yoo eny more questions to put to the Perfesser?" sed Joseph.

"No," replied the Ethiopian, "I hev sed my
say."

"Then," sed this Bigler, wich wuz gettin more
and more reckless every minnit, "I dismiss this congregashun, with this remark, that that nigger is under my protectin care, and ef a single lock uv his
wool is disturbed, I shel feel it a sollum but painful
dooty devolvin upon me, to put a ball into the car-
cass uv each uv the offishls uv this Church, commencin with the Paster, and continuin all the way
down to the scribe. Git!"

And pell-mell the congregashen piled out—one
over another.

It will be necessary to dispose of Joe Bigler
somehow. He lost wat property he hed in the
war, and is becoming exceedinly loose in his talk.
He can't be tolerated long.

PETROLEUM V. NASBY, P. M.

(Wich is Postmaster), and likewise Professor uv
Biblikle Politicks in the Southern Classikle &
Military Institoot.

VII.

Mr. Nasby does the ✕ *Roads a Service. — The Peace that reigns there, and the Cause of it.*

Post Offis, Confedrit ✕ Roads
(Wich is in the Stait uv Kentucky),
Janooary 20, 1867.

THERE is peace in the Corners! It reigns here, it does, with a sweetnis onparalleled since the Nashun launched out onto the sea uv trubles, which very near engulfed her. It comes about thro me. Biznis in the Post Orfis don't engross all my time. It don't take me very long to distribbit the paper which Deekin Pogram takes, nor the cirklers uv the gift enterprises which come here; neither does it consoom much uv my valyooble time directin the letters enclosin dollars back to em, besides which a good many uv em are insufficiently sealed, and the money drops out, and bein conscientious to a fault, ez I can't get em back into the right letters, why uv course I don't send sich at all. The only trouble I hev is in explainin why let-

ters containin such remittancis don't reach their des-
tinashen, but that has its rewards. I invariably tell
em that the managers uv the enterprises are ablishn
Yankees, and, uv course they'd be swindld, which
alluz intensifies their rage. A batch uv em sent for
tickets to Crosby's Opera House, which didn't reach
Chicago, ez I wuz behind with my board, and after
givin em the regular explanashen, they wuz so
enraged at the theevin ablishnists at Chicago, that
they sallied out and made it lively for wat niggers
they met. I forget now, but ef I remember right,
they hung two, or wuz it three? My memry is
failin.

But ez I wuz sayin, I hev plenty uv time, and I
put it in mostly studyin the caracteristiks uv human
nacher, ez developed in men and niggers. While
contemplatin a parsel uv niggers one day, I folleied
em, and overheard their conversashen. I wuz
astonished! They wuz notifyin one another uv a
meetin to be held that nite in Pennibacker's barn, to
which all wuz expected to be present. Here, thot
I to myself, is Guy Fawkes! Here is conspiracy!
Meetin! Wat rite hev niggers to meet! And I
hastened to Deekin Pogram and told him wat I had
heerd.

"Nasby," sed he, wringin my hand, "ef I ever

doubted the eternel fitnis uv things — the complete and entire adaptability uv one class to another — that doubt is removed. Here am I, a nigger owner — here are yoo, a Northern Dimocrat — a bloomin eggsotic ez I may say, wich hez took root in Southrn sile. I never wood hev overherd them niggers! — no Southner wood hev thot uv sneakin after em — for all sich work the Northern Dimocrat is precisely fitted. It's wat they've alluz done for us! alluz! alluz! alluz!"

And he wrung my hand again, and thanked me. I wuz too much overcome with emoshen at the compliment he paid me to reply. But we arranged the programme. We went to the barn, and overturned a wagon so ez we cood git under it and heer all that wuz sed without bein seen, and jest at nitefall the Deekin and me ensconsd ourselves in ou' hidin place.

The niggers gathered, praps thirty on em, and opened the meetin with prayer, in which exercise they hed the profanity to pray for the Government uv the Yoonited States and sich, and then the biznis commenst. It appears that they'd sent a man North to find a locashen for em, ez they hed made up their minds to run away from the blessins uv slavery wich we are preparin to re-open to em, and this nigger hed arrived, and they wuz assembled to hear his report.

"Brother Lee," sed the ringleader to the returned nigger, wich I knowd — he wuz nearly white, and wuz raised in Virginia, and hed bin four years in the army, on the Fedral side uv course, — " are yoo ready to report? Hev yoo found the Promised Land?"

Brother Lee replied, that ef he understood wat wuz the Ethiopian idee uv the " Promised Land," he cood safely and certainly say that he hedn't. He landed first in Philadelphy, and bein sumwat wearied by the long ride, he took a seat in a street-car which wuz empty. The condukter ordered him out, but sposin he wuz in a State where there wuz ekal rites he insisted on stayin, when the condukter and the driver bundled him out by force. His coat, he observed, showin wher the bloo blouse hed bin onskilfully mendid, wuz sumwat fraktered in the skuffle.

At this narrashen the niggers groaned, and it wuz all I·cood do to keep the Deekin from hollerin halleloogy !

In Noo York State he didn't fare so well. He diskivered that a decent nigger there isn't quite ez good ez a very ordinary white man. He happened ther on 'leckshin day, and narrated that he saw white men carried up to the poles so eggstremely drunk that them ez hed em in charge hed to put the ticket atween their fingers and anser to their names, while a 'spectable nigger hed to show that he wuz worth some property afore he wuz allowed to vote, and then a number uv gentlemen with red faces and clubs made it so onpleasant that but few attempted it.

The Deekin punched me in the ribs vociferously.

Next he went to Ohio, sposin, uv course, that a State so extremely opposed to bondage wood be the place he wuz in search uv. Agin he wuz disappointed. It wuz worse than it wuz in Noo York, for the Ablishnists wuz a going on the principle, he rather guessed, uv doin justis without runnin agin anybody's prejudises; or rather, uv lettin justice do herself, for they don't make any move towards helpin her. There the nigger uv no grade, no matter how much he pade taxes onto, or how long he served in the army, wuzn't allowed a vote. The Ablishinists, ez he understood, tho praps he wuz wrong, carried the state on the nigger question, but wuz now afrade to tetch it for fear they'd lose it agin. They've hed it, he remarked, 12 years, but

dn't, ez yit, got all the people edjicated up to the
it uv doin wat all the people knowd wuz rite.
His experience in the West wuz very similar.
e Ablishnists wuz everywhere very strongly in
majority, and every wun uv 'em he talked with
z in favor of givin the nigger his rites, but they
z all afraid ef they took hold uv it, they'd be laid
t by the Democracy, which wuznt in the majority
all. In Washinton, wher Congress hez give the
gers a vote, he wuz well treated, and it wuz the
ly place. A gentleman who wants to run for
yor next spring giv him his dinner, and quite a
mber of others who wanted small offises did like-
se, but he woodent advise emigrashen there, for
reason that ther wuz too many there now; and
sides it's possible that before the next elecshun
ngress may conclude that suffrage in the Dee-
ick will run 'em into the ground in the States
eir constituents, which are all Ablishnists, not
in edjucated up to the pint), and repeel it.
The Deekin nudged me agin.
"Wat shel we do?" then sed the niggers, all in
rious.
"Do!" sed the nigger, wich his name it wuz Lee,
lo! grin and bear it wher yoo are. Ez fo' me,

ef I hed my five yeahs back agin I shood do diffrent. Liberty is a gift hoss, wich, ef dis niggah
hed it to do ober agin, he wood look in de mouth,
shoah. I shood want to know whedder, I bein a
beggar, ef I mounted it I shoodent ride to de devil.
When I turned agin Massa, and went into de servis,
I wuz promised ef I behabed like a man I shood
be counted a man. I behabed like a man, but wat
now? Dar's de cibbel rites bill, which reads good,
but wha's de sogers to put it froo? Dar's all sorts
ob laws, but wha's de yoose ob em so long ez no-
boddy pays any tenshun to em? I go Norf, wha de
Ablishnists hab eberyting dah own way, and I find
de niggah is ez bad off dah ez he is heah, coz de
Ablishnis, wich is de champions uv ekal rites, ain't
eddicated up to de pint uv bustin unekal laws. We
can't stay heah and git our rites — we can't go dah,
coz ebry wun ob em will tell yoo his nabor ain't
eddicated up to de pint ob doin anything but holdin
de offises, and passin resolooshens dat dey bleeve in
de principles ob de Declarashen ob Independence,
wich principles reed bery well, but wat good is
dey to me ef dey ain't acted up to? Fo' fo'pence
I'd go hang myself."

They had other talk, and finally broke up, endin
with a prayer, the burden uv wich wuz that the

od Lord wood find some way, wat they didn't
e, to eddicate their friends North up to the pint.
Ez soon ez they wuz gone the Deekin and I
wled out from under the wagon, and I must say
old gentleman surprised me. Dashin his hat
wn on the ground, he execooted one uv the most
ntic Highland flings my eyes ever witnist. It
onished me to see how recklis the old man wuz
th his legs. Finally, out uv breath, he subsided
th a prolonged shreek uv exultant joy.

'Why so jubilant, my venerable friend?" sed I.
'Nasby," sed he, " it's better than I hoped for.
e Ablishnists bar em out — they ain't eddikated
 to the pint, and they drive em away. They
ke distinkshuns, and when the nigger's distinkted
nst in part, he's precisely the material uv which
make a servant unto his brethren. Ef the nigger
't git all his rites in the North, he'd better be
hout any uv em in the South. Up ther he hez
 the cussitood uv bein a free man, without any
the indoosements ; down here, ef he ain't got any
the blessins uv freedom he ain't any uv the re-
nsibilities. The nigger, uv course, will stay —
d be a cussed fool ef he didn't. Bless the Lord
 the Ablishnists wat ain't eddikated up to the
t !"

And the blessed old lunatic execooted another Highland fling onto his hat. Sharin his enthoosiasm, ez I alluz do everybody's I meet, that I may share whatever else they hev, we went to Bascom's, wher, before we separated, we wuz eddikated up to a pint, and considerable more. Bascom carried the Deekin home on a wheelbarrer, at a little past one.

Petroleum V. Nasby, P. M.

(Wich is Postmaster), and likewise Professor uv Biblikle Politicks in the Southern Classikle & Military Instituot.

5

VIII.

An Important Case at the Corners under the Vagrant Act. — The Decisions of Squire Gavitt.

POST OFFIS, CONFEDRIT X ROADS
(Wich is in the Stait uv Kentucky),
Janooary 28, 1867.

WUN uv the most important cases — important in a national sense — ever tried afore a court uv justis, came off afore Squire Gavitt at the court-house, at the Corners yesterday. It was important, becoz it involved the very eggistence uv the institution upon wich Kentucky is built — becoz, upon its decision hung the question whether or not the Bible shood be respectid and its holy injunctions obeyed — whether Kentucky shood, clingin to the Skripters, go on ez a Christian State, or denyin it, go back into infidelity and barbarism. I scasely need say that the porshens uv the Bible to wich I refer, is the ever blessid chapters relatin to Ham, Hager, and Onesimus — the only parts of the Skrip-ter we pay much attention to. But ef them is attacked successfully, wat follows? The entire strukter comes tumblin to the ground. Therefore, holdin to Aferkin slavery, we are orthodox believers.

The circumstances uv the case wuz suthin like this: A nigger uv the name uv Gabriel, wunst the happy and contented servant uv that eminent Christian, Deekin Pogram, becum possessed uv the spirit uv the devil, and sullen, becoz the Deekin sold his wife to raise the means to send his second son, Isaker, wich wuz a studyin for the ministry, to a Theolojikle Institoot, somewheres in Georgia; and also enraged becoz his female offspring, Elizer, happenin to attrack the attenshun uv his eldest son, Elijer, he run away in the fust year uv the war, and follered the Federal army, finally enlisting as a sojer. Durin the progress uv the struggle, he learned to read, and bein powerful in prayer and sich, he headed a revival, and hevin gifts that way, attracted the notis uv Genril Howard, or some uv them fanatics, who hed him instructed, and finally made him an agent uv a branch uv that accursid Freedmen's Burow; and sure enuff, after the war, he appeared in this vicinity, salaried by the society, and commenst unfittin the niggers for their normal condishun by teechin on em to read, and establishin

Sunday skools among em, and givin em advice generally, wich wuz aginst the dignity and peace uv the commonwealth. The citizens stood it with the pashense carakteristik uv the people uv Kentucky ontil last Monday. The Deekin hed a dispoot with a nigger relativ to a triflin matter uv wages. The nigger hed bin workin at the stipulated price uv $4 per month — the Deekin brought in, ez a offset, his board at $2 per week; and ruther than hev any fuss about it, proposed to let him work the balance out durin the winter months. To this ekitable arrangement the nigger demurred, holdin that board wuz inclooded, and this Gabrel advised the nigger to sue, and he did so.

Enraged at his interference, the Deekin went before Square Gavitt, and complained of Gabrel ez a vagrant, and employed me to attend to the case. Pollock, the Illinoy storekeeper, volunteered to defend the nigger, and there wuz a tremenjus eggsitement over it.

I opened the case by stating that the nigger's biznis wuz to prove that he hed vizable means uv support: Pollock insisted that it wuz our biznis to prove that he hedn't, but the court decided agin him.

The nigger then swore that he reseeved from his

congregashen $30 per month for services. I sub-
mitted that, ez he wuz a interested party, other
proof wood be required. Pollock interdoost the
elders of the congregashen, but I checkmated him
there, by submittin that the testimony uv niggers
wuzn't admissable, wich the court decided it wuzn't.

Immejitly Pollock submitted that whether or no
his client coodent be considered a vagrant, ez he
cood testify himself to the fact that he (Gabrel) hed
in his house $200 in greenbax — a suffishent sup-
port for a time, at least.

Ther wuz a immense eggscitement in the court.

" Wher duz he keep it? " asked the Squire, visibly
agitated.

" In his chist at the house wher he boards," sed
Pollock.

" This court stands adjourned for thirty minits,"
sed the Squire, boundin over the railin in front
uv him. " Hold on," sez he; " hold on, Deekin;
a fair start is all I want. Don't take advantage uv
my age to get ther first," and pell-mell over one
another the entire audience, ceptin Pollock, the nigger, and me, started on a keen run for the house.
In a few minits they returned, pantin and out uv
breath, when the Squire called the court to order
agin, wich bein restored, he remarked, —

Ef it cood be established that the nigger hed $200 in greenbax it wood nessessarily discharge him, ez no man with that sum cood be considered a vagrant; but he thot ef the prizner at the bar shood look in the direckshun uv his house, he'd find it wuzn't ther any more, ez a house, the materyal uv wich it wuz built wuz lyin permiskus. Likewise, probably, he wooodn't be able to find the $200 he hed in his chist. The place that knowd it wunst will know it no more forever — it hed been confis-cated by the enraged citizens. He wantid it under-stood that no such triflin impediment in the way uv justis ez the possession uv $200 cood be allowed within the jurisdickshen uv this court. The nigger not bein able to prove his means uv support, and ez the court knowed uv its own knollege that he ain't now got any $200, the court wood ask the criminal's counsel wat other nonsense he hez to plead.

Sed Pollock, the Illinoy storekeeper, —

" I wood beg leave to state to this court that, under the Civil Rites law, the defendant cannot be arrested ez a vagrant, ez the law under wich the accused is arrested only menshuns persons uv color, makin a distinkshen agin em."

Never, while memry retains her seat, shel I for-

get the scene that ensood. Filled with a sense uv
the responsibility restin onto him, the Squire rose
slowly from his seat, his face uv a deathly palenis,
wich hed the effeck uv hightnin, by contrast, the
intense rednis uv his nose, and risin to his full hite,
remarked that the court hed expectid that objeckshen to be urged, and hed, therfore, prepared fur it.
That law doesn't bind this court to any alarmin extent, considerin it ez infringin onto the reserved rites
uv the States.

" Will the court be so good ez to menshun for the
informashun uv the populace, wat the reserved rites
uv the States are? " sez Pollock.

" The court insists that it shel not be interruptid
when it's deliverin itself uv an opinion. Considerin
it ez infringin upon the reserved rites uv the States,
uv whom Kentucky is the cheefest and the loveliest
among ten thousand " — at this pint his nose glowd
redder, and it seemed to me ez tho a halo uv lite
encirkled his frosty head, ez he fearlessly continued
— " the court holds that law to be unconstooshnel,
end ez sich, shel not regard it. Hez the counsel
anythin more to remark? "

" Nothin," sed Pollock. " And knowin the court
so well ez I do, I wonder at my makin sich an ass
uv myself ez to hev remarkt anything at all."

" Hez the counsel for the State anything to say?"

" Nothin," sed I. " I am willin to trust the case in yoor hands, feelin confident that justis — genooine Kentucky justis — will be done."

Wareupon the Squire hed the prizner stand up, and, drawin on a black cap, in a very impressive manner, sentenst him to eighteen months hard labor, breakin stone for the turnpike, wich we are buildin from the Corners to the stashen, at the conklushen uv wich Pollock very profanely added, " And may the Lord hev mercy on your sole."

The nigger wuz immejitly stript uv his good close, wich the Squire thot wood just fit him, and a soot uv vagrant's close wuz given him, and he wuz towunst put to his labor.

We hev hopes that this will end the nigger skools in this vicinity, ez well ez the diskontent that hez eggisted among the niggers ever since the disturbin Gabrel hez bin here. The Corners is now enjoyin a holy calm — more so than any period for a month.

PETROLEUM V. NASBY, P. M.

(Wich is Postmaster), and likewise Professor uv
Biblikle Politicks in the Southern Classikle &
Military Institoot.

IX.

Mr. Nasby is despatched by the President and Secretary Seward upon an important Mission, similar in its Nature to that of Mr. McCracken. — His Report.

Post Offis, Confedrit X Roads
(Wich is in the Stait uv Kentucky),
Febrooary 11, 1867.

IT wuz a crooel necessity, after all, wich druv me into the servis uv His Eggslency A. Johnson. Crooel, I say; for whenever he hez a partikelerly mean piece uv work to perform, suthin so inexpressibly sneakin that Seward nor Randall won't undertake it, they alluz send for me. Welles is alluz willin; but while he hez the disposishen to do anything in the line, he lax the ability. The uthers, however, hev the ability to do anythin and the disposishen to do most things, and therfore I hev bin employed in only eggstreme cases.

The success wich attended McCracken's mishun, endin ez it did in the resinin uv Motley, stimyoolated Seward to prossekute similar researches into the actooal opinions uv the home krop uv offisers regardin him, and his, ez well ez my sooperior, A. Johnson. Randall wuz applied to to take a tour among Post Masters and sich. He declined the mishen indignantly, with the remark, "Is thy servant a dog, or the son uv a dog, that he shood do this thing?" And ez Welles isn't trusted out uv Washinton any more, I wuz sent for.

The biznis required uv me wuz statid by Seward in his yoosual loocid style. It wuz merely to cirkelate *incognito* (wich is Latin for sneakin) among the recently appinted offis-holders, and assertain ther views upon general politikle topics, but more espeshally ther feelins toward the President and Sekretary uv State. Jest ez I wuz startin, not at all pleased with the mishen, Welles put in his oar. He wuz agoin to give me instrucshuns ez to wat I wuz to do. Welles is a lunatik I never cood abide, and I felt it my dooty to wither him. Transfixin the venerable Sekretary with wun uv my most piercenist gazes, I remarked, — " Sir! in imitashen uv the man who inflicted yoo upon this country, wich wuz not the least uv his acts for wich the country cusses him, I propose relatin a little anecdote. Ther wuz wunst a man who wuz inebriatid; and that he

night present hisself in a state approximatin so-
riety to the pardner uv his buzzum, he wuz essayin
o vomit, tryin thus to ease his stumick uv the cause
uv the onpleasantnis therin; but he coodent do it.
He heaved and heaved, but there wuz no result.
At this critikle period another man approacht, who
remarked, kindly, that ef he desired to vomit, his
best holt wood be to run his finger down his throat.
The drunk individooal looked up indignant at this
unwarranted intèrference with his constooshnel rites.
Blast yoor eyes, sir,' sed he, ' are yoo or me bossin
his yer puke?'

" This, Sekretary Welles, is the anecdote. I
especk the posishun yoo hold, and dislike sayin
nythin disagreeable; but, sir, this *is* a puke, and
perpose to boss it myself."

I startid to-wunst, and found things in a highly
mixed condition. The followin is compiled from
my reports: In Noo York the Postmasters generally
re sound. The crops wer poor last year; and all
kinds uv biznis bein dull, the Postmasters are gen-
rally anxious to hold on. They are, therefore, out-
poken in their support uv the coz. Them ez wuz
men uv good standin and relijusly inklined, before
the rupcher between the President and the party
vich redoost him, say but very little in publick,

and that little they don't say very long. They generally can't see that ther is any partikeler differense
between the President's plan and the plan uv Congress, and ther bein so little, Congress ought to yeeld
for the sake uv peace. The Dimokrats, holdin sich
places, are loud enough in support uv the Administrashen; but, good Heaven! the endorsement uv
sich men is too heavy a load for any party to carry.
Now, that I think uv it, I hev at last solved the mys-
tery uv our wide-spread defeat last fall. In some
deestricks the Dimocrisy found Johnson too heavy
a load to carry, and in the balance the Johnson men
found the Dimokrisy too heavy a load to carry.

In Ohio, the first place I stopt at wuz Oberlin,
the place where the nigger college is located at. I
regret to say that the Postmaster at that pint is a
rantin Ablishnist; and in the two hours I wuz ther,
I coodent find a Conservative Republikin who wood
take it. I got one nearly perswadid; but jest ez he
wuz about to consent, his wife fell a weepin onto
his buzzum, and with tetchin pathos wantid to kno
ef he wuz willin, for sich small pay, to leave sich a
tarnisht name to the four children now born to em
and the wun wich wuz expectid? He repentid and
refoosed. I didn't investigate ez fully ez I might,
for ther ain't a drop uv likker sold ther; and ez my

flask give out, I felt that doo considerashen for my health woodent permit my stayin another hour. I recommend the abolishen uv the office, or the establishment uv a grosery, with a bar in the back room, ez a nukleus around wich the Dimocrisy kin rally.

The next place I cum to I found the Postmaster a suspishus caracter — very suspishus. Whenever he is drunk he speaks very highly uv the Sekretary uv State, but when sober he avoids politikle matters. I sejest a raise in the salary uv the offis, that he kin afford to keep drunk all the time.

At the next pint I interdoost myself ez a English nobleman in disguise, studyin Amerikin manners and customs, and menshund carelessly that I hed bin to Washinton, and hed bin presentid to the President and Sekretary uv State. The Postmaster wuz vizably affectid. Glancin furtively around to see that no one wuz lookin, he remarked in a low tone: "My deer sir, don't, I beg uv yoo, form yoor idea uv the public men uv Ameriky from them specimens. Don't, I beg. The first, sir, is a accident — sich a man cood never hev bin made on purpose. The second wuz suthin, in his earlier years; but now, sir, now — he's a degradid old man," and he busted into tears. " Bein determind to hold onto his place, he tried at fust to bring the President, by accident, up to his level; but that bein impossible, he deliberately let hisself down to the level uv the President, and the distance, sir, wuz so great, the Sekretary bein suthin, that the shock, sir, undoubtedly knockt his intelleck out uv him, for he ain't displayed any since. He literally fell among thieves. May the Lord forgive Willyum H. Seward for the shipwreck he made uv his reputashen, for — "

At this pint the poor man stopt. I happened to pull out my hankercher, and in doin so dropt upon the floor a piece uv paper, wich he seed. It read:

" Petroleum V. Nasby, Dr.

" To G. Bascom.
" To drinks doorin the month uv Janooary at 10
  cents per drink . . . . $30 00 "

He looked at my face, and seein that that bill reely b'longed to me, fell faintin onto the floor, shreekin, " I'm McCrackened."

I leave the case in the hands uv the Cabinet. It's aggravatin.

Another man openly defied me. He wantid me to take the offis off uv his hands. His children, he sed, wuz made mouths at and skoffed at, at skool, becoz ther father, wich hed bin a Republikin, held a Fedral offis, and his wife wuz defeeted for President uv the Sewin Sosiety, a posishen she hed alluz held, on the same akkount. He hed stood it long enuff. Ef he coodent git it off his hands, he'd commit sooicide, and by thus puttin hisself out uv the way make his abuzed family the only reparashen in his power. I sejest that he be removed. Sich talk may be safely set down ez incendiary.

Another hed the highest possible opinion uv the President, and worshipt the Secretary. He considered his plan uv reconstruction the best wich cood hev bin devised by mortal wisdom. He hed vainly striven to git a nominashen for an offis from the Republikin party for years, but failed, owin to a lack uv confidence. He wood have jined the Democracy; but ez they wuz hopelessly in the minority, it woodent hev helped him. He considered Johnson's idea uv fillin the offisis with Republikins bully, ther bein so few uv that persuasion who'd take em, and he didn't want any accessions to the party.

Ther wuz now jist enuff to hold the offisis in control uv the President, and them wuz all the offisis they cood git any how. I sejest that he be continyood. He isn't discreet; but we can't expect all the virchoos at so small a price. None uv us is perfeck — I spose I hev my failins.

I shell continyoo my investigashens, tho it is dredful tryin labor. Goin, ez I do, thro Abolition sections, I hev to carry my own whiskey ; and ez sad experience hez demonstrated, quart flasks won't do. Sometimes I hev to lay in one uv them towns for three hours. I respeckfully submit, that arrangements be made for the transportashen uv a keg uv sustenance to accompany me ; otherwise, I shel peremptorily resine. At my time uv life my regeler supplies is necessary.

PETROLEUM V. NASBY, P. M.
(Wich is Postmaster), and likewise Professor uv
Biblikle Politicks in the Southern Classikle
& Military Institoot.

x.

Mr. Nasby's Board commence the Compilation of a Series of School Books for the " Institoot," and the South generally, but are thwarted by the perverse Joe Bigler.

Post Offis, Confedrit X Roads
(Wich is in the Stait uv Kentucky),
Febrooary 20, 1867.

THE Institoot is, I may say, a success. Contribushens flow in slowly but shoorly, — fast enuff indeed to give each uv the Board a noo soot uv close ; and we, speshelly, who hev the fust handlin uv that money, sevral other comforts. But that corner-stun troubles us. Sum hundreds uv people saw that a bottle uv likker and a greenback wuz deposited under it, and regerly every nite it's bin overturned by persons in serch uv them relics. At great expense we built onto it a section uv wall ; but makin no account uv our expenditoor, they overturned it. We then histed a sign-board bearing this legend: " The whisky is gone, and the greenback also," signed by the Board; but one half uv the citizens uv that lokality don't read, and tother didn't hev the nessary confidence in the truthfulness uv the Board to prevent em from goin for the artikles, tho the very knowlege uv us wich brot about this state uv disbelief, shood, wun wood suppose, hev taught em that the greenback and likker coodent possibly be there after so long a period hed ensood. So, ez a last resort, we stuck two posts in the ground and drawd an iron chain over it. That got em. Force is about the only thing uv any account in this country.

The Board met last nite at the Post Offis, wich, ontil we git the Institoot built, will be the headquarters uv the Trustees, to consider the propriety uv publishin a series uv skool books, adaptid especially to the Southern intelleck, and calculated partikelarly to keep alive in the minds uv the buddin yooths uv the late Confederacy, wich is unfortunately deceest, a lively opinion uv themselves and a corresponding hatred uv Noo England and the North generally. We hev had serious doubts whether proper ideas cood be instilled into a yooth from a book written by a Boston man, and printed in Cincinnati, onto paper made in Noo York.

I submitted to the Board a example for a noo Arithmetic, to wit: —

" A Yankee sent a substitoot into the Federal army at a cost uv $1,000, passing off onto him two counterfeit ten dollar notes. To make up the expenditoor, he to-wunst swindles a innocent Kentuckian out uv $100 in a patent rite, a Alabamian out uv $200 in a western land trade, and the balance he makes up by sellin wooden nutmegs, wich he turns out uv basswood at a profit uv 4 cents per one. The grate moral question is, how many nutmegs must this ingenius but unprincipled cuss manufaktur, and how long does it take him, with the improoved machinery, they hev to do it?

" The Southern soljers, at the battle uv the first Bull Run, captured 18 Federals, one uv whom hed upon his person $12 in greenbax, and tothers $8 each. How many uv Johnson's Postmasters cood be bought with the proceeds uv the capcher? "

Deekin Pogram approved uv these examples; but he kept insistin that there wuzn't enuff in em to fire the Southern heart. The Southern heart wuz a perpetooal funeral pile wich needid continyooal firin. Onless fired it wuz a gloomy mass uv very onsightly black cinders. He proposed that the forthcoming book shood be coal oil on the slumberin embers uv the yoothful Southern heart. He hed a example :—

" The battle uv Chickamauga wuz fought a certain number uv miles from Chattanooga. One regiment uv Confedrit soljers druv a division uv Fedral mercenaries into the town. Allowin that each Fedral, ez well ez Confedrit, hed two legs, how many more steps did the Fedrals take to get em into Chattanooga, where they wuz comparatively safe from Confedrit rage and valor, and sich, than it did the Confedrits to drive em thar?"

Bascom remarkt that he hed one wich he felt it his dooty to perpose : —

" A strikly conscienshus grosery keeper starts in biznis worth four hundred dollars in clean cash. He pays for his whiskey two dollars per gallon in Looisville, and hez for a reglar customer a Postmaster, wich drinks forty or sixty times per day, and alluz tells him to ' jist chalk it down.' Required the length uv time nessary to bust him under them afflictin circumstances?"

Bascom remarkt that long before the book appears in print, he wood be able to furnish the anser to that little problem. Considerin the example a dig direct at me, I wuz uv a noshen to retort; but ther wuz sich a look uv injerd innosense onto Bascom's countenance that reely I coodent. Suthin must be done for Bascom, — I hev lived onter him too long. The next contribushen I reseeve from frends North shel be devoted to liquidating, in part, the debt I owe him. I cood bust him, by not givin him at least cost for his likker; but wat follows? There's the rub. Wood he who come after give me credit? Better bear the ills we hev than fly to them to wich we hevn't bin interdoost.

Joe Bigler, the drunken Confedrit soljer, happened in, and heard the last two examples, and remarkt that he cood furnish us any number uv examples at site. We never stop Joseph in anythin he perposes to do, for he hez a habit uv carryin a navy revolver slung to him, and he shoots. Joseph wuz, therfore, permitted to perceed.

" Ef a Southern man pants for his rites, and fites four years for em, gittin licked like the devil, how long after is it advisable for him to continyoo to pant, pervidid he didn't know at the beginnin wat his rites wuz?"

I vencherd to remark that a solution uv that problem wuz impossible, thar bein no pint to work a departure from, to wich Joseph remarkt that perhaps it wuz faulty in that partikeler; but he hed others: —

" Ef a Southern soljer kin whip five Northern soljers, why in bloody thunder, they hevin hed a suffishency uv opportoonities uv doin it, didn't the South gain her independence?

"Ef fitin four years, and loosin every doggoned cent's worth uv property a man hed wuz profitable biznis, how many struggles for independence wood a man uv modrit means be justified in goin thru with?

"Ef two gallons and a half uv Kentucky whisky kin be got from a bushel uv corn, how many Democratic voters, takin young men ez they run, kin be manufaktured from the produck uv an aker uv good land in a modrit year for corn?

"A high-toned shivelrous Virginian, twenty years ago, hed a female slave wich wuz ez black ez a crow, and worth only $800. Her progeny wuz only half ez black ez a crow, and her female grandchildren wuz suffishently bleached to sell in Noo Orleans for $2,500 per female offspring. Required, 1st. The length uv time nessary to pay off the Nashnel debt by this means. 2d. The number uv years nessary to bleach the cuss of color out uv the niggers uv the United States.

"Ef four old gray-headed jackasses, wich ought to know better, see fit to keep one sucker filled with whisky, how many suckers cood four iron-gray mules keep filled, they bein only half jackass?

"A. Johnson hed the idea uv carryin a certin number uv deestricks, by speekin in em with Seward,
all uv wich gave increased majorities agin him.
Required the number uv miles uv travel, and the
number uv repetitions uv the speech, to enable him
to carry out his policy?

" Ef two nips at Washinton wuz suffishent to perdoose the speech at the inaugerashen on the 4th uv
March, 1865, how many must have bin slung into
A. J. to perdoose the 22d uv Febrooary effort, and
how many must he hev taken between Washinton
and St. Louis?"

" These examples," sed Joseph, "I consider nessary for this book; and ef it is published without
em I shel take it ez a persnel affront, for which I
shel hold the Board persnelly responsible. The
Southern yooth must be properly instructed — my
orphans must hev proper notions instilled into em,
and these examples is necessary to that end. Let
this Board remember that, when this book is publisht, ef these examples is not in them, they hev me
to settle with."

And Joseph departed. We are in a quandary.
We dare not publish the book without his examples,
for he alluz keeps his word, and is a ugly cuss to
deal with; and uv course puttin em in coodent be

thought uv. We finally decided that Joseph must be got out uv the way ez soon ez possible, and therefore votid that Bascom give him unlimited credit at his bar for a week, chargin the same upon the account uv the Institoot. I know that a free run at his barrels would finish me or any one uv the Board in that time. Happy Bigler! He hez at least one satisfactry week afore him, — I cood almost wish the Board wood try it on me. It would be a short but glorious career.

PETROLEUM V. NASBY, P. M.

(Wich is Postmaster), and likewise Professor uv
Biblikle Politicks in the Southern Classikle &
Military Institoot.

XI.

Mr. Nasby desires Confirmation. — Is advised how to proceed by the President, but rejects the Proposition with Scorn.

Washington, D. C., March 20, 1867.

WASHINGTON agin! What changes hev been made in the last two years! Not in Washington, for this deliteful abode uv official purity hezn't changed a particle, nor never will. From the summit uv Willard's Hotel I kin see now, ez I did a year ago, the same signs uv "steamed oysters;" the Capitle, in front, towrin over the trees at the tother end uv the avenue, and behind, the Patent Offis and Post Offis buildings; the first the Mecca uv every Dimokrat and the tother uv every Yankee who comes here. No! Washington ain't changed, but I hev. Formerly, when I visited Washington, it wuz tite times with me. Willard's wuz my hotel then ez now. Chadwick, him uv the towerin hite, rotund abdomen, side whiskers, and round hat, wuz

then, ez now, my landlord. In them days, before
the happy return uv A. Johnson to reason put some
thousands uv Democrats, who hed more stumic than
money, and more appetite than small change, into
offis, and, per consekence, into condition to pay
their bills, I wuz a guest at this hotel; which is to
say, I slept on the steps uv the Capitol, and took,
or tried to take, my meals at Chadwick's bountiful
board. Ef I hed no currency, I hed taste; and ez
I wuz foragin for subsistence, I allus made it a pint
to forage on the richest paster fields. It's ez easy to
cheek a first class dinner ez it is a second class; and
besides, I felt that sich a hotel ez Willard's wuz
better able to stand sich boarders ez I wuz than them
of less patronage. I kept away from the tother
hotels out of sympathy for the proprietors. Never
shel I forget my last visit here. I hed run the dinin-
room guardian angel for a week, and wuz congratu-
latin myself on another week at least, when Chadwick stopped me hisself, and the follerin conversashen
ensood : —

"My friend," sed he, in winnin tones.

"Davis, Garret, is my name!" sez I, promptly.

"We hear enuff," sez he. "Listen! I've let you
run a week, coz it's my regler practis. Yoo hed a
hungry look, but by this time yoo ought to be filled

up and able to go at least a week without eatin. Ez yoo ain't uv no earthly yoose to any body, and make no pretensions to bein ornamental — Git!" and three well-directed kicks landid me onto the sidewalk.

But I hev forgiven him. He treats me well. He hes confidence in me now, ez I hev paid my board in advance. It's a rool he hez, he jocosely remarked, with men of my peculiar cast uv countenance, to hev em pay in advance. He says it's much the best way. After payin, sich men ez me feel more comfortable about the house, and so do the proprietors. It's me that is changed, — I hev money to pay my bills. Bless the Lord for Seward, Johnson, Randall, and other luxuries!

But pleasant ez it is to contrast my former posishen with my present proud one, I hev not time to dwell upon reminiscences. Life is short; I am a practical man, and tho it may be pleasant to linger for a moment onto memry's pleasant fields, I cannot. My biznis in Washington is precisely what every Democrat's biznis here is, to get confirmed. It ain't no trouble for a Kentucky Dimocrat to git appintid, for the President hez so far relaxed his rules in this pertikeler ez to appint them ez wuzn't never in the Confederit army; but to get confirmed is the pinch. There's the gauntlet uv a Ablishen Senit to run; and good Lord, wat a knowledge they hev uv the out-goins and in-comins of the appintees!

The President and Postmaster-General Randall wuz extremely anxious for my confirmashen, so much so, that they advised me to resort to the strategy now so common in the North.

"Go back on me for the time bein," sed that trooly great and good man who adorns the sofas in the Presidenshul Manshen. "Wilcox em. That's yoor only holt: Wilcox em. I advised him to do it, and see how it worked."

"My dear sir," sed I, carried away by this new and onexpected development uv greatness, "kin yoo bear to hev me who bears yoor banner in Kentucky bend the knee to a ablishen Senit, and repoodiate yoo, even for a hour? It is safe in my case, for my nateral affinities are with yoo, but don't, I beg uv yoo, advise all uv em to do so. My deer sir, two thirds uv em will go out for confirmashen, and, ef successful, will forgit to return."

But the great and good Johnson wood take no denials. "Draw up," sed he, "a letter to a conservative member uv Congress, explainin your connection with me, and —"

And overkum with emoshen, he burst into tears.

Sadly I undertook the task, and after four hours uv intense labor, the following wuz completed: —

"Hon. ——, House uv Reps.

"My dear Sir: My confirmashen by the Senit uv the Yooiited States to the posishen uv Postmaster at the Confederit X Roads, wich is in the State uv Kentucky, being somewhat jeopardized by my operashuns in the politikle field doorin the past two years, I hev the honor to explane that, notwithstandin the fact that I wuz a original Demokrat, early in the war I took up arms for the preservashen uv our beloved Yoonion. The precise date I cannot give, owin to the demoralized condishen uv my mind at the time; but that yoo kan assertane for yoorselves. It wuz about two weeks after the fust draft. That I laid down arms agin ez soon ez the regiment struck Southern sile will not, when the motives wich actooated me are known, be allowed to weigh agin me. It hez bin said I deserted to the enemy, — so it wuz sed uv John Champe, but history subsekently vindicated him; he went to ketch Arnold. I will not stop to reply to my defamers; but ef it comes out finally that I went for the purpose uv satisfyin rebels by okular demonstrashun that they hed nothin to hope for from the Northern Democrats, uv whom

I wuz a average specimen, what kin my enemies say then?

"I do not deny that I wuz a ardent supporter uv President Johnson from the beginning uv his career. I wuz filled with a drafted man's magninimity toward a conkered foe, and up to the very day I reseeved my commishen I favored consilatory measures. I accompanied him on his — I will not say disgraceful, for he is my sooperior officer — tour thru the Northern States, and slung my hat higher nor anybody else's at his — I will not say drunken, for reasons above mentioned — speeches, and aboozed the highly intelligent populaces at Cleveland, Injeanapolis, Springfield, and other pints, in a manner wich, now that I think uv it, wuz trooly shameful. Also, I organized the Postmasters uv various Northern States into a Johnson party, and vigorously supported members uv Congress pledged to the policy uv wich I wuz, at the time, a deceeved supporter. About this time I wuz appointed Postmaster; and, findin I needed confirmashen, my views undergoed a radical change. Time and observashen hev taught me that instid of consiliashen, coershen is our best holt; and that now military measures are necessary in the South ontil them rebellyus people completely acquiesce in terms imposed by Congris for restorashen. My views on this interestin topic is best defined by the recent speeches uv Hon. Charles Sumner, the eminent and trooly great Senator from the enlitened State uv Massachusetts, and also by the recent utterances uv them lovable Representatives, Hon. Thadeus Stevens, of Pennsylvania, Hon. & Gen. Benj. F. Butler, uv Massachoosetts, and Hon. James M. Ashley, uv Ohio, in all uv whose sentiments, sich as they hev now, and also them ez they hev alluz hed, as well ez them which they may hereafter hev, I most heartily and entirely concur.

" With this explanation, wich I hope will prove entirely satisfactory, and with the addishnel asshoorence that I am now a very warm supporter of the Congressional policy, and that when I look back and see what I hev bin a doin for the past two years, I so loathe myself that I kin hardly be restrained from sooisidin, may I ask you to personally urge my confirmation in the Senit?

" Trooly and Respectfully Yours,

" PETROLEUM V. NASBY."

I read this epistle to A. Johnson, who wuz pleased to approve it, and also to Randall, who wuz delited with it, and to Welles, who, after forcing me to read it twice over, wantid to know if it had anything to do with the Navy Department, and then returned to the President with my mind fully made up that *I never would send that document.*

"Wat?" sed he, startin back astonished, "not send it?"

"Never!" sed I. "Never! Sich things may do for Postmasters and Assessors wich you took from the Republican ranks, but not for me. I hev done many things wich perhaps woodn't hold out sixty pounds to the bushel — I voted for Peerce and likewise for Bookannon, and supported em in all their various dooins, besides other things too tejus to menshun; but my sensitive soul recoils at this, — my proud stumick revolts. I leave it for yoor Custers and Wilcoxes and sich, — no Kentucky Dimokrat kin. Let them refooze to confirm me at their peril. I am the only Dimocrat in ten miles who kin write, and they dare not, by turning me out, deprive Kentucky, wich never seceded, uv mail facilities."

"Brave man!" exclaimed Johnson, in a husky voice, and his eyes suffused with tears, fallin onto my neck and weepin profoosely down my back, "let em reject yoo. Ef they do, I pledge yoo my word, and will give yoo sekoority now if yoo desire it, that yoo shell hev a partnership with Mrs. Cobb, or Mrs. Perry, wich is worth a score uv post offices."

I hev allus noticed that virchoo is its own reward. By bein troo, wot a feeld is now open to me. Let the Senit do its worst.

PETROLEUM V. NASBY, P. M.

(Wich is Postmaster), and likewise Professor uv Biblikle Politics in the Suthern Classikle & Military Institoot.

7

XII.

Mr. Nasby takes a Retrospective View. — He considers the Situation, and is not satisfied with it.

POST OFFIS, CONFEDRIT X ROADS
(Wich is in the Stait uv Kentucky),
March 25, 1867.

BACKERD, turn backerd, O Time in yoor flite," is the fust line uv a song wich I heerd not long since. Wood that Time cood perform that back ackshen feat, and get us all back wher we wuz six years ago. But Time can't. Time is a perpetooal moshen, wich must go on, and on, and wich can't never retrace her steps.

The situashen ain't pertickelerly agreeable jist now. It hezn't a joocy look, nor does it promise an improvement in the future. The confidence uv the Dimocrisy uv Kentucky is shaken to the extent that it's lost its equilibrium and totters to its centre. When it falls, I shel be found under the rooins.

The passage of the Military Law may be sed to be the last feather wich reely ought to break the Kentucky camel's back. It's the deepest and finishnest stab at constooshnel liberty and ekal rites, inezmuch ez it not only blasts forever the hopes uv re-establishin slavery, but gives the nigger all the rites and privileges enjoyed by white men. We, who are chiefly interested, are not to be consulted in the matter. Fedral hirelins, whose very presence is pizen to the people uv these States, are to be quartered onto us to see that " justis " — wat holler mockry ! — is done to em. The governments established by Androo Johnson is overturned ef they don't play the fiddle to military satraps, and accept the Constooshnel Amendment, wich perhibits them who wuz our champions in the late effort to destroy a government wich we hatid, from takin hold uv it agin and runnin it. Wuz ther ever sich a mixter uv injustis and perscripshen? Wuz ther ever sich severity? Wuz ther ever sich a lack uv magnanimity? And all this time where is Johnson? He vetoed these bills, — but wherefore? He knowd that the Rump Congress hed a majority uv two thirds, and cood pass em over his veto ; why, then, when they set his authority at defiance, didn't he rise in his might and disperse em? Where, too, wuz the

Dimocrisy uv the North? Where are they in this crisis, when our dearest rites — their greatest care — is bein shiprecked on the iron-bound rocks uv despotism? Where are they, I say? Why don't they rally, ez they threatened, and demand that Johnson shel hurl them levelers from their usurped seats, and restore peace, on sich terms ez we shall consider ekitable, to this wunst happy, but now distracted, country. Alas! they hevn't time. I see them who breathed so much vengence and slawtrins afore Johnson hed offices to dispose uv, a neglectin us, and a runnin about gittin signatoors to applicashens for Post Offises, and hollerin to us ez they ketch their breath, "Accept the condishens — git back into the Yoonion, that we may elect the President in 1868, who'll give us all the patronage!" Their noose-papers all shreek, "Accept, and get back into the Yoonion, that we may elect the next President, who'll give us all the patronage!" And that ain't the worst uv it. Them wich we bought up with appint-ments diskivered on a sudden that a Abolition Senit hed to confirm em, and to sekoor that they hev gone back onto us. Custer is a shinin example, Wilcox is another, and I mite menshun hundreds uv others who hev slid back in the same manner.

Troy wuz taken by the strategy uv the Greeks,

who exposed a wooden horse, in the bowels uv wich wuz conceeled armed men, wich the verdant Troys pulled inside their gates. Androo Johnson wuz the wooden horse wich wuz sent into our camp by the Ablishnists, and the offices wuz the armed men in his bowels. They hev bin our rooin. So long ez they wuz in the dim distance, the Democracy wuz hungry and feroshus, and capable uv almost anythin — so soon ez they got em, they become quiet ez lambs. The Postmaster who holds a commishn sez to himself, " Wherefore shel I bust the Government under wich I hev a place? Kin I git another under the new one?" and he yells to us, " Accept the terms!" We capchered the camp uv the enemy, but are demoralized by the plunder we found. It's the old trick, over agin, these offices, which the white men yoost to play onto the Injins, to wit: — evacuatin a posishen and leavin a barrel uv whiskey behind, knowin that the Injin's instincts, like them uv a Kentucky Dimokrat's, wood lead him to git blind drunk, and make him a easy prey to the skelpin knife. The offisis wuz the whiskey wich intoxicated our braves; and our skelps, so to speek, hang at the belts uv our enemies. Sumner hez many, Thad Stevens hez many, and Butler is a gatherin uv em with a rapidity wonderful to behold.

But wat marks the demoralizashen uv the Dimocrisy the most, is the follerin extract wich I cut from the Noo York World, wunst our trusted orgin. I hev not the heart to re-write it. I paste the slip onto the paper; hence I am not responsible for sich errors uv orthografy and grammer ez may be discovered into it. Here it is:—

"As regards the popular notion of the odor of the negro, it may be positively stated that he, in this respect, is like the white,—a clean negro bein free from it, and a foul one cursed by it."

Ef this be troo — ef the nigger don't stink, then Noah got tite, and Ham wuz cust in vane — then Paul sent back Onesimus for nothin, and Hager is uv no more interest to the Dimocrisy than any other female who hez bin ded several thousand years. The Dimocratic party wuz built upon this stink; and ef that corner-stun is knocked out, the temple falls, and buries all beneath its rooins who are sheltered under it, uv whom I am the cheefest and the loveliest among ten thousand.

At one fell swoop the wind is knockt out uv the sales uv the Northern Dimocrisy. Wat is the nigger now to them ef he does not stink? " Popler noshen," indeed! Trooly it wuz a popler noshen. That stink led hundreds uv thousands uv Democrats by the nose. That "odor"—ez the writer styles it—wuz our best holt, and wun wich wuz everything to us. That stink wuz all that elevated the Demokrat over the nigger—that wuz our mark of sooperiority. *We*, at times, wuz not uv the precise odor uv Nite-bloomin serious. A Democratic mass convenshen, when in a tite room, with two stoves in it, wuz not the most odorous gatherin in the world; but we thanked God continyooally that the smell wich ariz ez the room got hot wuz not the pecooliar aroma uv the nigger, and we wuz comforted. But this writer redooses the whole thing—the whole difference between the nigger and a Democrat—to a matter of color and cleanliness. Wat heresy! Wat iconaclasm! (this last word meanin, I believe, idol breakin, or suthin uv that sort.) *Ef this be troo, then in the nite time, a nigger with his feet washed is better than a Demokrat!* For one, now I care not ef Dr. Cummins' "Last Warnin Cry" be trooly the last. I'm sorry that he rented his house for ninety-nine years, ez it hez a tendency to destroy my faith in his beleef that the world is about peggin out. The sooner Gabrel blows his horn the better I shel be sooted.

Here agin this matter uv state offisis comes in. The Dimocrisy uv Noo York see that nigger suffrage

is inevitable, and to sekoor their share uv it, they're
biddin in time; forgettin that while they're acheevin
a temporary success on that side uv the cirkle we're
losing all control uv the niggers on this. Wat did
the South ever care for Dimokratic successes, 'ceptin
ez it bolstered up their niggers?

I'm discouraged. I see afore me trouble. I see
but one or two streeks uv lite on my horizon. Ohio
won't let her niggers vote no how, and sum other
States are in the same fix, and possibly this ackshen
may be the sign uv returnin reason. Ohio may, after
all, be the rock agin wich the waves uv fanatakism
may beet in vane, and conservatism, gatherin strength
there, may finally assert itself elsewhere. May the
Lord send it, for ef this thing goes on, I'm a lost
and rooined man.

PETROLEUM V. NASBY, P. M.
(Wich is Postmaster), and likewise Professor uv
Biblikle Politicks in the Southern Classikle &
Military Institoot.

XIII.

The Negro Vote. — Mr. Nasby, in imitation of Wade Hampton, tries to conciliate the African. — The Result of the Venture.

POST OFFIS, CONFEDRIT X ROADS
(Wich is in the Stait uv Kentucky),
·March 28, 1867.

I HEV made many sudden and rather 'strordinary changes in politix — some so very sudden that the movement perdoost conjestion uv the conshence. I rekollect wunst uv advokatin free trade and high protective tariff, all within twelve hours (I made a speech in a agricultooral deestrik uv Noo York in the forenoon, at 10 A. M., and in a manufacturin town in Pennsylvany in the evenin, our platform bein so construktid that both sides cood find a endorsement in it), and hev performed many other feats uv moral gymnastiks ; but this last change I hev bin called upon to make is probably the suddenest. Last week Toosday, Deekin Pogram, Captain McPelter, and I, wuz engaged in riddin the Corners uv niggers. We hed endoord em ez long ez we thot possible, and determined on standin it no longer. Selectin three, wich we wuz satisfied hed too much spellin-book into em to be enslaved agin, we wuz preparin notises to be served onto em, orderin em to leave in twenty-four hours, when I reseeved in the northern mail a letter marked "Free — Alex. W. Randell, P. M. G." I knowd it wuz offishel to-wunst — that blessid signatoor is on my commisshun, and I've contemplatid it too often to be mistaken in it. Its contents wuz brief, and run thus : —

" To all Postmasters in the Southern States : The niggers hev votes — consiliashen is our best holt. See to it."

This breef, tho not hard to be understood order, wuz sealed with the offishel seal uv the Post Offis Department, stampt into putty instid uv wax, to wit: a loaf of bread, under a roll uv butter, with ten hands a grabbin at it. I comprehended the situation at site, and set about doin my dooty with both Roman and Spartan firmness. "Deekin," sez I, tearin up the notises, " these niggers we hev misunderstood. They are not a inferior race — they are not descendants uv Ham and Hager — it wuzn't

Paul's idea in sendin back Onesimus to condemn him to servitood — we hev misunderstood the situation, and must make amends. The nigger is devoid uv smell, and is trooly a man and a brother!"

"Wat?" said the Deekin, tippin back in amazement.

"Jest wat I say," sez I. "Read that," and I flung him the letter.

The upshot uv the conference wich follered wuz the callin uv a meetin the next nite, at wich all the Ethiopians uv the Corners wuz invited and urged to be present.

The trouble wuz to git the niggers to attend the meetin. The fust one I spoke to lafft in my face, and askt me how long it wuz sence I hed helpt hang a couple uv niggers, by way uv finishin off a celebrashen. Pollock, the Illinois storekeeper, got hold uv it, and told Joe Bigler, and Joe swore that ef the niggers hedn't any more sense than we give em credit for, in sposin we cood bamboozle em so cheep, he shood go back to the old beleef, to wit: that they wuz only a sooperior race uv monkeys, after all; and by nite every nigger in the visinity wuz postid thoroughly, and out uv all uv em I cood only git four who would promise to attend, and them the Deekin hed to pay $2 apiece to. To give it eclaw I promised one uv em $5 (to be paid at the close uv the meetin) to sit on the stand with me, wich, bein a very poor man, and hevin a sick wife in a shanty near by, who wuz suffering for medicine (wich he coodent git without money), he accepted.

At this pint an idee struck me. I remembered Philadelfy, and determined to hev a scene rivalin the Couch and Orr biznis. "Another thing, Cuff. Understand that it's a part uv the bargain that when in my speech I turn to yoo and stomp, yoo must rise and embrace me."

"Wat?" sez he.

"Fall into my arms, lovin-like — you understand —jist as tho we wuz long-lost brothers!"

"Scuse me!" sed he. "I'se a mity low nigger, and wants to buy de old woman some quinine, and wood do most anything foah dat; but, golly, dat's too much!"

"Not a cent," sed I, sternly, assoomin my most piercinest gaze; "onless this is included!"

"Well," returned he, sulkily, "ef I must, I speck I must; but, golly —"

The nite arrived, and the meetin-house wuz full. We thot fust uv holding it in the chapel uv the College, but give up the idea ez impracticable, ez, owin to the dillytorinis uv our Northern friends in forwardin sich subscripshens ez they hev raised, we hevent got no furthei with the bildin than layin the corner-stun. In the front wuz the four niggers, all in clean shirts, and on the stand wuz the nigger I hed engaged. Over the platform, wuz the follerin mottoes : —

" In Yoonion ther is strength — For President in 1868, Fernando Wood. For Vice President, Frederick Duglis."

" In the nigger, strength — In the Caucashen, beauty — In the mulatter, who is trooly the noblest uv the human species — both."

In addishen to these, we dug up all the old mottoes wich Jefferson writ, about yooniversal liberty and sich, wich hedn't bin quoted in Kentucky for twenty years, and postid em up; in brief, hed Wendell Phillips' blessed sperit bin a hoverin over that meetin-house, it wood hev smiled approvinly.

I spoke to em elokently on the yooniversal brotherhood uv mankind, holdin that whatever else cood be sed, Adam wuz the father uv all mankind, and that the only diffrence between a white man and a nigger wuz, the nigger wuz sun-burnt. The nigger, I remarkt, wuz, ondoubtedly, origenally white; but hevin bin, sence his arrival in this country, addicted to agricultooral persoots, he hed become tanned to a degree wich, tho it marred his physikle beauty, did not interfere with his sterlin goodnis uv heart Ther hed bin diffrences between the races — at times ther hed bin onpleasantnises wich no one regretted more than I. The whites uv the Corners hed not alluz bin ez considrit ez I cood hev wished. They hed flogd sevral uv em, and hung many more, and in times past hed held em in slavery and sich; but that shood not be thot uv at this happy time. It wuz constooshnel to do these things then, and Kentucky wuz eminently a law-abidin State. "Here," sez I, "on this platform, with the flag uv our common country over me, I declare eternal friendship to the colored man, and to seel the declarashen I thus embrace — "

The obstinit nigger didn't stir a step.

"Come up and fling yoor arms around me, you black cuss," sed I, in a stage whisper. "Come up!"

"No yoo don't, boss!" sed the nigger, in a loud voice, wich was audible all over the church, and holdin out his hand. "I can't trust yoo a bressid minit. Gib me de $5 fust. Yoo owe dis chile foah dollars now fo' sawin wood fo' yoah post offis, and ef we's a gwine to hab our rites de fus yoose I shel

IN YOON ON THER IS STL
PRESIDENT
1868
FERNANDO WOOD
FOR VICE PRESIDENT
CK DUGLIS

put mine to be will be gittin dat money. Pay up fus, and de 'brace afterward. I can't do sich a disagreeable ting widout de cash in advance."

This ruther destroyed the effect. The unities wuzn't preserved. The niggers in front bust out in a torturing laff, and Pollock and Bigler rolld in convulsions uv lafture, in wich half uv our people joined. Me a standin petrified, in the attitood of embracin, and that cussed nigger standin with his hand extended for the money, with the Deekin and Bascom horror-struck jist behind, formed a tabloo wich wuz more strikin than pleasant.

The meetin wuz to-wunst adjourned, for it wuz evident to the dullest comprehenshen that nothin more coodent be done that nite. Ez yoosual I failed for want uv capital. Hed I bin possesst uv the paltry sum uv five dollars, how diffrent wood hev bin the result! Perchance we may, thro that defishency, lose Kentucky. It must never occur agin — my salery must be raisd. I can't make brix without straw.

Joe Bigler met me next mornin and remarkt that he regrettid the occurrence, ez he ardently desired to see the two races a pullin together. " The fault, Perfessor," sed he, " wuz in not managin properly. The next time yoo want a 'spectable nigger to sit

on the platform with yoo and the Deekin, or kiss
or embrace yoo — git him drunk. He'll do it then,
probably — I know he will. Ef he's drunk enuff,
he'll hurrah for Johnson, and it's possible to git em
down to the pint uv votin with yoo. Lord! how
whiskey drags a man down. See wat it's brot yoo
to!" and the insultin wretch rolled off, laffin bois-
terously. "Git em drunk, Perfesser!" he yelled ez
long ez he cood see me.

We don't intend to give it up. Bigler's advice
wuz given in jest; but, nevertheless, I shel act upon
it. Whiskey is wat brings white men to us; and
ef a white man kin be thus capchered, why not a
nigger? The Afrikin hezn't got ez far to fall to git
down to our level, and it'll take less to bring him.
Bascom ordered five barrels to-day, wich I spose the
Administrashen will pay for. We hev yet the Noo
York Custom House, and more uv the perkesits
must be yoosed for politikle purposes.

PETROLEUM V. NASBY, P. M.
(Wich is Postmaster), and likewise Professor uv
Biblikle Politicks in the Southern Classikle &
Military Institoot.

XIV.

The Connecticut Election. — The Effect it produced at the Corners, and likewise at Washington. — A Proposition to remove the College rejected.

WASHINGTON, April 7, 1867.

THE news uv the election in Connecticut created the most profound sensashen at the Corners. It cum to us so onexpected, so like a clap uv thunder from a clear sky, or ruther so like a gleam uv sunlite thro a mass uv overpowrin black clouds, so like the first streak uv sunlite in the mornin after a long nite uv cholera morbus with no brandy in the house, that we wuz overpowered with it. The Corners hevn't experienct sich a satisfactory spasm uv joy sence the receet uv the news uv the Fort Piller affair. It perdoost a very singler effect on Deekin Pogram. When I cum up to him with the news, he wuz engaged with all the elokence he possest a trying to convince a nigger, wich formerly belonged to him, that, after all, the Southerners themselves wuz the only ones wich the niggers cood trust; and that when the time cum for em to exer cise the 'lective franchise, ef they hed any regard for their own interests they wood turn their backs on the Ablishinists, who wuz, to a man, hory headed deceevers, and trust them and them only who knowd em.

"Samyooel," sed the Deekin, in a affecshunit tone, with one hand on the nigger's shoulder, "why shoodent we love yoo? Yoo are bone uv our bone, and flesh uv our flesh — we are uv one blood — " (this remark the Deekin got into a habit some years ago uv gittin off when speekin uv the Dimocrisy North, and alluz uses it. It is ruther effective, tho in this instance, ef I hed bin in his place, I shoodent hev slung it out, owin to the pecooliar con- struckshen wich mite be put onto it) — "and our interests is one, Samyooel."

"Deekin," sez I, interruptin him. "Deekin! Connecticut hez spoken in thunder tones, and hez gone Dimocratic!" —

"Wat!" sez he, "Dimocratic!"

"Verily," sez I. "A Governer, and three Con- gressmen out of four."

Ther wuz a sudden rupcher uv the friendly rela- shens existin between the Deekin and Samyooel the dark complexioned. If he wuz uv the Deekin's flesh, the Deekin wuz in favor of mortifyin it; for never wuz flesh so belabored ez wuz that unfortunit chattel's. The flesh wuz imejitly lasserated. He pitched into him feroshus; and after pummelin the astonished Aferkin, who didn't see why the result of a eleckshun shood work sich a change, till he wuz out uv breath, he condenst wat strength wuz remainin into one vigrous kick, exclaimin —

" Take that, yoo black swindler. I've talked sweet to yoo under false pretenses. I've bin betrayed into wastin soft sawder onto a nigger — into coaxin wher I hev a ondeniable rite to command — into — "

" Wat does all dis mean ? " sed the nigger, faintly.

" Mean ! " sed I to him; " my frend, this is the reaction we've heard so much about — it 's arriv. It means that there is a exceedinly good chance uv yoor bein redoost agin to yoor normal speer; uv yoor comin down from the high hoss yoove bin a ridin, and uv bein agin a servant unto yoor brethren. It means that Connecticut hez spoken, and that yoor a good deal more valyooable to us now than yoo wuz a hour ago. Go, my friend, and buy salve for yoor brooses; for unless yoor heeld yoor valyoo will be less in the markit. Yoo'd be ashamed to sell for a low price — woodent yoo?"

I left the Dimocrisy jubilatin and come on to Washinton, feelin that I must go where I cood find kindred soles. The nite I arrived there wuz high carnival at the White House. The President wuz in tall feather. Ther wuz Connecticut visible all over him. He hed a wooden nutmeg for a buzzum pin — a minatoor bass-wood ham hung from his watch fob, and in honor uv the occashun they wuz drinkin punches made of Noo England rum, with small slices uv Wetherfield onyuns in em insted uv lemons. Randall sprung toward me ez I entered the room, and clasped me by one hand, the President by tother, and we then — not altogether onlike the three graces — embraced. They hed the advantage uv me, ez they hed one odor — the onion — wich I hedent, but I stood it. Why not, when that odor wuz from the breaths of those hevin the apintin power? I wood hev stood it hed they bin eatin assafœtida.

At this juncter Sekretary Welles come in.

"Ha!" said he, "why this unwonted hilarity! why this joy wher greef generally holds her court!"

"The Conneticut elecshun," said Seward.

"O, to be sure," sed the venerable old man,

vacantly; " I remember. Hawley, wuz it, or some other man who wuz elected over — over — wat wuz his name? — our candidate? "

" That wuz last yeer! " sed Seward, angrily.

" Well, perhaps it wuz. When did that State vote agin? " asked he, innocently, to wich no anser wuz given. But very little attention is paid to Sekretary Welles by any one 'ceptin Seward, and the fact that he occasionally undertakes to keep him postid in current events is ginerally taken ez evidence that he's breakin up. Poor William, it's evident that he's passin into his dotage.

Ther wuz a pleasant gatherin. Cowan wuz ther, and Saulsbury, and Garret Davis, and Doolittle, and Seymour, and Brooks, and more congratulatory letters wuz read than wood fill a page of the Noo York Herald. John C. Breckinridge hoped this auspicious event wuz the beginnin uv good feelin, presagin, ez he trusted it did, the evenchooel triumph uv them wich he hed alluz bin proud to call his friends. Mayor Monroe, uv Noo Orleens, hoped that, after this evidence uv returnin reason, President Johnson wood not hesitate to remove that second Butler, Gen. Sheridan, who wuz ojius to every friend the President had in the city uv wich he wuz lately Mayor. Gen. Wise sent his congratulashens; but ez they okkepied thirty-eight pages uv legal cap paper, closely written, they wuzn't read. Mosby sent a allegoricle pipe made uv a corn cob, onto wich wuz carved a symbolicle nigger, with the American eagle, a clawin vishusly into his wool, with his congratulations; and Fernando Wood, and Jesse D. Brite, and Dan Voorhees, sent theirn, and Vallandigham wanted to know now whether or not the President wuz a goin to accept the situ-ashen, and take the Dimocratic party to his buzzum? Ef so, he hed a list of apintments for Southern Ohio, wich he wished made. At this pint the question arose whether or not I hed not better move n y Classicle and Military Institoot to Connecticut? I am a practicle man, and I to-wunst asked, ez pertinent to the question, whether or not ther wuz a distillery in Connecticut; and sekond, whether or not ther wuz a vacant post offis within four miles uv it.

Sekretary Randall replied. He woodent hold out indoosements that he coodent fulfill. He wuz honest. Honesty wuz his best holt — simple, child-like strate-forwardniss in his deelins in politix wuz his cheef failin, and had well nigh been his rooin. The first query was easy to anser — the eleckshun returns wood indicate to any man uv ordinary intellek that ther wuz distilleries either in Connecticut or very handy to the State; but ther wuz no Post Offisis to spare. To carry the State every wun of em had bin solemnly promised.

The President remarkt that he reely shoodent think that triflin circumstance wood interfere with givin uv em to other men.

At this pint I broke in. I told em firmly that onless I cood hev a better post offis than the wun I hed, I woodent go. I cood go and cood move wat there is of the College bildins. It woodent cost much to pay freight on that corner-stun. I spose a better one cood be got in Connecticut at less than the cost uv transportin it, but wherever that Dimocratic College is built that must be the corner-stun uv it. That stun is hallowed. Ther are tender assosiashens hangin round it. It wuz the corner-stone uv a nigger school-house wich we burnt to the ground the nite we heard uv the veto uv the Civil Rites Bill. But I won't go to Connecticut onless my subsistence is asshoored. Ther is more money ther than in Kentucky; but I doubt whether they wood support me ez well. I speek frankly. I kin understand why a man kin be a Dimocrat in Kentucky — he's interested in niggers. I kin appreciate the Dimocrisy uv Suthern Injeany, Illinois, and Ohio, coz they come from that region, and the sekond generashun ain't got to be voters. I kin understand the Dimocrisy in Heenan's and Fernando Wood's deestricks, but pardon me — I want to keep very clear uv Connecticut Democrats. A people anywhere in Noo England wich kin deliberitly ally theirselves to us is just the kind uv people I don't want to be among. I instinctively mistrust a Yankee who hez dickered away his intrest in Bunker Hill. I hev notist that a Noo Englander wich come South and married an old maid, or a widder with a plantation, wuz never to be trustid; and it's my experience that a demoralized Yankee — one who hez shed his early trainin, and took up anybody else's moral close — is about the meanest specimen uv a white man on the face uv the green earth. He hez the acootnis wich is born uv a barren soil, without the Puritanism to keep it within bounds; he possesses the ability to make a livin on his native rox, but his laziness impels him to a easier subsistence in milder climes; and instid uv fishin for mackrel he goes South and fishes for men. A Noo Englander, unrestrained by grace, is pizen, and I bleeve Connecticut is full uv em. I hev heerd Massachoosits religion aboozed, but its suthin we may well be thankful for. I hev alluz bin thankful that the Mayflower brot over religion ez well ez brains and will.

Among the Connecticut Democrisy I shood stand no show; and, beside, I hev too much self-respeck to 'soshiate with em on terms uv equality. Instid uv foragin on them, they'd manage to live on me. I hev lambs to shear in Kentucky, and I don't care about changin em. I don't want to throw any cold water onto this festive occasion, it being a element we all despise; but, hev we any asshoorence uv her continyooin troo? Ef I understand it, we won by means uv patronage, and running a War Democrat — a bein I, in common with all the troo Democricy, despise. We can't do it agin. The next blast that sweeps from the North will bring to our ears a story uv another kind. One swaller don't make a spring. I hev knowd uv calves being born with two heads. This eléction, I fear me, is one uv these monstrosities wich Nacher sometimes perdooses to show what she is capable uv. It ain't normal. I hev no objeckshun to yoor feelin good over it — it rejoict me, coz it'll give our friends South courage, and may skeer the Radicals into givin us better terms, but —

My remarks wuz interrupted by Saulsbury, who hed bin sureptitiously drinkin punch with the ladle,

and the odor uv the onions overcomin him he rolled
under the table, and very shortly thereafter the
meetin broke up. I leave for home to-morrer, or
ez soon ez I kin draw my mileage.

PETROLEUM V. NASBY, P. M.
(Wich is Postmaster), and likewise Professor uv
Biblikle Politicks in the Southern Classikle &
Military Institoot.

XV.

The Russian Purchase. — How it was done. — Mr. Nasby really the Originator of the Speculation.

WASHINGTON, April 14, 1867.

IT'S done ! Seward did it — him and me ! The American Eagle hez coz now to screem with redoubled energy. Ef the Nashnel bird wuz a angel, I shood remark to it, " Toon yoor harp anoo ; " but it ain't, and therefore sich a rekest wood be ridiculous. This rapsody hez refrence to the Rooshen purchis.

The idea originatid in these massive intelleck. When I wuz here afore, the Blairs, all uv em, wuz a crowdin the sainted Johnson for a mishun. Cowan wantid a mishun, and so did Doolittle ; and that day pretty much all uv the delegates to the Cleveland and Philadelphy Convenshens had bin there, wantin some kind uv a place ; wat, they wuzn't pertikeler. One gentleman, whose nose (wich trooly blossomed ez the lobster) betokened long service in the party, urged that he hed bin a delegate to both Convenshens. "Thank God!" sed Johnson. "Wood that both them Convenshens hed bin made up uv the same men. I wood then hev bin bored for places only half ez much ez I am."

I wuz a helpin him out in my weak way. When the crowd wantin places become too great for human endoorance, I wood say, in a modrit tone, "Let's go out and git suthin;" and to-wunst fully half wood exclaim, "Thank yoo, I don't keer ef I do!" It wuz a great relief to Johnson, but wuz pizen on me. With the most uv em, the anguish, anxiety, and solissitood in the gittin uv offises and free drinks wuz about an ekal thing. The offisis they wantid wuz merely the means to that pertikeler end; and so long ez they wuz gittin the latter without the trouble uv the former, they wuz content. A good constooshen and a copper-lined stumick carried me thro this tryin ordeel, until I came across a Boston applicant, who, in consekence uv the perhibitory law, hed bin for some time on short rashens, and wuz keen set. Napoleon hed then met his Wellington, and I succumd. The man's talent wuz wonderful.

Sekretary Seward wuz in trouble about the Blair family pertikerly. He hed did his level best for em. He hed appinted em to Collekterships and furrin mishuns; but the crooel Senit, wich hed no respeck for us, took delite in fastening uv em onto us by perpetooally rejectin em. Jest after a long siege by Montgomery and the old man, I sejestid the purchis uv the Rooshen Territory, to wich not only they cood be sent, but a thousand uv others wich we hed on our hands; and the Sekretary wuz so pleased at the idea that he wept like a child. With a vigor wonderful in one so old, he set about gittin testimonials ez to the valyoo uv the territory, to inflooence the Senit in ratifyin the treaty he was agoin to make. And he wrote to a naval officer about it, who answered more promptly than I ever knowd a naval offiser to do, ez follows: —

" It's trooly a splendid country! The trade in the skins uv white bears kin be, ef properly developed, made enormous. There is seals there, and walruses so tame that they come up uv their own akkord to be ketched.

" P. S. — In case the purchis shood be made, a naval stashen will be necessary. May I hope that my long services on the Floridy Coast would prove suffishent recommendashen for the command uv the depot? May I?

"I hev the honor to be," &c.

A distinguished Perfessor wrote:—

"The climate is about the style uv that they hev in Washinton. The Gulf Stream sweeps up the coast, causing a decided twist in the isothermal line, wich hez the effeck uv making it ruther sultry than otherwise. Anywheres for six hundred miles back uv the coast strawberries grow in the open air. I recommend strongly the purchis.

"P. S.—In case the purchis is made, a explorin expedishen will be necessary. May I hope that my scientiffik attainments are suffishently well known to yoo to recommend me as a proper person to head the expedishen? May I?

"I hev the honor to be," et settry.

The President wuzn't favorably inclined. He wuz full uv the old fogy idea that it wuz rather chilly there than otherwise. He hedn't faith in the Isothermal Line, and wuz skepticle about the Gulf Stream. It wuz his experience that the further North yoo got the colder it wuz. For instance, he remarkt, that while the people wuz warm toward him in Virginny and Maryland, last fall, they became very cold ez he got North. Wher wuz the Isothermal Line and the Gulf Stream then?

Randall, who will hev his joke, remarkt that the isothermal line twisted. He notist that the people made it ez hot for em ez he wantid it ez fur North ez Cleveland ; to wich Sekretary Welles replied, that it only confirmed him in the opinion that for platin vessels uv war, iron wuz preferable to pine plank any time.

Seward removed the President's objections to-wunst. He read his letters, wich set forth the beauties and advantages uv the country twict over. Here wuz whales, and walrusses, and seals, and white bears, and pine-apples, and wheat, and sea-lions, and fields uv ice the year round, in a climit ez mild and equable ez the meridian uv Washinton. The isothermal line wuz more accommodatin ther than in any other part uv the world. It cork-screwed through the territory so ez to grow fine peaches for exportation to the States, and ice to the Sandwich Islands, side by side. He drawd a picter uv the white bear a rushin over the line, and dis-portin hisself in fields uv green peas ! Imagine, he remarked, the delicacy uv Polar bear meat fattened

on strawberries; think uv the condishn the sea-
lions must be in which leave their watery lairs to
feed on turnips wich grow above the 60th parallel;
think uv —

"It won't do," sed the President.

"Think uv," retortid the Sekretary, with a quick-
nis uv intellek remarkable, "*think uv gettin rid
uv the Blairs forever!*"

"Will the Ablishn Senit ratify the treaty?" askt
Johnson, eagerly.

"I converst with many on the subjick, and they
sed ef we cood promise that the Blairs would accept posishens ther, they wood do it cheerfly. For
sich a purpose, sed one uv em to me, $7,000,000 is
a mere bagatelle."

"I'll do it," sed Johnson. "I agree with the Senators for once. Rather then hev it fail, I'd pay it
out uv Mrs. Cobb's share in our jint spekelashens.
Freedom from the Blair family! Good Hevings!
kin one man be so blest? Is ther sich in store for
me? $7,000,000! Pish!"

My opinyun being askt, I give it. Ez hefty ez
the vencher is from a commershl stan-pint, in a
politikle pint uv view, the advantagis will be still
heftier. The Rooshn territory will finally be the
chosen home uv the Dimocrisy. Ther is already

a populashen there adaptid to us, who kin be manipulated without trouble, and the climit is favorable to a strickly Democratic populashen. The trouble with us here is that the amount uv likker necessary to the manufakter uv a Democrat kills him afore he hez a opportoonity uv votin many times, wich keeps us in a perpetooal minority. Our strength is, for climatic reasons, our weaknis. Far diffrent is it in Roosha. Ther the happy native may drink his quart per day — the bracin atmosphere makin it abslootly nessary for him. Ther is the troo Democratic paradise. How offen hev I sighed for sich a country. Then, again, ther are posishens uv profit. The delegates to Congriss will, ef I hev figgered it rightly, draw about $15,000 per session, mileage, wich is $30,000 per year, $60,000 per term. He cood afford to serve without the paltry $5,000, wich wood be cheep legislatin, indeed.

And so it wuz agreed upon, and the treaty wuz made by telegraph at a expense uv — I forgit eggsackly — but I think it wuz summers in the neighborhood uv $20,000. Before it wuz finely conclooded, some other little incidentals wuz inclooded by the Zar, wich run the price up to $10,200,000, but that wuz nothin for us. Seward went at his work with great energy. The Purchis wuz divided up into six territories (for the number uv dele-gates to our convenshuns wuz large, and they all hed to be provided for), wich wuz named, respec-tively, Johnson, Seward, Cowan, Doolittle, Randall, and Welles. For the one in the extreme North, the furthest off, Frank Blair wuz appinted Governor; for the next, Montgomery; and the next, the old man, and the other three wuz held in reserve for the pure but unfortunate patriots wich might be hereafter rejected for the Austrian mishun. A list wuz prokoored uv the delegates to our various con-venshuns, and them ez hed bin martyred by the Senit; ther names wuz put into a wheel ez at Gift Enterprises, and the Judgeships, Marshalships, Clerkships, et settry, wuz drawd by lot. This ijee was sejested by Postmaster-General Randall, ez bein the easiest way of doin it. He statid that the appintments from his department hed alluz bin made in this manner, ez it saved time in eggsaminin petitions, cirtifikets uv fitnis, and sich. In this way, about ez near ez I kin estimate, two per cent. uv those claimin posishens at our hands hev bin pro-vided for.

The idea is capable uv unlimited extension. The Administration feelin the releef it hez gin em, are already negotiatin for the British Provinces. This territory kin, by makin uv em a little smaller, be divided up into — say, forty — which, by makin a few more offises for each, and bein libral with explorin expedishuns and sich, will be sufficient to give places to all who really have claims upon us and who are pushin us.

The President breathes easier, and the Secretary is placid ez a Summer mornin. He hez cut the Gordian knot; he hez releeved hisself uv the boa constrickter wich wuz crushin him in its folds. Happiness pervades the White House.

PETROLEUM V. NASBY, P. M.

(Wich is Postmaster), and likewise Professor uv
Biblikle Politicks in the Southern Classikle
& Military Institoot.

XVI.

The Radical Change. — A slight Alteration in the Name and Policy of Mr. Nasby's " Institoot."

POST OFFIS, CONFEDRIT X ROADS
(Wich is in the Stait uv Kentucky),
April 22, 1867.

TIMES changes, and men change jist ez fast ez times. I should like to see the times wich kin change faster than I kin; but this last shift I hev bin forced to make, ruther took my breth. It wuz sudden. The Connecticut eleckshun didn't do us much good after all. We felt well over it for perhaps a day; but ez we begun to git other indicashens from the North, we didn't jist see how that little spirt wuz agoin to help us. Cincinnati went Ablishin stronger than ever. Chicago ditto; and most everywhere the Dimocratic rooster wuz flattened. The cabinet, when they heerd uv Deekin Pogram's assault upon the nigger, on the receet uv the intelligence uv the election news, notified me officially that a repetishen uv sich loonacy wood be equivalent to a reseet uv my resignation, even tho the post offis shood be discontinyood. "*The nigger vote must be capchered. It's essenshel. Wade Hampton sez so,*" wrote Randall to me, and I reprimanded the Deekin for his recklessniss, and borrowed four dollars uv Bascom, who is the only man in the vicinity who hez any ready money, to make it all right with him.

We held a meetin uv the Drecktors and Faculty uv the Southern Military and Classicle Institoot last evening, to decide wat course that instooshn wuz to take in the grate work uv surroundin the Ethiopian and attachin uv him to us. In sich a time ez this, ez I menshend to Captain McPelter, it won't do for our institooshuns uv learning to stand back. These great levers, the molders uv public opinion, must be ez progressive ez the progressiveist, and must change like other things to meet the requirements uv the times. We hev commenst our march into Africa, and thus far hev we gone into the bowels uv the land without impediment, to speak uv — let us persevere. Let us capcher the Ethiopian, stink and all.

The meetin wuz held in the back room uv Bascom's, owing to the fact that it wuz rainin, and the roof uv the Post Offis leaks. I hed an appropriashn some time since from the Department for repairs; but bein in doubt whether it wuz intended for repairs on the Post Offis or the Postmaster, I gave the prizner the benefit uv the doubt, and got a new pair uv boots. I cood better endoor the slite inconvenience uv occasional rain than to go barefoot.

I made a statement uv the case, and sejisted a radical change in the Institoot. Captain McPelter agreed with me. He felt that ther hedn't bin that complete, hearty recognition uv our Afrikan brethren as there ought to be. He had on several occasions allowed his nateral vivacity to git the better of his proodence, and hed waded into em alarmin. The old ijee of Ham and Hagar and Onesimus hed bin so drilled into him in his yooth, that he hed to wrestle with it to keep it in control, and in spite uv himself it often got the better uv him. He sejisted that the name uv the Institoot be changed from "The Southern Military and Classikle Institoot," to "The Ham and Japheth Free Academy for the Development uv the Intellek uv all Races, irrespectiv uv Color."

That he thought would anser the required end. The colored men who choose to avail theirselves of the priviligis afforded by this institooshn, when it is finished, kin find in this no cause uv complaint. They are recognized. They are given the precedence. They stand first in the matter and foremost. Wat more kin they ask?

Bascom hed a series uv resolooshuns wich he desired to present. He sed it mite be looked upon ez strange that he shood favor the concentrashun uv free niggers at the Corners, but he hed good and suffishent reasons. First, he hed faith that constant contact with the Board wood bring em to the pint uv patronizin his bar; but ef it didn't, he knowd perfectly well that the Board and Fakulty wood manage to git all they hed, for board and tooition, wich he was perfectly certin he'd git in the end. Wat he wanted wuz people here : to yoose an illustration borrered from his biznis, the offishels uv this Institoot wuz the funnel through wich the wealth uv all uv em wood be conducted to his coffers. I fell onto his neck in rapcher, and then vowed that I wuz willin to die for his good — that I cared not how much uv other people's money run through me to him ef 'twas thus dilooted. The resolooshens presented read ez follows : —

" *Resolved*, That the name uv the Southern Military and Classikle Institoot be changed to ' The Ham and Japheth Free Academy, for the Development uv the Intelleck uv all Races, irrespective uv Color.'

"*Resolved*, That in makin this change, we, the Board uv Directors, do so, assertin,

"1. That in this emergency we are justified in doubtin whether Noer got tite at all, the statement in the Skripters to that effect bein ondoubtedly an error uv the translators.

"2. That ef he did git tite, he didn't cuss Ham at all.

"3. That ef he did cuss Ham, the cuss wuzn't intended to extend beyond Canaan at the furthest, and hence his descendants go scot free.

"4. That ef the cuss wuz really and trooly intended to attach to all uv Ham's descendents, irrespective uv color, to the end uv time, it ain't uv no effeck in Kentucky, ez that State hez allus run irrespective uv any code, 'ceptin sich ez hez bin adopted by her Legislacher.

"5. That the theory that the nigger, irrespective uv color, is a beast, is a deloosion, a snare, which we hev alluz practically held, no matter what we may, for effect, hev sed, ez the number uv mulattoes, to say nothin uv them still farther bleached in Kentucky, abundantly proves.

"6. That the Ethiopian, irrespective uv color, 's

trooly a man and a brother; and the female Ethiopian, also irrespective uv color, trooly a woman and a sister.

." *Resolved*, That this Institoot, whose name is now so happily changed, shel be conducted upon the principles uv strict ekality, irrespective uv color.

" *Resolved*, That when we reflect that the bloated aristocracy uv England interdoost, and the early settlers of Massachoosets sankshund, slavery on this continent, forcin it really onto us, we bile with indignashun towards em, and kin hardly restrane ourselves.

" *Resolved*, That at the tables, in the choice uv rooms, and in all matters where there is a choice, the African man and brother, irrespective uv color, shel hev the precedence.

" *Resolved*, That Oberlin College, by not givin the sons uv Ham, irrespective uv color, the precedence, shows clearly that it is actooated by narrer-minded prejudice, wich deserves the reprobashen uv every lover uv his kind.

" *Resolved*, That the Ethiopian, irrespective uv color, kin change his skin, and that his oder, ef he hez any, is rather pleasant than otherwise.

" *Resolved*, That we look with loathing upon the States North, wich, alluz professin friendship for the noble black man uv the cotton fields, refooze to take him to their buzzums, irrespective uv color.

"*Resolved*, That ef Massachoosits and Vermont, and Northern Illinois, and the Western Reserve in Ohio, are honest in their professions uv love for the negro, they will come down with donashuns to assist in the completion uv the Academy."

Deekin Pogram didn't know about all this. He hed bin edikated in Ham and Hager, and wuz a bleever in Onesimus. He doubted. Sposen after all this concession the nigger shood play off onto us? Sposen he shoodent vote with us after all, but cling to his Northern friends? Or spose he shood vote with us, and we shood, thro his vote, git control, wat then? How cood we redoose em to ther normal condition agin after all this palavrin?

Bascom replied that he wuz surprised at the Deekin's obtoosnis. First, ef they did vote with the Ablishnists, we wuz no worse off, ez that wuz wat they proposed to do any how. Ef, on the other hand, they didn't, what then? The trouble with em now is, they know too much. "Let em," sed Bascom, warmin up, "let em associate with us a year, let em vote with us, et cettry, and in twelve months they're precisely fitted agin to be servance unto their brethren. Look," sed he, " at the Northern Dimocrasy, and see to what we may hope to bring these men in time."

But little more bizness wuz transacted. Beverly Nash, of South Caroliny, was unanimously called to a Professorship ; and a young gentleman uv color, who, from his strong resemblance to Elder Gavitt, ought to hev biznis capacity, wuz unanimously elected a member of the Board. The yoonyun is perfect. Ham and Japheth hev shaken hands, and are embracin each other.

May prosperity attend the nupchels, and may the isshoo be fortunate. I hev got over the disgust attendant upon the fust chill, and am consekently feelin well.

Petroleum V. Nasby, P. M.

(Wich is Postmaster), and Professor in the Ham and Japheth Free Academy for the Development uv the Intelleck uv all Races, irrespective of Color.

XVII.

Mr. Nasby Preaches a Sermon on Universal Brotherhood, the Effect of which is destroyed by Northern Democratic Papers. — He remonstrates.

POST OFFIS, CONFEDRIT X ROADS
(Wich is in the Stait uv Kentucky),
April 25, 1867.

WE are in continyooal trouble down here with these cussid niggers. They are harder to manage than pigs. Pigs don't express ther pecoolyarities. Mules come nearer. Ther is sich a method in their obstinacy — sich a wilful cussidnis, that I reely hev made up my mind that I don't understand em at all. They cuddle up to us ez kind ez a bloomin maiden does to her first adored, and they fling us just ez natral ez that same guileless maiden does when number two heaves in site. They behave well for a season, aperrently for no other purpose than to enjoy our discomfiture when they finally throw us. I hev bin a gittin a suspishen thro me that they ain't half ez stoopid ez they look; and that, after all, we are not fur from the trooth when we say, in our resolooshens, that they are the ekals uv the whites. Why shoodn't they be? Ah! why, indeed? Why shoodent the nigger boy, wich is now crossin the street, wich hez Deekin Pogram's feechers ez like ez a photograff, hev ez much sense ez the Deekin? I hev egsamined into the pedigree uv that nigger, and I find that his mother hed the hawtiest and best blood uv Virginny coursin toomulchusly thro her veins — and that stock the Pogram mix coodent materially depreciate in one generashen.

I hed the niggers uv the X Roads very handsomely in tow up to yisterday. I hed em attendin services last Sunday at the meetin house, and by private arrangement hed em seated miscellaneously among the awjence. Dekin Pogram hed a wench, wich weighed at least 250 pounds averdupoise, atween him and his wife, while four other niggers ornamentid his pew. Bascom, with alacrity, consented to three; and Elder Gavitt provided seats for four. It wuz a pleasant site! White and black wuz alternatid like the spots on a checker-board — niggers and whites wuz spread out together like the fat and lean in pork; and ez I seed it I stood hardly restrane my emoshuns. There before me wuz the regenerashun uv the Democratic party — there wuz wat wuz to bring us out uv the valley and shadder uv death into wich we hed fallen, up on the high ground uv offishel life. I preached that memrable day from two texts, to wit: "Uv one blood did he make all the nashens uv the earth," and "All ye are brethren;" and I orated a movin discourse. I demonstrated with great fervor the loonacy uv the idea that the Almighty wood take the trouble to create two or more races when one wood do ez well — wich idea is alluz well receeved in this region. All men form their idea uv the Deity somewhat from themselves; and I never knowd a Confedrit Cross Roader to make two things when one wood anser. I refuted the theory, advanced by some writers, that there wuz more than one head to the race, by quotin the texts wich treated uv the creashen uv Adam and Eve, and demolished the Ham doctrine at site. "Ef," sed I, "Noer did cuss Ham, and condemn Canaan to be a servant unto his brethren, how do we know that our colored brethren and sistren *is* the desend-ants uv Ham and Canaan? It may be *us* for all we know! Is it his color? Is not black jest ez con-venient a color ez white?"

"More so," murmured Mrs. Pogram, half asleep, "more so — it don't show dirt."

"Is it his shape? O, my brethren, I ain't a handsome man, nor wood I exactly anser for a model for Apoller. Ef beauty, or comeliness, or shape, or style, is to decide the pint, may the Lord help us! Is it his smell? My brethren, the New York World asserts that the nigger hain't no smell, and ef he hez, why shoodent he hev? Standin under the common flag uv our country, with his hand upon that magna charta, the Deklarashen, and his beamin eye turned exultinly toward our nashnel emblem, the eagle, shall not our Afrikin brother be allowed to smell jist ez he chooses? Ef smell must be uniform, then let our Government establish a Burow uv Perfoomery to-wunst. Besides, I take high religious grounds in this matter. Ef he hez a natural odor, the Lord give it to him. Let us not fly in the face uv the Lord by condemin it. Judge not, lest we be judged. The odor uv the colored gentleman or lady is the work uv the Lord — the odor uv yoor unwashed feet is yoor own — wich shood stand the highest?

"My brethren and sistren, I acknowledge that I hev not long held these views. I hev showed the common prejudis, and hev contemned our friends uv color; I hev despitefully used 'em; I hev gone for 'em, and banged 'em like old boots. But it wuz becoz I didn't know 'em. I didn't see the kernel of meat under the rough shell: I didn't recognize the glitrin diamond in the ebony coal. My eyes hev bin opened. Like Saul of Tarsus, I see a lite. Sence the passage uv the Military Bill I hev diskiv ered many things too tejus to menshun. I hev mostly found out all these things sence that occurrence. But let us accept the situashen, and bless the Lord that it hez resultid in developin excellences where we didn't expect to find 'em."

There wuz an affectin scene after service wuz over. Deekin Pogram, Captain McPelter, and Elder Gavitt shook hands with em with a degree uv corjality I didn't expect. Trooly, them are great men. They develop a degree uv adaptability to circumstances wich I didn't look for. I really bleeve if I'd a told em that it wood hev a good effeck to kiss the nigger babies all round, that they'd a done it. But I spared em this. There is such a thing ez laying it on too thick.

But all this wuz spiled the next day. There wuz an eggstraordinarily heavy mail that day. In addition to the paper wich Pollock, the Illinois storekeeper, takes, ther wuz eight others; and to my surprise they wuz all directed to niggers. "Wat is this?" thot I to myself. "Hev the Ablishnists uv the North determined upon proselytin these men, and are they goin to flood this country with their incendiary readin? Ez a Federal officer it's my dooty to look into the matter!" Jist imagine my delirious joy at findin that they wuz Democratic papers from Noo York and Ohio! "Thank Heaven!" sed I, "our people hev awakened to a sense uv the necessity uv doin suthin;" and I handed the papers out to em with impressive words, exhortin uv em to read em, ez they wuz trooth, and nothin but the trooth.

I ruther think they read em, for from that time out they avoided me ez though I hed the plague. Ef I wuz a goin down the street, and one uv em wuz a comin up, he'd cross the street; and the pecoolyer expression uv his countenance indicatid that it wuzn't my majestick presence wich awd him. They hed loathin depicted on their classick feechers. Unable to endoor this, I seezed one uv em, and asked why I wuz treated thus?

Delibritly he pulled out uv his pockit one uv them cussid Northern papers, and openin it, pintid indignantly to a editorial article. It wuz perfoosely headed in this wise : —

Shel niggers vote? — Shel the prowd Cauca-shen be redoost to a ekality with the disgustin Afrikin? — Is this a white man's government or not? — Ameriky for white men!

Sed this Ethiopian, with his fingers on this headin, " 'Pears like ez ef dah wuzn't jist dat good feelin towards us colored men on de part ob de Dimoc'sy ob the Norf dat dah ought to be. 'Pears like as dough up dah wha de niggah ain't got no vote, dat dey don't intend he shel hab it. 'Pears like, ef Dimoc'sy's one ting all ober de country, dar's a cussid site ob humbug a goin on down heah ! "

Wat cood I say? Wat cood I do? There it wuz in black and white ; and from papers whose Dimoc-risy could not be questioned. I wuz dumbfoundid. The nigger stalked hawtily and proudly away in one direckshen, while I sneaked off ruther sneakinly in another.

I hev one word to say to our brethren in the North. Yoo'r doublin our troubles, and makin our burdens harder to bear. Why can't yoo understand common sense? Wat hurt wood nigger suffrage do yoo up there wher ther ain't no niggers, and how much wood it benefit us down here wher ther's millions uv em? Can't yoo see it? We can't play the same game on the niggers that we used to play on the sturdy yeomahry uv Berks County, Pennsylvany, and other localities. On all questions heretofore the Dimocrisy hez allowed a liberal license. We hev bin Free Trade in Noo York and Tariff in Pennsylvany the same year, and we cood do it. Sich Dimocrats didn't git ther asshoorences from papers, owin to their inability to perooze em rapidly, it bein so long afore they got a word spelled out that they forgot the one precedin it, wich destroyed the connection, the continuity uv the narrative, ef I may so speak, and wat we told em wuz gospel. That won't do with the nigger down here. He reads, he does; and ef he don't, ther's alluz everywhere some sich sneakin cuss ez Pollock, who reads for him, and they know wat they know jist ez well ez anybody. Let em stop hammerin the nigger. It won't do. Ef he's to be a man and a brother here, he must be a man and a brother there. Ef the Dimocrisy must hev a race to look down on, let em turn their attenshun to the Chinese or the Injuns, but from this time out the nigger is sacred.

PETROLEUM V. NASBY, P. M.

(Wich is Postmaster), and Professor in the Ham and Japheth Free Academy for the Development uv the Intellek uv all Races irrespectiv of Color.

XVIII.

The Decease of Elder Gavitt. — Mr. Nasby announces the Death of his Friend and mourns. — A touching Obituary.

POST OFFIS, CONFEDRIT X ROADS
(Wich is in the Stait uv Kentucky),
May 2, 1867.

A BLITE hez fallen o'er my soul. My eyes, albeit unused to the meltin mood, hev distilled nothin but tears for twelve hours. A Piller hez fallen! In the meetin-house there is a vacant pew, and a chair at Bascom's is without a setter. Last nite, at precisely nine P. M., Elder Abimileck Gavitt departed this life, aged 63 years and some odd months.

I weep ez I write. The Elder wuz snufft out jest ez the flowers uv spring wuz cumin — jest ez the weather wuz a gittin warm enough to go barefooted — jest when it wuzn't nessary to bother about getting fire-wood, or be concerned about feedin the stock — jest when it begins to be comfortable a settin onto the grocery stoop — jest at the threshhold uv six months' enjoyment. Why wuz he taken? Ekko ansers. The ways uv Providence is inskrootable.

Elder Gavitt wuz a native uv North Karliny, wich State he left in the blush uv early manhood, jist after he wuz married. Wat he left North Karliny for, I never wuz able to assertane percisely; but I hev understood that it wuz suthin in connection with a smoke-house, and the hams wich did hang therein. He wuz in a Whig naberhood — his naber, the proprietor of the smoke-house, wuz a Whig — ther wuz sum hams mist — the rinds wuz found in his possession — Whig intolerance and persekooshen. Upon sich slite evidence he wuz adjudged guilty of theft, and wuz ignominiously rid on a rale, and ordered to leave the country in twenty-four hours, wich he did, driftin nat'rally to Kentucky. Thank Heaven for sich outrages! But for sich, Kentucky wood hev bin a Republican State, or wood hev remained unsettled to this day.

Elder Gavitt wuz alluz a Democrat uv the strictest sect. He voted for Jackson, and reglerly for every Democratic candidate sence. He didn't read very much; indeed, ef I remember right, he coodent do it at all, and wuz, consekently, stedfast in the faith. He wuzn't shook about, and driven hither and yon by every wind, but remained thro life fast in the groove into wich he hed bin origenelly sot. His politikle creed wuz made up uv this one idee, to wit: Hatrid uv Noo England. He hatid Noo England becoz Noo England hatid whiskey, wich he coodent git along without, and slavery, uv wich he hed a hundred niggers. He votid agin Noo England all his life reglerly, and ez many times on each eleckshen day ez he cood without risk.

My acquaintance with the deceest commenst about three years ago. It wuz at his house I stopt on my advent into these parts. Ther wuz no need uv formel introduckshens — ther wuz already a bond atween us wich knit our souls together. His eye, ez it lit onto my nose, lighted up with a smile; and ez I gazed on hizzen, I felt that he wuz indeed a man and a brother. He took me in— he sheltered me — he gave me whereof to eat and to drink and to make merry, and with him I tarried till I wuz reglerly installed ez pastor uv the Church, and thereby reglerly pervided for.

The cause uv the Elder's death wuz a broken heart. He wuz a ardent Confedrit, and manfully bore up under the reverses of the war. His courage wuz unshaken doorin the repeated successes uv the Federal armies; and even when emancipation deprived him uv his slaves, he still hed faith that, evenchooally, all wood be well. "We may be beeten now," wuz his constant remark, "but the Northern Dimocrisy are all right, and thro them we'll yet conker!" Confidin in em, bleevin in em, he held out brave up to the passage uv the Military Reconstruckshen Bill.

I then saw a change steel insensibly over my venerable friend. His head bowed with supprest grief — his bosom throbbd with the emoshen that wuz strugglin for uttrance. He wood come over to my offis five or six times a day, and ask me to read him that passage uv the law givin the nigger the ballot. I wood do it, when, without sayin a word, he wood reel off, with tears flowin down his wasted cheeks, to Bascom's. I wood foller him, to see that no harm came to him. The old man wuz so broken that he'd pay for his own likker and mine too, without noticin. Fearin to awaken unpleasant emoshens in his-mind, I never menshend the latter circumstance.

Things grew worse with him. When Mr. Randall wrote me to consiliate the niggers ez Wade Hampton wuz a doin it, the old father in Democrisy obeyed without a murmur. Democrisy wuz his first idea, and he obeyed her behests, tho 'twuz consoomin his very sole. He shook hands with niggers at my rekest, tho the touch wuz ez red hot iron ; he took two of em into his pew, tho his promoxity to em set him a shakin like the ager; and he votid to change the name and objects uv the Institoot, tho the convulsive workins uv his face showd wat the struggle cost him.

Day by day the Elder faded. The iron entered his sole, and it wuz corrodin! corrodin! corrodin! and eatin him up by degrees. He walked the streets listlessly, his eyes suffoosed with teers, and his lips movin ez ef mutterin suthin to hisself. I become concerned for him, and so did the entire cirkle. Bascom figgered up his akkount at his bar, and went to the records to see whether his farm wuz unencumbered, and sich uv the neighbors ez hed lent him small sums sot about gittin em.

Last Sunday the pitcher went to the well for the last time. I hed four niggers in his pew, upon whom he looked vacantly, but sed nothin. After servis, I stopped him. "Elder," sez I, in a whisper, "it wood hev a good effeck ef yoo cood kiss them little nigger girls."

"Parson!" sed he, tremblin like a leaf, "is it abslootely necessary?"

"It is," sez I firmly, "a dooty evry Dimokrat

owes to his party, in this crisis, to kiss ez many nigger children ez possible."

A strange expression lit up the old man's countenance. In a frenzied manner he kissed all there wuz in the church, and, ez ef insane, commenst on the adult femails uv that persuasion. With difficulty we restrained him; but breakin loose from us, he startid down the street, a running down and kissin every nigger child his eyes restid on. Finally he sunk to the erth eggsaustid, and we bore him to his house and put him to bed. From that bed he never ariz. He wuz a goner. We hed to give him his likker in a spoon, and I never knowed a Kentuckian to recover who wuz past drinkin out uv a bottle.

Slowly his strength wasted. Yesterday he rallied and asked for me, ez the candle uv life flickered feebly in the socket.

"Perfesser!" sed. he, with an effort, "is Kentucky to rool the niggers, or the niggers to rool Kentucky? Has the Dimocrisy swallered the nigger, or the nigger swallered the Dimocrisy?"

And all wuz o'er! He fell back a piece uv clay, wich never cood rally to the poles agin.

Bascom and I turned aside and wept. Sed Bascom, "Hed he lived two years more I wood hev hed his farm."

"Not any," sed I, bustin into teers. "I wood hev hed it to endow the Institoot."

"In that event it wood evenchooally hev bin mine," gasped Bascom, relapsin into a fresh spasm uv grief.

We buried him yesterday. It wuz the biggest funeral ever knowd at the Corners. It was a tetchin site. Standin around his bier, wuz his four children by his first wife, and his six children by his second wife, and twelve or fifteen other children uv all colors, from that uv a new saddle up to dark. molasses, who insisted upon bein counted in ez mourners. It wuz the tightest place I wuz ever in in my life.

"My friends," sed I to em, "is this seemly? Is this proper?"

They replied that it wuz. "I mourn a father," sed one; "not much uv a father, but he wuz the only one I ever hed." "I mourn a husband," sed the mother uv the first speaker, "not legally a husband, but morally, or rather, immorally." "We weep," sed all these various shades in korus, and they bustid out into a torrent uv greef wich completely extinguished them on the tother side uv the grave, wich hed the legle rite to mourn.

Ez a matter uv coarse, it ended in a row. Issaker Gavitt swore that no cussid bleached niggers shood shed teers at his father's funeral ; and Amandy flew at a quadroon wich wuz cryin too prominently, and Mrs. Gavitt attacked the quadroon's mother who wuz displayin altogether too much white pockit hankercher. In the melee I left, satisfied that Democrisy hez altogether too many rough pints to git over pleasant.

I feel it my dooty to erect a monument to the memory uv this good and true man — this martyr to Democrisy. Demokrats, feelin an interest in the matter, and wishin to contribute to the work, may send by mail sich donashens ez they see fit, to me, with perfect confidence that they will be yoosed. Let em remember that but for his devoshen to the coz he wood hev bin livin to-day. Ef we cannot do much for the livin, let us not forgit the dead.

PETROLEUM V. NASBY, P. M.
(Wich is Postmaster), and Professor in the Ham and Japheth Free Academy for the Development uv the Intellek uv all Races irrespectiv of Color.

XIX.

Triumphal Progress of J. Davis from Fortress Monroe to Richmond.

THE " SPOTTSWOOD," RICHMOND, VA.,
May 13, 1867.

IN castin a retrospective glance backerd over the pathway uv the past, I kin see many mistakes wich I hev made. I hevn't alluz made the most uv opportoonities — I hev doubtid when doubtin wuz a crime, and I hev stood shivrin on the brink and feared to lanch away, when on the tother side uv the Jordan wuz pelf and profit. Our foresite isn't alluz ez good ez our hind-site. The great error uv my life wuz in not plungin headlong into the war ez a Confedrit Major-General, distinguishin myself for crooelty to Fedral prizners, and bein, at the close uv the fratrisidle struggle, reseeved and embraced ez a long-lost brother by the Northern people (lettin em kill fattid calves for me), and uv coorse bein the objeck uv sympathy ez a marter by the Southern people. In this sitooashen a man hez

two strings to his bow. He brings to his support
the two' extremes. He fetches together Horris
Greely from the one side, and General Boregard
from the t'other — they embrace, and standin onto
both their sholders, he hez wat may be called a soft
thing uv it.

I wuz led into these train uv reflections by the
experience I hev hed with our sainted cheef, Jefferson Davis. I wuz sent hither by the President to
see that everythin wuz done for the comfort uv the
illustrious man that cood be done, on the occasion
uv his contemplatid trip to Richmond. Partikelerly
I wuz charged to see that everything calkelatid to
jar onto his sensitive feelins be removed — everythin wich cood wound his sense uv hearin, seein,
or smellin.

The grate man had consentid to go. He hed
bin, he felt, illegally deprived uv liberty — uncon-
stooshnelly in fact — and ef he shood consult his
own feelings he wood remane; but to forgive wuz
divine. Viewin these perceedins in the lite uv an
apology, he wood go.

The day hed arrived. The steamer wuz at the
Fortress carefully prepared to receive its illustrious
burden. It hed been thoroughly cleaned and fumi-
gated, the cabins hed bin nooly furnisht, and speshel

alterashens made for the President and party. Ther wuz Yoonited States officers and soljers aboard; but out of respeck for the feelins uv their illustrious "prizner," ez he is technically called, they kept theirselves carefully out of his site, that the color uv their uniforms might not awaken onpleasant refleckshens. So perfeck, indeed, wuz the arrangements, that the railin uv the boat, which wuz originelly bloo, wuz kivered with gray cloth, and the eagle figger-head uv the craft wuz sawed off. This wuz sejested by a eminent Conservative uv Noo York, who hez a large Southern trade wich he didn't prejoodis by his course doorin the war. The ladies' cabin wuz originelly assigned to the party; but a female passenger hed no more regard for the comfort uv the marter than to die on the passage, an they were deprived uv it. The Conservative merchant insisted that the corpse be chucked overboard; but Mr. Davis, with a magnanimity wich wuz alluz characteristic uv him, refoozed. "No," said he, "let her rest there. I kin endoor the inconvenience, severe as it is. It is but one more attempt to break my sperit."

All the way up there wuz the most tetchin deference shown him. At every landin the people were assembled to greet him, wich he acknowledged with a condesenshen I never saw off the stage. He conversed but little on the passage up. Ez the boat was a sweepin majestically past pints made historicle by the events uv the great struggle, his eye wood brighten, ef they wuz sich pints ez a Confedrit cood take pride in, and dim with teers ef they wuz pints at wich ther had bin reverses.

The most considrit preparashens hed bin made for his resepshen. Ther wuz no irons onto him: the only guards in site wuz them wich wuz detailed to keep the crowd from annoyin him, and a carriage wuz in readiness, into wich we seated ourselves, and wuz driven off at a dignified pace to that resort uv the aristocracy uv Virginny — the Spottswood. Here, more considerashen wuz shown. Mr. Davis being averse to walkin up stairs, a suite uv rooms hed bin prepared for him on the fust floor, and the presence uv General Burton, uv the Federal army, bein obnoxshus, he wuz assigned by the Ex-President a room at the further end uv the corridor. His nerves bein very sensitive, heavy mattin wuz laid down in all the halls, and the servants uv the house wuz especially directed to wear list slippers, and to walk on their tip toes.

I wuz invited to his room, and wuz favored with a few minutes' conversashen with the first of Amerikens. Glancin out uv the winder, his fine, soft, gray eyes restid on the roof uv Libby. "Lies! lies!" sed he, angrily.

"Wat speshel lies hev yoo reference to?" askt I.

"Them wich wuz publisht in the scurrillous reports uv the Committees uv a unconstooshnel Congris regardin the treatment uv prizners in Libby. They asserted that the officers died becoz they hed but ten feet by two for sleepin, washin, cookin, and eatin. They hed that space, and wat more wuz necessary? Why give 'em room to cook when they hedn't anythin to cook? Wherefore room to eat ef they hedn't anythin to eat? No, its false. It wuzn't the crowdin that perdoost the mortality."

Only wunst wuz his buzzum wrung, and that the Government cood not pervent. He wuz a standin at the winder, gazin out upon Richmond, his mind revertin to the time when it wuz the Capital uv his Confedracy, when a procession passed with moosic, and flags, and banners. With a shreek uv anguish he buried his head in the curtins, and wept aloud. I rusht to the winder. It wuz ez I feared. Filin slowly by wuz a percession uv niggers who hed past that way perposely. "Merciful Heaven!" sed he, "hez it come to this?" and he wuz very reserved and deprest the balence uv the day.

The next day the President wuz taken to the Court. Ez he entered the room, and glanced proudly over the awjence, it wood hev bin very difficult to hev decided whether he wuz a goin to try the Court or the Court him. But repressin hisself he took his seat. Techin solissitood wuz displayed in the Court Room for his comfort. A crack in the winder-casin let in a draft uv cold air; he shuddered, and a shudder run thro the entire assemblage. The shudder uv the Conservative merchant from Noo York wuz trooly artistic. Cotton wuz called for, when the Conservative merchant's wife tore off one uv her buzzums and stufft the apertoor. Wuz ther ever more techin sacrifis? The President wept ez he beheld it. On assertainin the temperatoor wich best sootid his system, a thermometer wuz brot, and the room wuz kept at that precise degree.

There wuz sum triflin legal formalities gone through with, and the President's counsel made a motion that he be admitted to bail. There wuz a stir in the Court. "Make it a million!" sed one, "so that the craven North shel see how we kin take keer uv them we love!" But Judge Underwood fixed it at $100,000, and, brisk ez bees, Schell, a Noo York Dimocrat, several Richmond

Dimocrats, and Horris Greely, stept forrerd and signed it.

Never shel I forgit the shout that assendid ez Horris wuz a signin his name.

" Three cheers for Jeff'son Greely and Horris Davis — one and inseprable, now and forever ! " shoutid one enthoosiastic confedrit.

" Immortality is yoors ! " sed another, seezin him by the hand corjelly. " Jeff'son Davis is the big dog uv the age, and yoo, my deer sir, are now the tin kittle tied to his tale ! Wat joy ! Wat happinis ! When posterity speeks uv Him, they'll speek uv Yoo ! "

I coodent restrane myself no more. Bustin into teers, I fell onto Greeley's buzzum, and we embraced. Ez he hedn't his spekticles on, he sposed it wuz Davis hisself, and he bustid into teers also, and there wuz wun uv the most strikin tabloos ever exhibited. I got away afore he diskivered his mistake.

Here wuz the endin uv our troubles — the consummashen uv our hopes. Davis wuz free ! The pent-up emoshens uv the people found vent. Ez he stept into the street the people crowded to the carriage wich contained us, and rent the air with cheers. We reacht the hotel, and after embracin his wife, a season of religious exercises wuz held. The clergyman who hed excloosive charge of Davis's piety doorin the war wuz present, and he offered prayer. He prayed fervently that the Lord wood forgive the people of the North for the wrong they hed done our sainted head; that he wood forgiv, ef possible, the late head uv the Fedral Government who hed opposed him and the glorious coz; and ef Divine mercy could stretch so far, that he wood forgive the Colonel uv Michigan cavalry wich hed hunted down the Saint who wuz now in our midst, and made uv him a captive. He prayed for forgiveness for the reckless men of the North who invaded Virginny; for the noosepaper condukters who had aboozed him who is now with us, and particklerly Horris Greely, who hed this day, in some measure, atoned for his previous wickidness. He prayed that the blessins uv Heven might rest, first, upon the city uv Richmond, then upon the balance uv Virginny, and afterward upon the rest uv the Southern States; and he wound up with a fervent appeal that the Ethiopians, wich coodent change their skins, might see the error of their ways, and return to their normal condishen.

After this the President received his friends.

I am not permitted to give more uv the President's plans than this: He will remain in secloosion, and will take no part watever in politics until after his final acquittal in November. He don't feel at liberty to take hold uv the Government, so long ez ther is even a technikle charge agin him. Our friends in the Northern States, who expected him to take the stump in their behalf this fall, will be disappintid. I return to-morrer to Kentucky.

PETROLEUM V. NASBY, P. M.

(Wich is Postmaster), and Professor in the Ham and Japheth Free Academy for the Development uv the Intellek uv all Races irrespectiv of Color.

XX.

A Provision for the Ex-President of the Confederacy. — Mr. Nasby tenders him a Professorship in his " Institoot."

POST OFFIS, CONFEDRIT X ROADS
(Wich is in the Stait uv Kentucky),
May 26, 1867.

TO JEFF'SON DAVIS, LATE PRESIDENT UV THE LATE SOUTHERN CONFEDERACY.

THE undersined, yoor ardent admirers, who follerd willinly yoor lead in the late tour the South took for addishnel rites, wich unfortnitely resultid in the loss uv sich uv em ez we had, beg leave to tender yoo, ez a testimony uv their esteem, the Presidency uv the Ham and Japheth Academy for the Development uv the Intellek uv all Races, " irrespective uv race or color," uv wich I hev the honor to be one uv the Fakulty.

We worshipt yoo, before your untimely capcher in female apparel, for the dignity with which you bore yourself doorin your prosperous days, your manliness doorin yoor long and unconstitooshnel incarcerashen in a Fedral bastile, and your hawty though silent assershen uv the natral sooperiority of the Southern man doorin the annoyin perceedings wich endid in yoor triumfant release from yoor abasht persecooters, and we feel confident that in yoor hands the interests uv the Institoot will be entirely safe.

Many reasons impel us to this course.

First. We assoom that yoo are poor in this world's goods. Troo, yoo hed oceans uv money passin thro the Treasury doorin the fratrisidle struggle forced onto us by the North; but wat chance hed yoo for steelin, with Benjamin and Mallory, and them fellows with yoo, who hed the benefit uv practice doorin Pierce and Bookannon's administrations? A man coodent make day's wages peculatin in a Treasury wich them men hed gone through.

Second. Yoo wood be uv benefit to us. With yoor name at the head uv our Faculty, the Northern Democracy would shell out their stamps with a libralty never before witnest, and the Institoot wood be endowed heftier than any similar institooshen in the country. The King's name is a tower uv strength. Remember that the Democrisy uv the North giv the exil Vallandigum $30,000 in ten cent contribooshens. Ef they'd do that for him, and sich, wat woodent they doo for yoo? The greater swallers up the less. There never will be sich a favorable opportunity for yoo to become a ten center, wich is trooly equivalent to bein a hed center.

Ez a matter uv coorse yoo will hev objeckshuns. Knowin wat they will be, we anser em in advance.

1. The incomplete state uv the Institoot. We acknowledge that it isn't in sich a state uv completidnis as we cood desire. Not to put too fine a pint onto it, it ain't built at all. But the corner-stun is laid. There's a good deal in that. A corner-stun is a good thing. The corner-stun uv the Institoot is laid. From the laying of corner-stuns great results follow. President Johnson laid a corner-stun at Chicago, and your release followed. He didn't get very far into 'the affeckshuns uv the people North, but he got yoo out uv Fortress Monroe. Jist let us fling our banner to the breeze with the name of "J. Davis" onto it, and how quickly wood the means to finish the Institoot be forthcomin! Ah, indeed! Ther wood be tournaments held all over the South in its behalf. The Knite uv the

Sore Eyes would tilt agin the Knite of the Cropped Ears; the Knite uv the Bandy Legs would run a course and be glorified agin the Knite uv the Released Cheef, for its benefit, and the Queens uv Love and Beauty wood bid em, more fervently than ever before, to lay their fish-poles in rest and run their course at the Injy Rubber Teething Rings, and do their devours manfully, in sich a cause. Ther wood be fairs held in Noo York for this fund, and C. Chancey Burr and Henry Clay Dean wood deliver lekters all over the North in its behalf, workin a double benefit, viz., affordin us a little money, Burr, clean paper-collars, and Dean, clean socks. In fact, the coz uv the ill success the Institoot hez met with thus far, may be found in the fact that ther hain't bin nobody connected with it but me. The Southern Democrisy don't take to me kindly coz they see me every day; the Northern Democrisy hev no confidence in me becoz they know I wuz originelly one uv em.

2. Its name, indicatin ez it does, that the institooshen admits the ijee of Nigger Ekality. This objeckshen kin be easily ansered. The name wuz, originelly, the " Southern Military and Classikle Institoot," and the title expressed fairly its objects. That's it yet, and nothin shorter. The change of

title was strategy. That change wuz Pickwickian, in the most comprehensive meanin of the word. It wuz done for effeck upon the Ethiopian. They hev votes in the States which supported yoo in your effort to perpetuate em reliably in their normal condition, and it wuz deemed necessary to conciliate em. I need not say wat a trial it wuz for our people to forego the ecstatic delite uv wallopin uv em, and wat agony it wuz to be forced, by circumstances over wich we hed litrally no controle, to recognize em, even in fun, ez ekals, but we hed to do it. After they hev voted wunst, and boostid us into Congress, it is eggstremely probable that a change will come over the sperit uv their dreems. After that happy day — Well, State Legislachers hev yit powers, and States hev yit rites. In breef, this nigger biznis is an effort to flank John Brown's sole, which hez bin marchin on for sevral years. You hev witnist, no doubt, in your gayer moments, the sole-inspirin and elevatin performances of nigger minstrels. Certainly. On the stage they resembled niggers; after the play wuz over, the curtain dropped, they washed off the cork, and went and took their well-earned nips ez white men. Precisely so. When this little play is over, probably we may wash off the cork, and ez Caucashens assert our rite to be, as uv old, the governin class.

3. Pay.   On this hed nothin definit kin be statid. Yoo must doo ez I hev done — hev faith, and take wat comes.   I hev hed contribooshens ez low ez ten cents, and that even in counterfeit postal currency, wich wuz no objeckshen to it down here, ez among our people it passes just ez well ez any. I hev lived on it for some time; the Institoot hez eked out the livin afforded me by the offis I hold from the Guvernment.   Ef contribooshens should be insufficient for yoor support, after my livin is taken out, wat uv it?   Is Johnson dead, and does Wade reign in his stead?   Do yoo hev any idee that he wood let yoo suffer?   Is ther not a sine-coor for yoo ez well ez for me?   Is ther a Confedrit officer, who wood accept it, who is not pervided with a posishen uv some kind?   Hevin pervided generously for every one uv the principal sufferers in the late fratrisidal struggle on the Confedrit side, is it probable that he wood make yoo an excepshen?

I hev ansered all the objections to the place wich yoo kin urge, and I beg leave to state some uv the reasons why you shood accept.

A full year intervenes before the meetin uv the

Democratic Nashnel Convenshen, and two before you kin be finally inoggerated. Pendin that event yoo must go into dignified retirement. It's the regler thing. Forrest did it, and he succeeded so well in masterin his nateral proclivities that, ef I remember ritely, he hez killed but two niggers sence he reverently folded up the stars and bars. Longstreet hez did it, Price hez did it, and so hez all uv em. Lee hez done it better than any uv em. There's suthin pecoolyerly fittin in the cheeftain uv an unsuccessful "rebellion," ez the Northerners call our struggle for our rites, takin the Presidency uv a college, in seekin shelter in academic groves, in trainin the noble young men uv his seckshen, and instillin into em a more perfeck knowledge uv the doctrin uv State rites and a higher revrens for Virginny, a deeper hatrid of ablishnism (wich is all that a Southern yooth hez a call to know), and a gittin rifled cannon from a tyranikle government to teech em artillery practis. That's the dodge for yoo. We hain't got the academic grove for yoo to walk pensively in at the twilite hour, a musin onto the eventful past, but we kin easily move that corner-stun into one. That corner-stun is ez easily shifted ez Democracy.

There's another reason why yoo shood do it.

The edjucashnel interests uv the South shood be entrusted to them ez knows how to manage em, and who to edjucate. We don't want it too common. It's too much power. I know the power ther is in it. I'm about the only one here who kin rite — were ther more, it wood hurt my standin.

Look at wat miscellaneous education hez done for the North! Noo England is a cloud bustin with educashen. That black cloud hez swept over the North, and all over that country its drops hev fell in the shape uv schools, academies, and colleges, and sich. Consekently, there's no Democracy ther; and the heavier the shower a locality received the less Democracy there is. In yoor hands it wood be safe. Niggers woodent git it, nor poor whites; but the sons uv the chivalry, uv the dominant race, they alone wood tread the flowery path with yoo.

We heven't the society at the Cross Roads in wich yoo hev bin accustomed to move, but wat uv that? Let it be known what yoo are, and the Democrisy uv the North will make this a place uv summer resort, and of winter recreashen. This will be their Mecca — yours will be the shrine at which they will come and worship.

Then come. To yoo the Cross Roads opens her arms, and offers her bosom for yoo to repose onto.

Come! Erect here yoor alters and yoor fires, ontil an ashamed nashen bids yoo take the highest place in its gifts, in reparashen uv the wrong they did to you two yeers ago.

On behalf uv the Trustees,

PETROLEUM V. NASBY, P. M.
(Wich is Postmaster), and Professor in the Ham and Japheth Free Academy for the Development uv the Intelleck uv all Races irrespective of Color.

his
GABREL X POGRAM,
mark
his
G. W. X BASCOM,
mark

HUGH McPELTER,

his
ISSAKER X GAVITT,
mark

Administrator uv the Estate uv Abimilek Gavitt, late deceased.

XXI.

A Vision of the Next World. — Mr. Nasby (in a Dream) is present in the Lower Regions during the Consideration of Mr. Greeley's Case.

Post Offis, Confedrit X Roads
(Wich is in the Stait uv Kentucky),
June 1, 1867.

THE Corners wuz in a most pleasant frame uv mind last Friday nite. So important a event ez the release uv our saintid Davis cood not be allowed to go by without commemoratin, and we accordingly commemoratid. The rejoicins wuz held at the Church, tho they commenst at Bascom's. Ez the heftiest part uv the rejoicin hed bin done at Bascom's, taperin off, ez I may say, at the Church, the speeches were very short, ef not to the pint. When, how, or wher it adjourned, I know not. I wandered orf into the realms uv Morphus in the middle uv Deekin Pogram's sekondly, and afore I got back I hed taken a rather long journey.

I dreamed a very curis dream. Methawt I wuz in the regions that are populerly supposed to lay below us. Onto his burnin throne sot Lucifer a reading the Noo York Triboon, with the most puzzled expression onto his face I ever witnest. Laying it down with a sigh, ez tho he hed gone bumpin onto a stunner wich he cood not comprehend, he remarkt, sadly, " To biznis!" and demandid uv his book-keeper the sitooashen of things. Reports were read to him, wich, in the main, pleased him. A shade uv sadniss becloudid his classikle countenance ez the statement that Napoleon and Bizmark hed made up, but his face illuminatid serenely ez it was statid that the Christian nashens hed decidid to let the Turks go on a butcherin the Cretans, wich wuz replaced with a frown agin when he wuz informed that there wuz a prospeck uv the English common people gettin a vote. After goin thro the rest uv the world, the United States come in.

" Kentucky," sed the book-keeper, lookin over a bundle uv fresh reports, " is all rite. Helm is electid Governor by a whackin majority, and McKee and Rice is defeetid."

" Good!" sed he, fetching his tail down in a ecstasy uv joy. " The next time I swing around the cirkle I must visit Kentucky. No State does so well for me with so little uv my assistance. I alluz like to visit Kentucky. Noo York city is ruther pleasant, tho it's so near like my own place that I don't enjoy it much when I'm there. I don't feel ez tho I'm away from home a visitin. But Kentucky I love — the people reely charm me. But go on, wat next?"

"Jeff'son Davis hez bin liberatid by Horris Greeley becomin his bale. This balein by Greeley, the reporter stashened at Washington considers a most momenchus event, and a most happy okkurrence for yoor majesty."

"That reporter's a ass, and don't know the secret springs wich actooate men. Recall him to-wunst for making sich a foolish remark."

"But," sed the Sekretary, who seemed to me to be a imp uv some consekence, to be permitted to argoo with Lucifer hisself, "I consider it uv importance. Did yoo wish Jeff'son Davis to die in prizen?"

"Ef yoo wuzn't uv desided yoose to me, hevin bin a Noo York Alderman, I'd redoose yoo. Want Jeff'son Davis to die? Not I. I'm not the yooth wot killed the goose wot laid the golden egg. He's bin the best recrootin lootenant I ever hed.

He hez the happy knack uv controllin everybody
he hez anythin to do with, and he turns em all
to'ard me.   He rooined Polk, he swampt Pierce,
he sedoost Bookannon, he dazzled Johnson, and he
hez now caught Horris Greeley.   But ther wuzn't
any danger uv his dyin in prizen.   Men ain't in the
habit uv dyin on panned oysters, briled beefsteak,
and milk toast ; they hev a trick uv peggin out
faster on diet suthin the opposite uv that ; for instance, the variety that Jeff'son furnished em at
Andersonville.   He wood hev got out any how.
Johnson is, after all, a poor white man, and he
cood bully them uv that class well enuff; but he
felt ashamed uv keeping a real gentleman like Davis
in prizen, and he wood hev releast him."

"Shel I put Horris down on our books?" askt
the Sekretary, eagerly, dipping his pen into bloo
flame ez Hertzog does in the Black Crook.

"Let us consider!" sed Lucifer, musinly. "Wat
hez he did?"

"Bailed Jeff'son Davis!" returned the Sekretary,
confidently, givin his pen a fresh dip.

"Very good.   Horris hez made uv hisself, to
speak figgeratively, a post for a drove uv hogs to
scratch themselves agin.   They are scramblin out
uv the slough uv secession in wich they wallered

till the droppin out uv the bottom made it dangerous; they find Horris a standin on the bank, and
agin him they rub their sides to clean off the mud
wich adheres. I speak figgeratively in likenin
Horris to a post; literally in likenin the secesh to
swine. They wuz jest ez senseless and jest ez
crooel. They wuz the wuns afore wich pearls wuz
cast.

"I hev jest finisht his defence of hisself. It's a
curious dokeyment, and puzzles me. I'm disposed
to consider him honest, — but wat a week showin
he makes! First, he sez he's honest, wich is alluz
agin a man, for a trooly honest man kin alluz find
enuff others to say it for him. 2d. He tries to prove
it, wich is very bad, for the honesty wich needs
provin is uv a rather scaly order. He instances his
spilin his chances for the Senit last fall by writin
that universal amnesty letter. Horris, in this matter, is, I fear, playin ostrich. He hez his hed in the
sand, and, bein blind hisself, fancies the balance uv
his anatomikle strukter, wich ought to be in the
background, ain't visible to the rest uv mankind.
Or, he is reely a loonatic!

"I never hed any idea that he wantid the seat in
the Senit. He wuz in Congress wunst, and the
terrible failure he made ther wood, ef he wuz con-

scious uv it, hev deterred him from seekin that per-tikeler place agin. Then, ef he wuz reely *compus mentus*, he wood hev knowd, or ought to hev knowd, that he hedn't the ghost uv a chance for the place, and coodn't hev got it ef he hed written a letter urgin the hangin of every rebel, from Jeff'-son Davis down to Commodore Hollins. It looks to me very much like ez ef Horris wuz playin the old game uv declinin wat hed never bin offered him. His letter wuz soundin brass and tinklin cymbals."

" Shel I enter him or not?" askt the Sekretary.

" It's a curis case," said Lucifer, not mindin him. " He hez bin agin me, by spasms, and when he he done things wich I could approve, I hev alluz, so far, entered it up to the account uv loonacy; for I am pertikler about puttin my claw onto any man who don't belong to me. I hev a clear rite to every one I git. This last trick uv his staggers me! Kin it be that the old man wuz, all along, opposin wrong and sich, not from any deep-seated dislike to the artikle, but becoz opposin things wuz his best holt? Kin it be — hevin bin in the minority all his life, and found therein profit because it so happened that the minority wuz rite — that he is now anxious to git into that fix agin? Does Horris spose, that hevin the strength uv a successful career to back him, and hevin a hundred thousand more or less, who are in the habit uv readin him — the people will follow him through the stinkin slums uv error jest ez lively ez they did over the breezy hills uv trooth? Hez his vanity got the better uv his discretion at last? Hev the hangers-on, wich alluz puff incense into the face uv success, been burnin hasheesh afore him, and hez it intossicatid him? Is he, at his advanced age, in imitashen uv Sut Lovingood's daddy, goin tō play hoss, forgittin the hornet's nest into wich his great exemplar plunged?"

"Shel I put him down or not?" askt the Sekretary agin, rather impatiently.

"No!" replied Lucifer, drawin hisself up decisively. "Ef he splits up the Ablishnists, we shel be so deep in his debt that he will deserve to git clear uv us. Ez it is, he hez done enuff to entitle him to our gratitood. He hez restored Jeff'son Davis to me; he hez even enlarged his field uv usefulnis. He is a demonstratin the theory that there ain't no sich thing ez treason, and ez a matter uv course, that there ain't bin no crime committed by my friend Davis's friends. Ez Horris is establishin the fact that the war agin my friends in the South wuz unjustifiable, I shoodent be surprised ef the next thing he does, in order that justis may be done, will be to insist that their niggers be returned to em. After all, I speckt that's wat he's drivin at. Now that slavery's abolisht, I bleeve he'd like to hev it restored, that he. may hev suthin to do. His okkepashen's gone. He's short uv a subjict now. His pen hez bin so used to writin slavery! slavery! slavery!—that he's reely at sea now that he kin write it no more. He wants that joocy old sin set up for him to batter at agin. He wants Lovejoy shot over agin, and bleedin Kansas to be repeetid. Wat's a perfessional Reformer ef ther ain't nothin to reform? Wat's a corn doctor in a country wher they wear big boots? No! let him go. He's shoor uv punishment enuff any how. He's a Universlist, a doctrine the mistake of wich he'll diskiver some day; but he's very likely to realize his ijee uv punishment on earth, for Wendell Phillips is after him, and wat wuss can he suffer? Set this last act uv his'n down ez honesty streakt with loonacy; or ruther, the loonacy bein the biggest, ez loonacy streakt with honesty, and leave him out— Go on with the reports. Where's Davis now? and particulerly, where's Johnson? Ef he does anythin agin me, he does it thro mistake. Keep track uv Johnson; don't let—"

At this pint I wuz aroused by somebody shakin me. It wuz Bascom. It wuz 8 o'clock, and ez I had not bin over for my mornin bitters, in wich dooty I'm very regler, the good man hed gone out in search uv me. How pleasant 'tiz to have somebody to care for yoo, even ef ther solisitood springs from a ten-cent motive.

Petroleum V. Nasby, P. M.

(Wich is Postmaster), and Professor in the Ham
and Japheth Free Academy for the Develop-
ment uv the Intellek uv all Races irrespectiv
of Color.

XXII.

A Faithful Account of the Trip to Raleigh, including the Discussion before the Start.

POST OFFIS, CONFEDRIT X ROADS
(Wich is in the Stait uv Kentucky),
June 10, 1867.

I ACCOMPANIED the President to Rawly. The President doesn't feel safe at goin anywhere without me to arrange the details, and do the nice financeerin wich is necessary.

The Rawly trip wuz the occasion of a serious truble in the Kabinet. The President wuz in favor uv it. Ez he sed, he wuz essenshelly uv a filial persuasion. He hed alluz experienced a most consoomin love for his parents, pertickelerly for them on his father's side. He hed swung around the entire cirkle uv offishel honor, and hed found traitors on all sides; but he could lay his hand on his heart and say that he hed never knowd a troo man but who, at some period of his life, hed a father.

Why, then, should we not honor our fathers? How
could it be better dun than by layin corner-stuns?
His father deceest in 1812, and it wuz time that
this dooty was attended to. Besides, at this crysis
in the affairs of the country, with Wilson and Kelly
a snortin through the South, he felt it wood be a
good thing to show ourselves.

Seward felt that it wuz well to go. Filial love
wuz charmin. Shakspeer, who wuz ez justly celebrated ez a dramatist ez one he cood menshun wuz
for diplomatic telegraffin, remarkt, " How sharper
nor a serpent's tooth it is to hev a thankless child,"
— the truth of which he hed experienced, ez he hed
been styled the father uv the Republican party : but
that wuz not to the pint. It is the dooty uv every
son to lay corner-stuns. In this case it wood, perhaps, hev been more creditable hed it been dun
fifty years ago ; but wat difference is it? It is natral
ez we are about being gathered to our fathers, that
we shood remember em. Besides, he hed a little
speech wich he felt he'd like to deliver. He wanted
to bear testimony to the patriotism uv the son uv
Jacob Johnson — particularly to our colored brethren in North Carliny, who hev bin listenin to Kelly
and Wilson.

Randall didn't bleeve in it at all. He made bold

to say that ez the deceast Johnson hed slept without a corner-stun for fifty-five years, he'd manage to git along a while longer.   It wuz rather late in the day. He bleeved in feelin sorrowful over the decease uv our relatives, but he didn't go much on doin it fifty-five years after date.   It wuz too much like bustin into tears over the suffrins uv the last illness uv yer wife's great grandmother.   The speeches he didn't bleeve in at all.   He hed seen some uv it — he hed accompanied one toor uv the kind.   He hed bin on it.   He wuz at Cleveland, at Indianapolis, and Springfield, Illinoy.   He begged to be excoosed. He didn't keer about tailin sich a kite agin.   Ef the people uv the South shood receive us ez corjelly ez the people uv the North did, he preferred to consult his feelins and be absent.   He wuz a sensitive plant, and disliked sum things.   Ef his memory served him rite, the demonstrashens coodent be considered flatterin.   The people didn't fling dead cats at us, but they did wuss.   Ef they wuz cold, they wuz rather too cold.   Ef they wuz in a volatile humer, they wuz rather too lively.   He hed about made up his mind that it wuzn't uv any yoose to fite it out on that line ef it took all summer.   Success is a dooty; but when success is ez impossible ez water in the great Sahara, wat's the yoose?

Wherefore struggle? Let us go slow, draw our salaries to the end uv our 'spective terms, and so live that wen the summons comes to jine the innoomerable caravan that moves out uv Washington to'ards their 'spective homes, we go not like the dusty slave at nite, wat's bet his all on two pair, but soothed and sustained by wat we saved, — go like one who's got the wherewithal to live. It wuz a source uv comfort to him to know that the worst uv men wuz soon forgotten. Who ever speeks uv Tyler, or Peerce, or Bukanon, now? Benedict Arnold is only spoken uv on Fourth uv Julys, and Judis Iskariot on Sundays. It will be so with us in time, for wich thank the Lord.

But it was determined to go, and I was sent to Rawly to find where the grave uv the honored father of our honored President was reely locatid, and to make sich other arrangements ez the eggsigencies uv the case demanded, wich I did. I hed difficulty in locatin the grave, and ain't jest shoor that I found the right one. The people uv Rawly wuz anxshus to hev it come off, ez trade was dull in the retail line; and for fear that I wood report that the grave coodent be found, and thus nip their budding hopes, they giv me the choice uv sum twelve

fifteen.   Selectin the most eligible, I made the
ier arrangements and returned.

The eggscurzion contrasted very favorbly with the
e we took last fall.   The people receeved uz at
ery stashen with the most affectin demonstrashuns
luv. "Johnson! Johnson! Johnson!" they yelled
each stopping-place, wich sounded sweeter in
ears and mine than the damnable iterashun of
Grant! Grant! Grant!" wich greetid us at every
it North.   The President wuz sorry he hedn't
in Grant with him, to show him that ef he wuz
most popular in sum localities, we hed the
arts uv the people in uthers.   But ther wuz draw-
x to our enjoyment.   No sooner wood the Presi-
nt commence, "Fellow-citizens!" than Randall
od pull the bell-rope, and off the trane wood
rt.   He wuz determined that the President
uldent speek, wich put me to a grate deal uv
uble, ez after we arrived I hed to write out and
egraph to the papers the speeches the President
od hev made.

At Rawley, General Battles welcomed the Presi-
ntial party, and the President responded.   He
narked that in Rawley he first opened his tender
es, a penniless boy.   Here is the scenes uv his
ildhood; here is everything to bind man to his

fellow, and to associate him with that with wich he is associated ; here is where the tenderness uv heart hev taken holt upon everything to wich it hez attached itself. But he was wandrin from his subjick. His mind went back to the day he left this city a penniless boy. Where is them wich he left behind him? He begged to inquire where is the scenes uv his childhood? Where's the Haywoods?

" Killed at Antietam ! " shouted a returned Confedrit. " I wuz by William's side when he wuz shot."

" Where is the Hunters? "

" Running a distillery at Waxhall Court 'ouse," sed this same fellow, who thot the President really wantid to know. He wuz choked down, and the President proceeded : —

" Wher is the Roysters and the Smithses, the Brownses and the Joneses? Wher is the long list of men that lived at that day, and who, like me, command respeck for constancy of devoshen ? I feel proud of this demonstrashen — I feel proud of any demonstrashen. Ez alloosion hez bin made to my boyhood days, when I wuz a penniless boy, I may say here, ez pertinent to that subjeck, that I hev adhered to the fundamental principles uv the gov'ment, and to the flag and Constooshen. But to return to my subjeck. When I went out from among yoo a penniless boy, I adoptid the Constooshen ez my guide, and by them I have allus bin guided. To the young I would say that they will be safe in takin me ez a model. Leavin here a penniless boy, it is not for me to say whether or not I hev succeeded. I am no longer a penniless boy, nor is them wich are round me. Mrs. Cobb ain't a penniless boy; nor is — But this is a wanderin from the subjeck. For the encouragement uv the young men afore me, I wood say, that I hev enjoyed all I care about. I am no aspirant for nothing, and therefore the way I now open for em. All places uv honor is now before em. I thank you for this corjel welcom. North Caroliny sent me out a penniless boy, and did not afford me sich advantages ez, considerin my merits, I ought to hev hed ; yet I luv her. It's better ez it wuz. Goin out a penniless boy, and returnin after holdin every offis, from Alderman uv my adoptid village up to President, shows my qualities to much better advantage than ef I hedn't gone out a penniless boy. I thank you for this tribute to my many good qualities."

And he startid to go down, when Randall whispered suthin in his left ear.

Risin promptly, and drawin out his hankerchief,

the President assoomed a look uv subdood greef, and resoomed.

"I hev come among yoo to participate in the dedicashen uv a monument to a man which yoo all loved, tho it hez taken suthin like fifty yeers for yoo to diskiver it. He wuz poor and humble, wich akkounts for my goin from among yoo a penniless boy; but uv him I am proud, — for hed it not been for him, I woodent hev returned the shinin example to yoor young men wich I am."

The corner-stun wuz laid, and the monument set on it. It is uv red limestone, ten foot high. It's ez good a ten foot uv stun respeck ez there is in North Carliny. Ez the monument was elevatid, there wuz the appropriate speeches, and then my little arrangements cum in. A nigger woman I hed took with us from Washington rushed for'ard, and sed, " Bress de Lord, I'ze bin a waitin for dis day to see de President, — OUR President!" at which a squad of niggers I'd picked up and drilled, hollered "'Ror!"

This little affectin sceen over, two quadroons, wich I'd also bro't with us in a privit car, cum for'ard with a expression of profound greef, at wich the President wept, and tenderly slung bokays uv the choicest flowers we cood buy in Washington, upon the tomb.

It wuz reely a techin tabloo. The ancient nigger woman a holdin the President's hand; the young quadroons a slingin the bokays; the President with his head bowed, apparently a dreamin uv the days uv his boyhood; me with an expression uv thankfulness that the niggers hed at last recognized their Moses; Seward with a saintly smile on his face; Welles tryin to look ez near like Seward as possible, but failin miserably to look like anything but the eggrejis old ass he is, and Randall with his handkercher to his eyes ez ef onmanned by the movin sceen, but keepin one eye cocked over the handkercher to see how it took among the niggers. It wuz a sceen easier to be imagined than described.

Ther wuz several incidents which occurred wich did not appear in the telegraph. When his Excellency wuz speekin uv himself, and remarkt that his race wuz nearly run, a unregenerated nigger yelled out " Tank de Lord! " And when the quadroons wuz a strewin flowers on the grave uv His Excellency's father, I observed rather more titterin among the niggers than I approved uv on so sollum an occasion. I askt Randall what he thought of the

spekelashen, and his answer, "It don't pay!" struck me ez havin a vane uv trooth running through it.

On our return, the President wuz allowed to speek more, for Randall got tired of watching him. We returned in good health, and some uv us in good spirits. Seward feels well, for he hez an abidin faith that the mere showin uv hisself alluz hez an effeck for good upon the people, and ez a matter uv course Seckretary Welles thinks so to.

PETROLEUM V. NASBY, P. M.
(Wich is Postmaster), and Professor in the Ham and Japheth Free Academy for the Development uv the Intelleck uv all Races irrespective of Color.

13

XXIII.

The Boston Excursion. — An Account of the Preparatory Discussion.—The Start, and the Progress up to the beginning of the Masonic Festivities.

TREMONT HOUSE, BOSTON
(Wich is in the Stait uv Massachoosets),
June 25, 1867.

THE Raleigh trip scarcely over, His Serene Highness determined upon acceptin the Boston invitashen. His corjel recepshen in North Karliny give him a sort uv appetite for popler applause, and he determined upon tryin it in the North agin. At the Cabinet meetin held to discuss the question, Seward expressed a desire to go. Welles follered Seward; but Randall, who, sence the decease of Sir Isik Newton, is considered the strongest man connected with the Administrashen, and therefore assooms diktatorial airs, opposed it.

"But," sed Johnson, "I feel ez though I must make one more effort to save our errin Southren brethren."

"Mr. President," retortid Randall, "I recently went to raise a coruer-stun to the memry uv yoor lamentid father, who deceest in 1812, onto wich wuz engraved these words: —

'*Jacob Johnson; died from the Effex uv a Disease superindoost by a over Effort to save his Friends from drownin.*'

"Now, ef yoo persist in yoor loonacy, I shel be compelled, after a time, in my quiet Wisconsin home, where an appreciative constitooency will permit me to forever stay, to indite an epitaff for the corner-stun over your politikle grave, wich I shel do thus: —

'*Hic jacet* Andrew Johnson,
Who died from the Effex uv a Disease sooperindoost by over Effort in a great many Attempts to save his Politikle Friends from bein strangled.
'*Poskript.* — *The Friends wuzn't wuth the savin.*'

"But upon sekond thot I've no objeckshun to this toor. Yoo kin do us no damage ef yoo deliver only sich speeches ez we determine upon before hand.

Yoo go thro Delaware, which is ourn; Noo Gersey yoo've bin thro wunst, and they know wat to expect; New York will give a enthoosiastic recepshun ef Morrisy and Wood will take holt uv it, — Seward, telegraff em, — and in Connecticut yoor certain uv a corjel resepshen. That State is full uv demoralized Yankee Dimocrats, who hev bin out to Michigan, and left there all ther Puritanism, bringin back with em, in its stead, all the cussidnis indigenous to that soil, wich cussidness, grafted onto ther natral cutenis, makes em rather enterprisin in ther worthlisnis. In Boston itself, the prospeck is good. There'll be a immense crowd present to dedicate the Masonik Temple, wich we shell claim the credit uv bringin, ez we did the throngs which come to see us on the toor north, but wich wood persist in hollerin 'Grant!' The trooly good men uv Boston are Ablishnists; but there's some thousands wich want offices, and them, with a sprinklin uv Demokrats and Conservatives, ought to make us a handsome recepshen. There is yet men in Boston who used to return fugitive slaves, and ther is besides the eminently respectable gentlemen who are so conservative that they hold onto sin becoz it's old and established by precedent, and so aristocratic that they won't do right, jist becoz doin rite is a quite common thing in that secksun;

who hold onto the cote-tale uv progress, and holler 'Stop!' and who, ef they tie theirselves to a good cause, load it down with their dignity. Like the 2d Lootenants uv '61, their baggage is worth mor'n they are. But the trip won't hurt us. You can't make the Ablishnists more Ablishn, and them ez foller us for the loaves and fishes we dispense, wood still foller us, ef the road we took led ez strate through perdishen ez a pigeon wood fly. It may be that it's the method by wich we shel finally carry Noo England. Pope sez, —

> ' Vice is a monster uv such hidjus mien,
> That to be hated needs but to be seen.'

" Now, ef we follered the poet no further, we shood never go, but each one wood keep ez close in his respective apartment ez possible. But, knowin man kind, he goes on : —

> ' But seen too oft, familiar with its face,
> We first endoor, then pity, then embrace.'

" That's it. We must be seen too oft. We must make em familiar with our face. Ef we stay long enuff, I don't despair uv seein Boston givin yoo an ovashen, and seein yoo locked in the arms uv Wendell Phillips. Ef they commence pityin you, the reackshen will take them to the embracin, and it seems ez though they ought to be at that pint by this time. And then ef yoo make this toor, and say nothing ideotik, the very novelty uv it will direct attention from wat we've desided to do with Sheridan, Sickles, Pope, et al. It will bewilder the people."

And so it wuz desided to go. Thro Delaware the resepshens wuz all that we desired, and in Maryland the people come in crowds to greet us; tho the cheers partook so much uv the nacher uv the cheerful yells wich the Confedrit soljers employed when they charged, that Sekretary Seward's nerves wuz somewat shockt. Ez Philadelphy didn't offer us the hospitalities uv the city, we didn't stop ther at all. The train run around it, the President's nose bein elevatid all the time ez tho he smelt suthin. When it had finally passed, Mr. Randall announst the fact, and the Presidenshel face assoomed its yoosual benine expression ez we glided into the sacred soil uv Noo Gersey.

In Noo York, Morrissy hed done his part. Ther wuz spectable bodies uv cheerers at the pints agreed upon, and, ez they hed bin paid librally, the spontaneous enthoosiasm wuz ez good in quality ez it wuz large in quantity. Occasionally a cheerer, wich hed taken too much uv his wages in advance,

wood yell for Jeff'son Davis, but it wuzn't notist.
It didn't mar the pleasant uniformity uv the pro-
ceedins, or strike anybody ez bein singler. They
tried terrible hard to get a speech out uv us, and
the President wuz willin; but Randall, seein that
the Herald and Triboon hed reporters present, supprest him, and got him off to bed comparatively
sober, and very early.

Arrivin at Boston, I wuz surprized at the length,
depth, and breadth uv the enthoosiasm wich greeted
us. Ez ef to show ther greef at the death uv Presidents, we notist everywhere the portraits of our pred-
ecessor, Linkin, draped in mournin, at wich the
President dropt a tear, sayin, " See how they mourn
us wen we're everlastinly gone!" Ther wuz a sort
uv subdood enthoosiasm, a kind uv half-mournin
gladnis, ef I may say so, wich wuz gratifyin.

We wuz receeved by Gov'nor Bullock, whose
speech wuz a noble triboot to the President. " I
welcome yoo," sed he, " to Massachoosits. Many
Presidents hev visited Noo England, and this visit,
like theirn, excites devoshen to the Yoonion, and
respeck for them, wich, in their offishel posishen,
respeck the government uv the whole country. Our
desire is to manifest our regard for those who, in
offishel capacity, respeck the Nashnel Yoonion,

wich is to say, we respeck the Nashnel Yoonion. I trust the President will stay long enuff to enable us to manifest our high regard for — (here the President's face brightened up) YOOR OFFIS! (the President turned frightfully red, wich Bullock, whose principles wuz a rasslin a back holt with his politeness, notist, and he added) — AND TO YOO, PERSONALLY!"

Ez them last words ishood slowly and despritly, the President's face lighted up. He tendered him thanks for the resepshun. He woodent undertake to conceel emoshens which agitated him at this personel welcome upon the soil uv Massachoosits. It wuzn't necessary for him to go into the histry uv Massachoosets ez he wuz in the habit uv doin further South, ez those afore him wuz probably ez familyer with it ez he wuz; but he wood ashoor em, for their encouragement, that the histry uv Massachoosits, in conneckshn with the histry uv these States, hez become a part uv the histry uv the country; and therefore, in visitin Massachoosits under sich pekoolyer circumstances, it is pekoolyerly gratifyin to receeve sich a welcome. In regard to yoor remarks tetchin the preservashen uv these States, I trust I may say without egotism, a vice wich I hev never bin accused uv, and from wich I may say no

one is more singlerly free than myself, I yield to no
patriot, livin or dead, in my devoshen, to that purpose. I dislike speekin, ez I kin trooly say that I
am not loquashus; but when trooth, wich I love,
and the coz uv humanity, wich I tie to, is at stake,
I hev spoke. I may say, without egotism, that I
live for principle; and I thank the people uv Massachoosits, wich my visit hez drawd to Boston, for the
outburst uv regard wich greets me. Without egotism I may say, that it's a outburst ekalled by few
and excelled by none ever given a President in the
Yoonited States or elsewhere; and it is my prayer
that comin in contact with me will do the people
uv Boston good. Yoor remarks, not referrin di-
reckly to me, on the Rooshn purchis, and a more
economical collecshin uv the internal revenue, also
meets my corjel approbashen, lovin ez I do my common country."

Randall pulled at his coat-tale, when the President remarkt that he might say, without egotism,
that he didn't desire to make a speech, and stopt.
We brought him off in comparatively good order.

We stopt at the Tremont House. It is a good
hotel, and the waiters are ez they ought to be, niggers. It's soothin to a troo Dimekrat to be waited
on by a nigger. Yoo kin damn a nigger waiter,

but put a white man in that posishen and yoo feel a delicacy about it. When we retired, the President insisted that I shood sleep lyin across the doorway uv his room.

" Why?" asked I.

" I am in Boston," replied he, " wher they stun the prophets. Boston dislikes me. Boston wears to-day a smilin face; but wot kind uv a hart does that smilin face conceal? Sumner lives in Boston, and so does Phillips. In Boston they elect niggers to the Legislacher, and are tryin to stop the sale uv whiskey. Wot kind uv a place is that for a Dime-kratic President to trust hisself into? Yoo sleep across my doorway, and ef a band uv Ablishnists, deemin me their foe, shood strive to enter, they wood hev to first sheath their daggers in yoor body. Meanwhile I wood escape, and continyoo to live for my lovd country. You cood, by preparin be-forehand a few impressive last words, make a gorjus death uv it, and do the coz good. For instance, ez Sumner stuck yoo, yoo cood gasp, " Slay me, but spare A. J., the hope uv the Republic." Or, ez Wilson struck yoo down with a bludgeon, yoo mite exclaim, " I die willinly for the Constitooshen with 36 stars onto it." Any little quotashen from any uv my speeches, joodiciously throwd in under sich circumstances, wood do good. Yoo will sleep ther to-night; and remember, in case you are called upon to die, the proper quotashens."

Seward concurred, but Randall objectid. He didn't anticipate any sich danger. Ef Boston wants to git rid uv the President, they hev a shorter way than assassinashen. Rash politishuns only assassinate them wich they can't find cause to impeach. But he wuzn't afraid uv Boston. We stood a better chance uv dying of excessive hospitality in Boston than uv bein stabbed. Our stomachs mite protrude in Boston, but our bowels never. Boston wood feast us, for ther are enuff men in Boston who want posishen to keep us a goin a year or two. He feared dyspepsia more than daggers, and hed no fears uv the wine bein pizened.

Nevertheless, I wuz forst to sleep in that posishen, wich I did, wakin up in the mornin ez sore and stiff ez a plow-hoss. I don't know how far the trip will be extended.

PETROLEUM V. NASBY, P. M.

(Wich is Postmaster), and Professor in the Ham and Japheth Free Academy for the Development uv the Intellek uv all Races irrespectiv of Color.

XXIV.

Mr. Nasby dreams a Dream, caused, probably, by the New England Atmosphere which he was breathing: Prefaced by some few Incidents of the Visit of his Grand Seigneur to Boston.

TREMONT HOUSE, BOSTON
(Wich is in the Stait uv Massachoosets),
June 29, 1867.

I HEV alluz hed an incorrect idea uv Boston. I sposed Boston to be strate-laced, moral to a degree not to be understood by a Dimocrat, and Puritanicle. I wuz mistaken. Ther is ez heavy a per cent. uv men in whom His Eggslency and I kin take delite ez ther is in any city in the country, ez the followin incidents, which came under my notice, will show : —

Ez we wuz a goin through Franklin Street, a man stepped up to the carriage rather hesitatinly.

" Mr. President," sed he.

" Well," sed His Eggslency, turnin full upon him.

The site uv the nose uv the Step Father uv his Country reashured him.

"Mr. President, wood yoo like some punch?"

"Punch! Certainly. But hevn't yoo suthin stronger, to lay a foundashen with?"

"Certinly!" and he pulled a bottle uv brandy from his right hind-pocket, and the great man took an observashen uv the sky thro the bottom uv it, wich lasted a minnit. I never agin will doubt that the material to make Democrisy uv exists in a country where they come at yoo with punch, and hev brandy bottles in their coat-pockets.

Bokays were showered upon us. One old gentleman, who sot two hours in a chair waitin to present us with his, finally histed it at us. The fact that ther wuz a note in it askin fur a posishen fur the genrous giver, don't detract anything from the valyoo uv the gift. When we got to the end uv our trip there wuz a dray-load uv bokays in our carriage, and in all but three uv em wuz tied-up recommendashens for the givers for places. It is better to hev sich missives enveloped in roses, though the most thorns we git ain't got roses round em.

The most techin incident was the number uv babies we hed to kiss. The mothers pressed to our carriage-steps to present their offsprings. Mistakin me for the President, I kisst half uv em. The rapcherus expreshun on the upturned faces uv the anxshus mothers affected the President to teers, showin, ez it did, the confidence reposed in him.

"Whisht, Teddy!" sed one uv em, "and howld yer mug up fer the man to kiss who doesn't kiss the dirthy nagers!"

"Musha, Phelim, be still. The Presidint, bless his sowl, won't bite ye!"

"Lind me yer apurn, Peggy, to wipe Terry's face wid. The Prisidint must kiss the darlin. 'Taint ivery Prisidint wood do the loike."

And the President kissed, and I kissed, till our lips wuz sore.

Sich is position.

That nite I received a letter from Deekin Pogram, in wich he desired me to ascertain whether or no there wuz eny bottom to the Northern Dimocrisy. Captain McPelter sed the Northern Dimocrisy wuz strong enuff to carry us uv Kentucky throo, while Pollock, the Illinoyer, swore the Northern Dimocrisy hed a considerable more to do to carry themselves than they hed bin able to accomplish for some time — that in a pullin match a corpse wuzn't uv much akkount, ef it wuz a big one. With this letter in my hand I fell asleep, and while asleep, drecmed.

Methawt I wuz in Noo Orleans at a gathrin uv the Faithful, who wuz called together for the purpose of considrin wat to do. Sum few — Longstreet, Gov. Brown, and Jeff. Thompson — wuz in favor uv submission, and hed got the majority uv the Southern people to agree with em that ther wuz no yoose uv further resistance, and they wuz jist about to so declare, when Vallandigham, Ben Wood, Toucey, Morrissey, Voorhees, and a score or two more uv that kind, rushed in and begged uv em to hold out. "Why submit?" sed Vallandigham. "We'll sustain yoo. The Northern Dimocrisy is a giant wich kin yet pertect yoo. He's in his prime, and strong enuff yit to carry yoo throo twice the troubles wich threatens yoo. Depend onto us — we'll carry yoo."

And the Southerners whopped over to their side and yelled fiercely, "No submission!" and immejitly the entire bilin uv em startid North with these men, to ascertain the strength and carryin capacity uv the Northern Dimocrisy. Methawt the party travelled and travelled until finally they come to a vast plain in Kentucky, onto wich wuz extendid prostrate the form uv a Giant. It was a Giant, immense in statoo, but emaciated to the last degree. His limbs hed bin strong, his teeth terrible, and his trunk massive; but it wuz plane to see that he wuz pegged out, and a look at its face showed why it wuz so. Dissipation had redoost him to helplessnis. His face wuz bloatid and bloo, his eyes wuz sot and ghastly, his chest was holler and sunken, his legs like pipe-stems, and ulcers, boils, sores, broozes, and contooshens kivered him from head to foot, and he drawd his breath with a effort.

He lay a groanin and a groanin. Randall wuz a tenderly feedin him out uv a huge bottle, labelled "Appintments," which appeared to give him temprary strength; but the effect of that wuz lost by President Johnson's dosin him with an offensiv smellin mixter, labelled "Policy," every swaller uv wich wood throw him into a spasm. Gov. English was rubbin one arm with a liniment Randall gave him, and hed succeeded in gettin up a little circulation in it.

"Wat is this?" askt the Southerners.

"Northern Dimocrisy!" sed English, rubbin away vigrously.

"Is this the Giant which is to carry us?" said the Southern gentlemen, viewin the disgustin objick doubtfully.

" Certainly ! " sed Johnson. " Now can't you git up ? " sed he to the prostrate bein, givin it a very large swaller out uv his bottle. The Giant made an effort, but flopped down agin like a dish-rag.

" Gentlemen ! " said Vallandigham, " we shel hev to call upon you to assist in settin him onto his feet, and then it'll be all rite with him. He's bin this way afore."

Accordingly, the Southerners gathered around him to lift him up. His arms, I notist, wuz marked respectively Connecticut and Delaware, and his legs Maryland and Kentucky, and in them there wuz strength, for ez soon ez the innocent Southerners got near enuff he wrapped them limbs around em, and sed, —

" Lift ! "

" We can't," sed they.

" Yoo must," sed he; " I got into this condishen fightin yoor battles, and doin yoor work. I was strong and vigorous until I got to runnin after yoor harlots; and for yoor sake I wuz druv out uv my native States into this accussid region. Yoo must carry me wat time I hev yet to live. Hist me ! hist me ! "

Those caught coodent get away, and the others

generously come to ther aid, and makin a terrible effort, they raised the half-dead bein onto their shoulders, holdin their noses meanwhile, and prepared to start. Ez the percession wuz about to move, Vallandigham remarked, " Stop a minit, gentlemen ! " and loaded ez he wuz with his war record, he clambered up ther shoulders and took a seat on the carkiss. Voorhees, jist ez badly encumbered, did likewise, and so did the Woods, both uv em, and poor Jimmy Bookannan, Seymour, Toucey, and a hundred or so more, the unfortunit bearers sweatin under this addishnal load.

" Is all ready ? " sed they.

" One moment ! " sed Johnson, and him and Randall, and Seward, climbed up.

This wuz the last feather. The bearers mite hev staggered off under the carkiss, and them wich climbed onto it first, but this last addishn to ther burden wuz friteful. It finisht em. Groanin under the weight, they swayed like a leaf in the wind, — like a majestic tree jist about to fall. They struggled a minit to maintain themselves — but all in vain. A breef struggle — a desprit gasp — they give up, and ther knees doublin up, the whole concern come to the earth with a squashin sound, wich letters can't express, and the half-decomposed mass sorter fell apart. Raymond and Thurlow Weed, wich hed bin hangin round, got out from under jist in time to save theirselves. The Southerners got out from under the putrid mass, tho almost smothered by the stench. Vallandigham and that class made lite uv it, ez they had bin around it. It staggered Johnson some, but he hed bin accustomed to suthin approximatin very closely to it in the old times, and it didn't serously affect him; but poor Randall, Seward, and Welles were smothered, and died.

I wuz tryin to pull Randall's corpse out, when the effort I wuz makin awoke me.

I ain't altogether certain but that that dream means suthin. When I think of it, it is rather preposterous for us to hope the Northern Dimocracy will carry us, when they can't carry a single State uv their own; jist about ez preposterous ez it is for them to look to us for help, when all uv us ez wood jine em hevn't got a vote. Pollock's remark, — "In a pullin match, a corpse ain't of much akkount, even ef it is a big one," — weighs onto my mind. Suthin can't come out uv nothin; tho ez in the case uv Seward, nothin may come out uv suthin. Ef we cood git — but, pshaw! we can't.   Thank the Lord, we kin hold the Post-offises two years yit.

PETROLEUM V. NASBY, P. M.

(Wich is Postmaster), and Professor in the Ham
and Japheth Free Academy for the Development uv the Intellek uv all Races irrespectiv
of Color.

XXV.

Mr. Nasby insists that the Democracy hold a National Convention at once, to define the Position of the Party upon an Important Question.

Post Offis, Confedrit X Roads
(Wich is in the Stait uv Kentucky),
July 12, 1867.

IN castin my eye carelessly over the politikle field, wich Seward and me do every sixty days, I think I kin spy into the horizon a bud wich is swellin into a most hopeful flower. It is spredin itself into a hurricane, wich threatens to sweep away the fabric uv Ablishnism and purify the politikle atmosphere. The Radikle party hev bin at last forced to adopt the legitimit endin uv their sooicidle principles, — nigger suffrage, — and from that the Dimokrisy, ef they are wise, will snatch a triumph litrally from the jaws uv death. WE HEV EM NOW. In Ohio that question is to be voted onto this fall; in Noo York and Michigan it's raisin a breeze in ther Convenshuns; and in Pennsylvania, Illinoy, and Indiana, it can't be long put off. It's our best holt. The proud Caucashen, wich votes the Dimecratic tikkit, hez no objeckshun to bein jossled by the Nigger in the rush to pay taxes; but his hawty soul recoils at the idee uv bein elbowed by him at the polls. Besides, the Dimecratic voters don't want the ballot given to any other lower class. It wood make undoo competishen. Ez I remarked, WE'VE GOT EM. Wat the Demokrisy want now is to so handle this delikit subjick ez to make the most uv it.

The great trouble with the party is, that there is no uniform style uv meetin this question. On the main question we are all agreed. We all oppose nigger suffrage. It's a part and parcel uv a Demokrat's nacher to oppose nigger suffrage. The leaders uv the party opposed it at the beginnin; for seein how the ballot wuz abused by ther followers, they trembled for the Republic ef it wuz entrusted to the hands uv any more uv ekal capassity, and the masses uv the organization opposed givin it to the nigger, becoz that one privilege, and color, wuz all that distinguished em. It's a pecoolyarity uv unregenerated human nacher that it must alluz bear down on somebody. The poet sez, —

> "Even the lice hev smaller ones to bite em,
> And they still smaller ones, ad infinitum."

Fortunately, the Dimokracy hev the nigger for their smaller lice. The sturdy yeomanry felt it to be a soothin thing to find, wunst each yeer, that in wun thing at least he wuz sooperior to someboddy; and so it will be so long ez there is a Dimokracy. The troo Dimokrat promotes hisself, not by liftin hisself above the level onto wich he finds hisself, but by shovin some wun down to a lower level; and ez ther wuzn't anybody else on this Continent wich they cood git hold uv, the nigger wuz, long ago, selected fur that purpose.

The great trouble is, we oppose nigger suffrage now from too many stand-pints. Some oppose it on the skore uv the inferiority uv the Afrikin; but that never wuz a popler idea with our people. They may hev assented to it outwardly, but in ther own minds they objected. "Ef," sez a reliable Dimokrat to hisself, "ef that's the rool, WAT IN THUNDER IS TO BECOME UV ME!"

Likewise the idea uv onfitness, wich others uv our apossels advance. "They can't read nor rite!" shreeks a injoodishus cuss, speekin to a audience, two thirds uv wich go to him reglerly to reed their ballots to em, and who, when they sign promissory notes, put an ✄ atween their first and last names.

Anuther speeker quotes Noah to em, and boldy asserts that the nigger is the descendant uv Ham, and that he is the identikle indivijjle wich wuz cust by Noah; but he runs agin the fact that the rest uv em, wich is in Afrika yet, hev managed to dodge the cuss, ez they ain't servin ther white brethren, and them wich wuz brot here to be Chrischinized hev busted ther bonds, and are jest about ez free, so far ez servitood goes, ez anybody.

There is, ez I hev showed, all these conflictin ideas that work agin us. Therefore, I want a Nash-nel Convenshun. I want a convocashen uv the lights uv the party to set forth authoritively WHY we oppose nigger suffrage — to give a reeson for it, that all our people may act together, ez do other well-regulated machines. Let us cum together and ishoo our manifesto, that we may know percisely the pertikler line uv argument to pursoo.

I shel be at that Convenshun, and I hev made up my mind wot platform to lay down. I shel go back on Ham, Hager, and Onesimus. I shel turn from the inferiority idea, and take the broad ground that *the nigger is a beast; that he ain't a man at all;* and consekently he hez no more rites than any other animal. I put my foot onto him by authority of the decree that unto man wuz given dominion over the beasts; that we are men, and they are beasts. Ef they admit the first proposishen, they will the last. I shel assert boldly and brodly his onfitnis to mingle with us, becoz his fizzikle structure, his muscles, nerves, fibres, bein different, go to show that he wuz uv a different origin, and uv a lower origin. I shel plant myself on the stoopenjus, yet simple proposishen, that the Almity made him, probably, but at a different time and for a different purpus, wich I shel show by citin the color uv his skin, the length uv his foot, the shape uv his head, and sich other matters as I kin git together in time for the Convenshen.

Uv course this doctrine will meet with objectors. We hev a few thin-skinned perfessers uv religion, whose piety service in our ranks hezn't quite obliterated, who will say that these dogmas undermines the Christian religion, ez it destroys the doctrin uv the unity uv the races onto wich orthodoxy is built. To this I shel answer, that sposin it does, wot then? Uv wot comparison is any religion a Orthodox Dimocrat hez to a triumph uv the party? Wot hez Dimocrisy to do with religion any how? It hez never permitted it to mix in its pollytix. Dimocrisy bleeves in keepin Church and State ez far apart ez possible.

Shood the Ablishnists pint to niggers wich reed and write, I shood say to-wunst that there is different degrees uv instink, — that ez one dorg hez more instink than another, that so one nigger hez more than another; and then I shood wind this answer up by askin him, "Sir, wood yoo force yoor dawter to marry a nigger, even ef he cood reed and write?" This hez alluz done good service, pertikelerly ef yoo walk hurridly away before there is time for an answer.

Ther is one pint wich is a stumper — but only one. One man to whom I unfolded this theory, asked me, sneerinly, wat I wuz a goin to do with a mulatter who wuz half white and half black — half man and half beast — half instink, wich dies with him, and half sole, wich wuz to be saved and fitted for the skies, or lost? When a mulatter dies, wat then? Does the half sole uv the half man drag the instink uv the beast behind it in a limpin, lop-sided fashion, into heaven? or does the instink drag the sole into the limbo for animals? "Ef this latter idea be correct," sed he, "in that limbo how much Southern sole is floatin about, held in solooshen in animal instink!"

An old friend uv mine, in Kentucky, become indignant wen I propounded the beast theory to him, and he threatened me with corporeal punishment ef I didn't quit his presence — wich I did to-wunst. Alas, for the imprudence of zealous men! Before speekin to him on the subjick, I didn't notis the skores uv brite yeller children all about the place, rangin from the infant uv six months to the boy uv sixteen, and all uv em with his noze!

But, notwithstandin these drawbacks, it's the most healthy doctrine we've got, and the only ground upon which we kin stand sekoorly. It kivers the ground, and besides, it don't interfere with anybody else's idea. The orators wich implore the people ef they want to marry niggers, kin make the appeal with more force after assertin that the nigger is a beast; and the anshent virgins, who will this fall bear the banners onto wich will be proudly inscribed, "We want no niggers for husbands!" will bear em still more defiantly; for, if they reely bleeve the doctrine, they will be in earnest in it.

At all evence, let the Convenshun be called, that this question may be settled. Let us all stand on one platform, that we may make the most uv this God-send. Let us inscribe onto our banner the inskripshen, "Ameriky fur white men!" "Eternel hostility to Animel Suffrage!" and go in to win. Ef the Amerikin people don't shy at Nigger Suffrage now, they never will.

PETROLEUM V. NASBY, P. M.
(Wich is Postmaster).

XXVI.

An Autobiographical Sketch.

Post Offis, Confedrit X Roads
(Wich is in the Stait uv Kentucky),
April 22, 1867.

EDITOR TOLEDO BLADE.   Sir : Enclosed find photograff uv myself, ez you desired. To make a strikin picter, I flung myself into the attitood, and assoomed the expreshun wich mite hev bin observed onto my classikle countenance when in the act uv deliverin my justly celebrated sermon, "The wages uv Sin is Death." The $2.00 wich yoo remitted to kiver the cost uv the picter wuz, I regret to say, insuffishent. The picter cost 75 cents, and it took $1.50 worth uv Bascom's newest to stiddy my nerves to the pint uv undergoin the agony uv sittin 3 minits in front uv the photograffer. I need not say that he is a incendiary from Massachoosets. Ez the deceased Elder Gavitt's son Issaker hez expressed a burnin desire to possess his apparatus, it is probable that public safety will very shortly require the expulsion uv the incendiary. But I hed my revenge — in his pockit is none uv my postal currency. Sekoorin the picter, I told him I wood take it home, and ef my intimit friends, those who knowd me, shood decide it wuz a portrait, I wood call and pay for it afore he left the Corners. Will I do it? Will this picter-takin Ablishnist ever more behold me? Ekko ansers.

Yoo may remit the odd twenty-five cents, either by draft on Noo York, or money order, at my resk.

I wuz born in the year 1806, at — I will not say where. I hev reasons for conceelin my birthplace. I don't want to set any town in that State up in biznis. That town hez gone loonatic, and gives Ablishn majorities friteful to contemplate, and I don't want to benefit it by givin it a nashnel rep-utashen. I don't want to double the price uv its property — to be the means uv erectin a dozen, or sich a matter, uv first class hotels to accommodate the crowds ez wood make pilgrimages thither to visit my birthplace. The present owner uv the house into wich I first opened my eyes onto a world uv sin, is a Ablishnist of the darkest dye, and I hev no desire to enrich him. Never, by word uv mine, shel he cut that house up into walkin sticks and buzzum pins.

My boyhood wuz spent in the pursoot uv knollege and muskrats, mostly the latter. I wuz a promisin child. My parence wuz Democrats, uv the strictest kind, my mother in partikeler. She hatid eny one that wuzn't Dimocratic, with a hatred that I never saw ekalled. When I say that she woodent borrer tea and sugar and sich uv Whig nabers, the length, and breadth, and depth of her Dimocrisy will be understood.

Uv my childhood, I know but little. My father wuz a leadin man in the humble speer in wich he moved, holdin, at different times, the various offices in the town up to constable, the successive steps bein road supervisor and pound master. He wuz elected constable, and mite probably hev gone higher, but for an accident that occurred to him the first month. He collected a judgment for $18, and the money wuz paid to him. The good man wuz a talented collector, but wuz singlerly careless in payin over wat he collected. Ez showin the pekoolier bent uv genius uv the old man, I repeet a conversashen I wunst heerd. A man who hed an account to collect, wuz consultin one who knowd my father well, ez to the safety uv puttin a claim into his hands.

"Is he a good collector?" askt the man.

"Splendid!" sed the naber.

"Is he a man uv responsibility?" askt the man.

"Sir!" sed the naber, "he hez the ability, but yoo'll find when yoo try to git yoor money out uv his hands that he lacks the response."

Cood ther hev bin a more techin triboot?

He wuz like all men uv genius, unbalanced. His ability was all on one side. The grovelin plaintiff, who didn't admire sich erratic flites, raised a ruckshen about the paltry sum, and my father

> "Folded his tent like the Arab,
> And ez silently stole away."

From that time out, the old gentleman migrated —in fact, he lived mostly on the road. He adopted movin ez a perfeshun, and a very profitable one he made uv it. When his hoss died, the nabors, rather than not hev him move, wood chip in and raise him another. Appreshiatin the compliment they pade him, he alluz went. I menshun these pekooliarities uv my ancestor, becoz

> "The lives uv all grate men remind us
> We may make our lives sublime,
> And, departin, leave behind us—"

ef our talent runs in that direckshun, ez many debts ez he did, though it does require espeshel talents.

This hed its inflooence upon my yoothful mind. I saw not only a great deal uv the country, but much uv mankind, and I acquired that adaptability to circumstances wich hez ever distinguished me. Even to this day, ef I can't git gin I kin take whiskey, without a murmur and without repinin.

My politicks hez ever bin Dimocratic, and I may say, without egotism, I hev bin a yooseful member uv that party. I voted for Jackson seven times, and for every succeedin Dimocratic candidate ez many times ez possible. For Mick Lellan, I only got in four votes. I didn't approve uv the nominashen, and wuz not overly zealous. Hed he bin electid, wat wood it hev availed me? He hed enuff dismist army officers follerin him to hev filled every offis in his gift, and I hed at that time become too old to foller pollytix for the amoozement it afforded, or for the benefit uv any cause.

But this is a digression.

My Dimocrisy wuzn't partikerly confirmed; in fact, I wuz not a Dimekrat from any speshel principle, but more becoz those in the speer in wich I moved wuz, until I arrived at the age uv twenty-four. My father wuz intimately acquainted with me, and knowd all my carakteristics ez well ez tho he hed bin the friend uv my buzzum. One day, ez I wuz a layin on my back under a tree, contemplatin the beauties uv nacher, my parent, sez he, —

"Pete" (wich is short for my name), "ef yoo ever marry, marry a milliner!"

"Why? father uv mine," replied I, openin my eyes.

"Becoz, my son," sed he, "she'll hev a trade wich'll support yoo, otherwise yoo'll die uv starvashen when I'm gone."

I thot the idea wuz a good one. Thro woman a cuss come into the world, wich cuss wuz labor; and I wuz determined that ez woman hed bin the coz uv requirin somebody to sweat for the bread I eat, woman shood do that sweatin. That nite I perposed to a milliner in the village, and she rejectid my soot. I offered myself, in rapid succeshun, to a widder, who wuz a washerwoman, and to a woman who hed boys old enuff to work, with the same result, when, feelin that suthin wuz nessary to be done to sekoor a pervision for life, I married a nigger washerwoman wich didn't feel above me. Wood you bleeve it? Within an hour after the ceremony wuz pronounst, she sold her persnel property, consistin uv a wash-tub and board, and a assortment uv soap, and investin the proceeds in a red calico dress and a pair uv earrings, insisted on my goin to work to support her! and the township authorities not only maintained her in her loonacy, but refused to extend releef to me, on the ground that I wuz able-bodied.

Ez I left that nigger, I vowed to devote my life to the work of gettin uv em down to where they wood hev to support us, and that vow I hev relijusly fulfilled. I hev never failed, by my vote and inflooence, to reduce em to ther normal condishun; I hev never felt good, ceptin when they wuz put down a peg; I hev never wept, save when they wuz bein elevated. I hev bin bathed in tears the heft uv the time for five years past.

The offices I hev held hev not been many. I hed signers to a petishun for a post-office in Jackson's time, but I killed my chances by presentin it in person. The old hero looked at me, and remarked that it wuzn't worth while throwin away post-offices on sich — that when he wanted em, he cood buy em at a dollar a dozen. Bookanan wuz agoin to appoint me, but somehow my antecedents got to his ears, and he wuz afeerd uv his respecktability; and I never succeeded till Johnson returned to his first love and embraced us.

I hed bin drafted into the Federal army at the

beginnin uv the war, and hed deserted to the Confederacy. Procoorin a certifikit to that effeck, I applied for a pardon and a place. He didn't like to giv me the offis, but he wanted a party, and, ez his appintments everywhere show, he coodn't be very pertikeler. I succeeded! I bore with me to Kentucky a commishun ez Post Master, and I am now livin in the full enjoyment uv that posishun, and I may say, I am happy.

The sosiety is conjenial. Ther is four groceries, onto wich I kin gaze from the winder uv my offis, and jest beyond, enlivenin what wood otherwise be a dull landscape, is a distillery, from wich the smoke uv the torment ascendeth forever. I hev associates who reverence me, and friends who love me. There is nuthin monotonous here. I hev knowd ez many ez eight fites per day, though three or four is considered enuff to break the tedium. And in these deliteful pursoots, leavin behind me the ambishens uv wat mite be called public life, with my daily bread sekoored, with my other sustenance ashoored, with a frend alluz to share my bottle, or, to speek with a greater degree uv akkooracy, frends alluz willin to share ther bottles with me, I am glidin peacefly down the stream uv time, dodgin the troubles, and takin ez much uv the good uv life ez I kin.

The twenty-five cents menshuned in the beginin uv my letter, you may, ez I remarked, remit either in postal order or currency.

Petroleum V. Nasby, P. M.
(Wich is Postmaster).

P. S.—Don't remit the twenty-five cents menshund in postage stamps. I hev enuff to last me, ez they ain't in demand here, ontil the Dimocrasy strike agin for their rites. Uv course all I hev on hand at that time will be uv no akkount. Send it in currency. P. V. N.

XXVII.

*The Negro being found not Available, Mr. Nasby
and his Followers decide to go back on him. —
A Meeting, the Effect of which was spoiled by
Pollock, the Illinois Storekeeper, and Joseph
Bigler, late C. S. A.*

POST OFFIS, CONFEDRIT X ROADS
(Wich is in the Stait uv Kentucky),
July 28, 1867.

THE speculashen in wool, into wich the Dimocrisy uv the South embarkt some months ago,
hez, I regret to say, resulted disastrously.   The
nigger ain't fitted for co-operashen with the Dimocrisy.   Instid uv hangin onto us like the ivy onto the
oak, he diskivered that, in the South at least, he
wuz really the oak and we the ivy; instid uv lookin
up to us, he contracted a disagreeable habit uv
lookin down onto us.   There wuz other reasons
why he coodent be made available for our uses, and,
therefore, it wuz decided to go back onto the Afrikin,
and to agin attempt his reduckshen to ez near his

normal speer ez the abnormal condishn uv the times
wood admit. The directers uv the college met and
changed the name uv the Institooshn back to the
" Southern Military & Classikle Institoot," and the
Corners wuz itself agin.

Deekin Pogram lookt ez tho ten years hed bin
lifted off him. " How pleasant 'tis," sed he, " to
walk erect agin in front uv a nigger, and to pass
em ez tho they wuz niggers! O, ef I cood only
wallop one wunst more, methinks I cood die
happy! "

We hed a meetin last nite to consider this nigger
question, wich wood hev resultid in great good, and
hed a powerful inflooence towards strengthenin the
hands uv our brethren in the North, who are fightin
the heresy uv nigger suffrage, hed it not bin for that
irritashen, Pollock, and that pest, Joe Bigler. I
hed made my regler speech on the nigger, and with
much effect. I hed quoted from sumboddy's quotashen from Agassiz, which demonstrated the radicle difference there is atween the Afrikin and the
proud Caucashen, arguin from the length uv his
heel and arm, the thickness uv his skull, and so
forth, that the nigger wuz totally unfit to exercise
the rites uv free men. I wuz applauded vociferously, and by none more than Pollock and Joe Big-

ler. Ez I took my seat, and wuz a wipin the per-
spirashen from my classikle brow, feelin that I hed
settled that question, Pollock riz, and desired to say
a few words, and make a suggestion. Sed he, —

" I hev listened with interest to the elokent speeker, and am happy to say I hev learned fax wich is
new to me. Ef I hev ever doubted the inferiority
uv the nigger, them doubts are removed, pervidin
alluz, that the statements uv the speeker is troo, uv
wich I hev no doubt, ez the caracter uv the speeker
is a suffishent guarantee for the trooth uv wichever
he sez."

I bowed, stately-like, with the air uv one to whom
sich compliments wuz a every-day affair, wich they
ain't, by no means; on the contrary, quite the reverse.

" But I want it demonstrated to the satisfackshen
uv the most obtoose. I want rite here a measurement uv the average Afrikin and the average white
man, that all the world may know the diffrence. I
move that it be did."

I acceded. " Let it be done," sed I, " that the
vexed question may be settled forever."

Sevral niggers were askt to submit to the measurement, but all refused. Finally Joe Bigler sed
he saw Napoleon Johnson — a nigger wich wunst

belonged to Deekin Pogram — in the audience. "Napoleon," sed he, "will yoo contribbit yoorself to the great science uv ethnology? Ain't yoo willin to let us yoose yoo a while to demonstrate the grate and growin trooth, that yoor grandfather wuz a monkey? Step up, Napoleon."

Napoleon, nothing dasht, stept up, and Pollock, Bascom, Bigler, and I measured him, with the folldwin result : —

Heighth . . . . 5 feet 8 inches.
Weight . . . . 150 lbs averdupoise.
Length uv foot . . . . 12 inches.
Breadth uv foot . . . . 5 inches.
Length uv hand . . . . 8½ inches.
Breadth uv hand . . . . 4 inches.
Length uv forearm . . . . 11 inches.
Length uv bone from ankle to knee . . . 6 inches.
Projeckshun uv heel . . . . 4 inches.
Capassity uv skull, wich, bein the top
   or cap uv the vertebral column, so to
   speek, is, accordin to Hippocratees, a
   trooly scientific Greek, and Hon. Wm.
   Mungen, uv Ohio, a very important
   bone for pretty much all uv the races, 66 cubic inches.

"Now," sed Pollock, "let us examine in the same way a avrage specimen uv the Caucashen race, ez he is found in this delectable spot. Will Issaker Gavitt be good enuff to step forrerd? I perpose to demonstrate the sooperiority uv the Caucashen with a two foot rool. Figgers won't lie. Step up, Issaker."

And Issaker stept up, and wuz measured, with the follerin result : —

Heighth	5 feet 8 inches.
Weight	150 lbs.
Length uv hand	7½ inches.
Breadth uv hand	3½ inches.
Length uv foot	11 inches.
Breadth uv foot	4½ inches.
Projeckshen uv heel	1½ inches.
Length uv forearm	10 inches.
Length uv bone from ankle to knee	15 inches.
Capassity uv skull	97 cubic inches.

Pollock wuz delited! "Here," sed he, "it is in a nut-shell. Issaker hez a shorter hand, a more narrer hand, a shorter and narrerer foot, and his heel projecks less than the nigger's by 2½ inches! Good Lord, how I hev bin deseeved! Wat errors I hev bin nussin! How kin a human bein hev intelleck whose heel projecks four inches? How rejoict am I that I am at last set rite on these important pints!"

I smiled beninantly onto him.

Bigler riz. "I, too," sed he, "am satisfied that the nigger is not wat we, who wuz disposed to consider him fit to exercise rites, supposed him to be.

I held firm when the measurement uv his hands and arms wuz bein made, but the heel staggered me. It's clear that no one kin hev intelleck whose leg isn't set in his foot better than that. I shel persoo this investigashen. Hevin now a startin-pint, — a heel, ez I may say, to stand on, — I shel go on to prove the inferiority uv the nigger. With that heel for a fulcrum, I shel, with the lever uv trooth, proceed to upset the fabric uv nigger ekality, and carry confooshen into Boston. I shel assoom that Napoleon is a average specimen uv the lower, or unintellectooal Afriken type. Is it so?"

"It is! It is!" yelled we all, delited at the happy turn the thing wuz takin.

"I shell also assoom that Issaker Gavitt is a avrage uv the higher or intellectooal Caucashen type. Is it so?"

"Certinly! Certinly!"

"Very well. Now quake, Massachoosets! Napoleon, *kin yoo read?*"

I saw the trap into wich we hed fallen, and risin hastily, protestid that the examinashen hed bin carried far enuff, and so did Deekin Pogram; but Bigler swore he wuz a goin to kiver Massachoosets with shame, and I sot down paralyzed.

"Kin yoo read, Napoleon?"

"Yes, sah!"

"Read this, then," sed Bigler, handin him a noosepaper.

The nigger read it ez peert ez a Noo England skool marm, wich well he mite, ez he learned it from one uv em.

"Kin yoo write?"

"Certinly;" and takin a pencil he writ half uv the Declarashen uv Independence.

"Set down, Napoleon. It's a devilish pity yoor heels is so long; otherwise yood be credited with hevin intellek. Now Issaker, my bold Caucashen, *kin yoo read?*"

"I protest!" shreeked I, in agony. "Issaker don't answer the skoffer at ethnology!"

But Issaker, ez white ez a sheet, and tremblin under the eye uv Bigler, who knowd him from infancy, stuttered out, "No!"

"Kin you rite, my gay desendant uv the sooperior race?"

And, still under the inflooence uv Bigler's eye, he answerd, "No!"

"Kin yoo cipher?"

"What in thunder's the yoose uv cipherin, when the old man alluz kep a nigger to do his figgerin?"

"Set down, Issaker. We're done with you.

There's an error sumwher. The nigger's capassity uv skull is less by sevral cubic inches, but he seems to hev made a lively yoose uv wat he hez. But it's all rite, Parson. Issaker shel vote, and the nigger shan't. Reedin and writin never wuz a qualifica-shen for votin down here, any way. Possibly the seat uv the intellek is in the heel insted uv the brain, wich accounts for the nigger's hevin the most uv it."

And Pollock and Bigler, and the niggers present, left the meetin-house, laffin uproarously, and throwin all sorts uv adoos back to us.

I doubt whether the result uv the investigashen will help our friends North. The fact is, it wuz overdone. It wuz carried too fur. There is a pint at wich facts ought to stop — Dimekratic facts in partikeler. In this instance, the investigashen shood never hev bin carried beyond the heel. Hed it stopt there, we wood hev hed em. But carryin it to the radical pint, Bigler and Pollock took it, the founda-shen we built wuz upset, and we are all at sea agin. Wood, oh! wood that we wuz rid uv these jeerin fanatics.

Petroleum V. Nasby, P. M.

(Wich is Postmaster).

XXVIII.

A Consultation at the Corners, followed by a Dream, in which General Grant and other Individuals are mixed, with no Regard whatever for Time, Place, or Fitness.

POST OFFIS, CONFEDRIT X ROADS
(Wich is in the Stait uv Kentucky),
August 1, 1867.

LAST nite there wuz a convocashen uv the saints connected with the Institoot (uv wich Deekin Pogram is the cheefest and lovelist among ten thousand), to take sweet counsel together onto sevral matters connected with the institooshen uv learnin, the success uv wich is so dear to all uv us. The conversashen happenin to turn upon the conferrin uv honorary degrees, Deekin Pogram sed that he hed a suggestion to make. He hed notist that all the leadin colleges uv the country hed a practis uv conferrin titles, sich as "M. D.," "A. B.," "LL.D.," and sich, onto distinguished men, though he wuz free to say that he didn't know wat in thunder they meant, or wat they wuz good for; but he hed notist in a noospaper that no college hed yet conferred any sich onto Androo Johnson.   Considerin it a burnin shame, he wood sejest that as a rebook to the hidebound institooshens uv the North, this college do to-wunst confer all uv em, and ez meny more ez there is, onto Mr. Johnson.   Bascom remarkt that he didn't kno whether the President wood feel complimentid.   " You kno, Deekin," sed he, " that this ain't much uv a college."

" Troo," sed the blessid old peece uv innosence, " troo, troo ; but then, to balance that, Johnson ain't much of a President, you kno."

And so the honorary degrees wuz conferred, and notis thereof wuz sent him immejitly.   From this the question uv the next nominee uv the party for President came up.   Bascom, who isn't a far-seein man, asserted that it wood be necessary to nominate Grant.   The Deekin remarkt that he thought it wood be safe, but McPelter thought different.   He didn't bleeve, in the first place, that it become a Peace party, or at least a party wich, ef it dipped its hands in gore at all, did it mostly in Northern gore, to take up a Northern General, wich had dun his best towards sendin many thousands of Southners to their long homes; and besides, the General wouldn't take it.

Bascom wanted to know what the conference at Long Branch meant? Ef General Grant wuz in the control uv Weed, Raymond, and the Noo York Herald, wich wuz ekal to the World, the Flesh, and the Devil, he felt that he hed trooly found the broad, macadamized road to Democrisy. He begun to hev hopes uv him. Various opinions wuz expressed by various persons, when, without comin to any conclusion, we separatid. I retired that nite earlier than usual, and, dwellin on the chances uv my continuin in offis in case uv Grant's accession, I fell into a troubled sleep and dreamed a dream.

Methawt gathered in front uv the White House . wuz a galliant array uv our friends. There wuz Franklin Peerce, and Bookanan, and Vallandigum, and the Woods, and Magoffin, and Monroe, and Brite, and Breckinridge, and the leaders uv the Dimocrisy, all a standin ther lookin wishfully at the White House, and wonderin how and by what means they cood git in. Johnson, blessins on his head, stood onto the portico wavin to 'em to come, but alass! guardin the passage stood a mighty host uv Ablishnists, armed and clad in armor, and in such force ez to make the stormin uv it hopelis.

"How shall we get in?" sighed Belmont.

"Ah, indeed, how?" ansered Henry Clay Dean.

"That's the great moral question — how?" ekoed Ben. Wood.

"My friend," sed Thurlow Weed, "its easy enuff. When you can't sore like the eagle, crawl like the snake. Sorein is preferable, but crawlin will do at a pinch. Is there not the Lion uv the Republic? Can't you git him out and mount him? The Ablishnists hev a regard for that same Lion, and will never discharge ther arrers at you when yoor on his back, for fear uv killin him. Besides, yoor ridin him will in some degree doo away with the prejoodis they hev agin yoo."

"But how kin we mount him?" said they.

"Trust to us for that," said Weed, and him and Raymond trotted off together.

They got the Lion out, but ez soon ez he cast his eyes onto the crowd, he uttered a roar which struck terror into their soles, and lashed the ground with his tail, and cast up dust with his claws, in a manner fearful to behold.

"He'll never stand it!" said Weed, "onless he's blindfolded," and Thurlow wrapped Raymond like a wet dish-rag over his eyes; and that done, him and Randall pared his nails and blunted his teeth (so that ef the bandage should wriggle off and he shood see wher he wuz he coodent hurt anybody), and shaved his mane, till he looked like a very innocent Lion indeed, so that his appearance woodent startle them not used to his fiercenis, and in that condishen they led him very quietly down to the crowd and give the word to mount.

Lord! what a scramble ther wuz. Tha piled on from the tip uv his ears to the end uv his tale; and them wich coodent git on for lack of room, hung to the feet uv them wich had got on, until it wuz nuthin less than a pirrymid of Democrats.

Finally, when all wuz loaded, the word wuz given, and the lion moved off. They wuz delited. He hed strength enuff to carry em, and he wuz a a carryin em strate to the White House, and at a good pase, too.

Ez they approached the portals, the Ablishin defenders uv the place opened onto em.

"Hold!" said Weed, "wood you destroy the Lion of the Republic?"

"Stay yoor hands!" shreeked Raymond. "The savior uv the country is under us."

But they lafft them to scorn.

"It's Brite and Vallandighum, the Woods, et settry, we're firin at," shreekt they, singin, as they fought, " The Battle Cry uv Freedom," "John Brown's body lies a mouldin in the grave!" and sich other sacriligious odes. " It's them we see, and them we'll kill."

And they belted away, till the whole mass wuz stretched dead and dyin on the plain.

Then they came up and began to turn over the corpses, one by one, until at last they came to the body uv the Lion, which, peerced thro and thro, wuz ez dead ez any uv em.

"My God!" sed they, "*it is the Lion after all!*"

" And we've slayed him!" sed another.

" Well!" remarkt a third, " we couldent help it. He was so kivered up with this carrion that I coodent make out what it wuz they wuz a ridin. Let us give him a decent burial for the good he hez done, and forget, if we kin, the company he died in."

And at this kritikle juncture I awoke.

I hev an idea I can see a sort uv a warnin in this dreem. It occurs to me, —

1st. That if we do ride Grant, we'll hev to divest him uv his mane, teeth, and claws, wich is the identical qualities wich makes him valuable to us.

2d. That with us on his back, we will probably succeed in killing him without savin us. Grant might deodorize a dozen or two uv us, but the whole party! Faugh! It wood be a pint of cologne to a square mile uv carrion.

3d. That ef we wuz wrapt all around him, the people woodent be able to see him anyhow, and wat good wood he do us?

Interpretin the dream thus, I shel oppose the nomination. Besides, I doubt whether all the Weeds and Raymonds in the country kin so manipulate him ez to bring him quietly into our ranks. We mite possibly go over to him, and thus git the privilege of votin for him, but wherefore? How about the offisis then? Ef the Ablishnists vote for him, and we vote for him, the obligation is ekal, and between us is ther any doubt wich he'd chose? I don't want to take sich chances. I'm opposed to the movement. I care not what others may do, but ez for me, give me straightout Dimocrisy or nothing. McClellan was a vencher wich satisfied me ez to the propriety uv undertakin to set a roarin lion a convoyin a flock uv peaceful lambs into green pasters.

PETROLEUM V. NASBY, P. M.
(Wich is Postmaster).

XXIX.

The Kentucky and Tennessee Elections.— The Hopes of the Democracy of the former State. — How they expect to hold it.

POST OFFIS, CONFEDRIT X ROADS
(Wich is in the Stait uv Kentucky),
August 16, 1867.

IT wuz a conjenyel party. Ther wuz me, and Deekin Pogram, and Bascom, uv course, — for it wuz at Bascom's, — and Capt. McPelter, and Issaker Gavitt, and Joe Bigler, who wuz, naterally, mischeevusly intoxicated. We hed met to rejoise over the result uv the Kentucky eleckshun, and the removal uv Stanton and Sheridan, and we rejoist. We hed rejoist for several hours, when the Deekin, — blessins on his frosty pow, — perposed that we take one more drink, to wich we ackseeded with alacrity. Ez Bascom handed back the Deekin his change, the old man observed among it a most villainous counterfeit ten-cent postal currency. "Bascom," sed he, in an injoored tone, "really I can't take that — it's counterfeit." "Certin 'tis, Deekin," sed George W., "certin; but what's the odds? Ez a matter uv course, Deekin, I'll git it agin afore to-morrer. It's evenchooally my loss, ain't it, ez I git all the money that floats here? Carry it till it comes around to me, Deekin, in the nateral course uv evence. Let us bear each other's burdens, Deekin?" And Bascom smiled sweetly onto him.

I don't know when I felt so happy. Kentucky hed spoken. We hed elected Helm by a majority of forty odd thousand, and hed with him elected a strate State ticket, incloodin all the Congressmen. The Ablishnists hed no show watever. The candidates were strate Demokrats, every one uv em. Sum uv em hed bin accoosed uv leanin towards the Fedrel side, but they hed, by affidavits, proved theirselves troo to the Demócrisy. One candidate hed bin charged, by a envious cuss, uv hevin furnisht the Federal forces with hosses, but he indignantly repelled the charge. His enemies brought forrerd the documents, showin that he hed furnisht the Fedral forces with hosses, and I trembled for him. But he smilingly cum to the scratch. He *hed* contracted to furnish em with hosses — he *hed* taken their accursed greenbacks, — but wherefore? Wuz it to benefit em? Wuz it to add to the resources of the gorrila Linkin, or the reverse? Let the facts answer. When wuz the hosses delivered? Ha! ha! Did the Fedral offiser git em? He did. Did he keep em? Alars! That nite John Morgan, who seeled his devoshen to the Confederacy with his blood, scooped em, and them hosses, which the Fedrals paid for, did servis in the Confedrit army. He wood ask his maligners whether it was sinful for a troo Confedrit to take money uv the Fedrals for furnishin supplies to the Confederacy? Hed these hosses remained in the hands uv the farmers uv Kentucky, John Morgan wood hev felt a delicacy in takin em ; ez the farmers hed hed valyoo receeved he wuz free, and he took em. Sich reasonin cood not fail to convince, and the candidate wuz, uv course, electid. The shafts uv his enemies fell pintless.

Therefore I felt happy. The waves uv Ablishnism rolled over all the other States, but aginst Kentucky they struck harmless. Kentucky is a brite oasis in the desert. Built onto Ham and Hager, bleevin in the sooperiority uv the white race, and that same race holdin in their hands the privilege uv sayin who shood and who shood not vote, they wuz safe. And we sot in silence, contemplatin our happiness.

At last Deekin Pogram spoke. He sighed ez he spoke. He hed heard uv Tennessee. He hed seen the 'lection returns, and he wuz ez much afflicted ez we wuz rejoist. " Wherefore," sed he, " shood we feel good, while our brethren in Tennessee are wailin over ther woes? The nigger with us is in his normal speer. Sence this eleckshen they bow their heads in silence, and dodge by ez ef they were afraid uv us, wich is a good sign. They hev lost the airs they assoomed afore, and are more like slaves and less like men. I hev twelve uv em a sweatin on my farm, and four expatiatin the cuss uv Noer in my kitchen. The men yield to the power uv the stronger race, and the females bow meekly to ther destiny. Tom, my oldest son, is happy, and stays at home, and my other sons is ez contentid ez they kin be. But it is not so in Tennessee. There they are not normal. There white men bow beneath a power they can't resist. There the nigger holds up his hed, and the Confedrit white man sneaks. There the abnormel nigger hez a vote, and the white man, who follered his State, is disfranchised. My God! how kin a man be happy under sich circumstances? How kin a Dimokrat rejoice when jist across the line he sees Liberty weepin, prostrate, and the white man, who struck for his rites, pinin becoz uv his deprivashen uv the rite uv suffrage?"

He cood feel good over Kentucky, but he wept over Tennessee.

Bascom remarkt that he, too, felt for Tennessee, but he wuz consoled. Kentucky hed proved troo, and Johnson, one worthy son uv Tennessee, hed removed Stanton! Wat more cood we want? Kentucky hed gone Dimocratic, and Johnson hed removed Stanton —

"And Tennessee hed elected Brownlow, and Johnson hez appinted Grant," whispered Joe Bigler.

"And," spoke up McPelter, "and Sheridan is removed."

"Troo! Troo!" retorted Bigler, "and put Thomas in his place. The man who whaled us in the Shenandoah Valley is deposed to make room for the man wat whaled us in Tennessee."

This bit us. This griped us. This is wuss nor a cathartic to us. Ef Kentucky is oil, Tennessee is aquafortis. Ef Stanton is soothin, Grant is pizen. Wherin are we better with the one than with the other? is a question wich we askt ourselves over and over agin.

But we felt good after all. Tennessee is to the

Democracy a dark cloud, but Kentucky is the silver lining to it. Ef no Confedrits wuz allowed to vote in Tennessee, thank the Lord no other kind wuz permitted to hist in ballots in Kentucky. The troo, sterlin Democracy uv Tennessee may suffer, and it is probable that they will suffer. There the Ethiopian votes by State law, but Kentucky is herself alone. Kentucky will never be so afflicted. Kentucky hez yet the makin uv her own laws. She will let them vote ez she sees fit, and none others. Relyin on Ham and Hager, she will deny the niggers that rite, and will keep the power in her own hands. Congris dassent interfere. Thad Stevens may howl, but he's lost his holt. Congris dassent make a law prescribin the rite uv suffrage, and sayin who shel and who shel not vote, for Congris is Conservative. Thad Stevens may shreek, but Congris ain't eddicatid up to the pint uv keepin within hailin distance uv ther own principles. Congris hed ruther see them wich adhered to the forchunes uv the Federel Goverment sunk than to exercise its power, for so far the matter hez bin left to the States. Likewise wood it ruther see every nigger in Kentucky, no matter tho they wuz all survivors uv Fort Piller, redoost agin to ther normal condishen ruther than give em the means uv pertectin themselves. The nigger may be a man in Tennessee, but he shel be a nigger in Kentucky forever, becoz it alluz hez bin so. Bless the Lord! That idea uv holdin to form and clinging to precedent is our salvashen. I begged em all to dismiss ther fears. Ohio is hagglin and bogglin ez to whether it will give her niggers the ballot; and ef she refooses, how kin she interfere with Kentucky? Congris dassent mix in the matter, for half the men that's sent to Washinton hev a greater fear uv shadders than they hev uv substance, and they sleep with that old hag Precedent, when they mite ez well repose in the arms uv the virgin Progress. They've got holt uv the tail uv an idea that's too big for em, — they can't manage it from that end, and they're afraid to ketch it at the other.

We shell do well for a long time. We can't afford to shed tears over Tennessee — let us thank the Lord that Kentucky is safe. Here we kin flog our niggers, — here we shel hev the Institooshen in sperit, ef not in name, — here Dimocrasy kin flourish, ef nowhere else. Let us be thankful that it is ez it is. Let us praise the Lord for a Congris that acted ez a drag on the sperit uv the times, and hedn't pluck enuff to do all that the people wantid. Let us praise the Lord for the conservatism wich wood-

ent let em make votin a nashnel matter, instid of
leavin it to us who know so well who to give it to,
and who not. So long ez we're left to ourselves,
so long will Kentucky be troo to Dimocrisy.

They felt encouraged, and the convocation broke
up feelin good.

PETROLEUM V. NASBY, P. M.

(Wich is Postmaster).

XXX.

Mr. Nasby goes to New Orleans to acquaiut the President's Friends with the Contemplated Change.

Post Offis, Confedrit X Roads
(Wich is in the Stait uv Kentucky),
August 20, 1867.

I WUZ a settin all so pleasant in the Post Offis last nite, a musin onto the mutability uv human affairs, when I received the follerin despatch, per boy on a mule, from the stashen : —

"Washington, August 19, 1867.

" To P. V. Nasby, &c. :

" Hev determined to be President or nothin. Shel remove Stanton, and immejitly thereafter Sheridan, and ultimately the ballence uv em. Go on to Noo Orleens, and make this known to our frends. Draw on the general fund for expenses.   A. J."

Wat a thrill run thro me ez I red this! I never felt so good but wunst before in my life. I wuz in an inteerior town in Massachusetts four days, wher the most stimulatin bevrage wuz root beer. The occasion when I felt better than I did on the receet uv that despatch wuz the identikle minit I struck Noo York and stood afore a bar. O, wat a pleasin, soothin, magnetic thrill run thro my veins ez the golden likquid gurgled down my esoffagus! Jest so I thrilled at reedin that despatch. My thot-contracted brow smoothed agin, the wrinkles of care left my face, and I wuz a boy wunst more!

I left immejitly, and after a pleasant journey reached Noo Orleens.

I hed no trouble in finding them to whom I wuz accredited. If there's a divinity wich doth hedge a king, ther must be suthin also in the face uv a troo Dimekrat wich betrays him. I wuz follered to my hotel by a crowd uv the first men uv the city, and when they saw my name onto the register, the scene wuz terrific. They knowd me! they knowd my comin wuzn't for nothin, and afore I hed time to say nay, I wuz hurried to the "Lost Coz" Club Rooms, and made an onorary member for life, incloodin the freedom uv the bar, wich privilege I prized.

"Wat nooze from Washinton?" shouted they all with one akkord.

"Calm yourselves!" sed I, impressively, "and restrane yoor emoshens. Four days ago I receeved this," and I read 'em the dispatch. Never shel I witnis anuther sich a sceen. Old men danced like yooth, while young men wept like wimmen.

"Excoose us, sir," sed one; "this weepin is onmanly, but ah, did yoo know wat I hev suffered! Sence last Joon, a year, I hevn't killed a nigger nor a preecher, and hev only knocked two uv 'em down, and for them two I wuz imprisoned three months each. But, thank God, I'm free agin — I'm free!" and he fell onto my neck, and askt me to take a drink with him, which, fearin the effex uv irritashen on him, in his present eggsitable state uv mind, I did.

I wuz askt ef I hed ever bin in Noo Orleens, and, on sayin that I hedn't, my friend accompanied me to the many objeks uv interest in the city.

"Here," sed he, "is the buildins in wich Beast Butler receeved the surrender uv the city, and where he signed the order for the hangin uv Mumford. Subsekently, in this same room, the tother beast, Sheridan, took his orders from Mayor Monro and Abell. Ha! ha! 'twuz retribushen," and he smiled grimly several minits. "Here is the hall where Dostie and his Ablishn hordes gathered over a year ago, and from wich Dostie wuz carried a corpse.

At that angle in the bildin I, with this good rite hand, slew three niggers and a Burow preecher. Right here, where we are standin, a cart containin the killed came along. I wuz eggsited and infuriated at their obstinacy in holdin the Convenshen. In my revolver there wuz one load — in the cart under the corpses wuz a nigger, groanin. I mounted the cart, and turned over the corpses — the wounded nigger had on a bloo cote — inflamed with rage at the site I pulled the trigger, and he groaned no more."

"Glorious sperit!" sed I, in eggstacy, wringin his hand.

"Just in front uv wher we stand thirty odd niggers wuz killed, and one or two uv them Burow teachers. It don't become me to say how many I killed, but I wan't idle. In three weeks thereafter I received my pardon from the President, and am now, thank God, a citizen."

By this time we reached the Club again, and for hours I listened to tales of oppression on the part of the military satraps, wich made my blood run cold. A citizen hed shot a nigger — and forthwith he wuz torn from the buzzum uv his family and inkarserated in the common prizen! Another's wife hed throwd a buckit uv bilin water over a wench in the street, uv wich the perverse creacher died, and she, too, wuz arrested. Policemen hed bin discharged for refoosin to arrest men whose spirits coodent brook nigger ekality, and who hed banged em about somewhat; and others had bin dismisst for hurrahin for Jeff Davis and pullin down Fedral flags. Ther hed bin no liberty uv speech nor ackshen. This Club Room hed bin invaded, and pistols and shot guns hed bin taken out by these despots, wich wuz a grindin the citizens into the dust. But the most oppressive case wuz that uv one uv our first citizens, who hed a girl in his family who wood persist in attendin skools after he hed postively forbid her doin so. He tied her up, and in the most patriarchal manner gave her one hundred and fourteen lashes. She wuz obstinit and died. He gave her a Chrischen berriel, but nevertheless he wuz pulled up, and fined and imprizened! Fined and imprizend for wallopin a nigger!

Then biznis commenced. Lists were bein made out, the purport uv wich I comprehendid. "Enter up," sed one, oilin a revolver, "the nest uv niggers on the alley jist around the corner from my house. They hev ther a chapel, in wich they hev preechin Sundays, and skools doorin the week. Aside from the annoyance it is to my family, it's really dangerous.

Two hundred nigger children attend it, beside the adult nigger classes."

"Enter up," sed another, cleanin out a shot-gun, "a grocer on the same street. He is from Iowa, and teaches a Sunday skool class in that same chapel. Sich incendiaries we kin never tolerate."—"There's a nigger church two squares from me wich must be abated," sed another; "and, by the way, a agent uv the nigger missionary sosiety and two teachers from Connecticut boards next door. Put em down."—"In my part uv the city," sed another, "there's four nigger draymen who hev bin suffishently impudent to scrape together enuff to buy ground and build em houses. Don't forget to put em down —don't. They are niggers and hev houses. I," he added, bitterly, "I am a white man, and hev none. Put em down. When Sheridan goes! ha! ha!"

And so on. The sekretary entered the names ez fast ez they wuz furnisht him, until the name uv every man suspectid uv Yankee perclivities wuz registered. The niggers wuz not put down, 'ceptin them uv sich prominence ez they desired to make shoor uv. It is considered entirely safe to kill a nigger anywhere. Sum uv em desired to make excep-shuns in favor uv certin niggers who cood be dependid upon ez troo. One uv em kep a keno, and t'other a faro bank. But they wuz rooled out. The niggers, it wuz desided, wuzn't to be trustid. Their impudence, in persumin to keep faro banks, was friteful.

The next day, brite and early, I wuz at the Club, when I receeved another despatch. The members flockt around me. "Is it done?" shreekt they. "Is Stanton out?"

"He is," sed I, slowly, "he is, but—"

"But what? Oh, releeve our suspense!"

"But Grant is in!" returned I, droppin the message, and sinkin on a sofa in a brown study. But they wuz delited.

"It's better than we hoped," sed they. "Grant hez come over at last. Bless the Lord! His name will give the administration strength." They cheerd like loonatics.

Finally, one mornin I got a despatch that Sheridan wood be releeved that day, and the enthoosiasm biled up agin—this time I shared in it, for I felt that that wuz trooly suthin. It wuz impossible to restrane the gentle lambs uv the Club any longer. Ez a sort of a lunch, preceding the feast that wuz to come, they sallied out and made it lively for sich niggers ez they cood git safely near to. At noon

the next dispatch came to me.　The entire member
ship uv the Club wuz gathered around, impashent
to hear me sound the glad tidins over Egypt's dark
sea.　I broke the seal.

" Sheridan is removed this day !—"

" Ror ! Ror ! Ror !" cheered the Club.

" And Thomas is appinted in his place !"

So read the despatch.　There wuz nary a cheer
follered it.　The most death-like silence pervaded
the rooms.　One by one the members skulked out
to settle with the niggers whose heds they hed bustid
in the mornin, and to ashoor em it wuz all a joke.
The lists wuz destroyed, and the revolvers and shot-
guns wuz all packed away.　At a meetin held immejitly, the follerin resolooshens wuz passed : —

" *Resolved*, That it is possible for men whose
faith is bigger nor a grain uv mustard seed, to
hev confidence in President Johnson, but ourn is
gin out.

" *Resolved*, That we asked him for bread, and he
give us a stone ; we asked him for an egg, and he
give us a scorpion.

" *Resolved*, That a committee uv two be appointed to toss up for the difference between Sheridan
and Thomas, and another to figger up wherein we

are better off under Grant than we wuz under Stanton.

"*Resolved*, That the President, in awakenin hopes only to dash em to the ground, is guilty uv a crooel disregard uv our feelins.

"*Resolved*, That if he is ever goin to do anything for us, why don't he do it? and—"

At this pint another despatch came. I was too much affected to read it, and I passt it to the President. "Hell!" sed he. "Gentle sirs, hunt yer holes. Thomas is sick and won't come, and Sheridan is goin to stay after all."

Concludin that my offishel duties prevented me from makin a longer stay in Noo Orleans, I hastened North agin with all speed. Jest ez I wuz leavin the city I got another despatch, statin that Hancock wuz appinted to Sheridan's place. I didn't consider the nooze suffishently cheerin to indoose me to go back agin. I feel that men uv my opinions is safer in Kentucky than any where else. Kentucky didn't secede, and therefore within her borders secesshenists are safe. Thank the Lord for Kentucky.

They don't do Johnson justice down there, tho. He wood help em if he cood, but he can't. Congris tied his hands. He kin appint this man or that man, but both this man and that man are bound to execoot the law. Wat kin the President do?

PETROLEUM V. NASBY, P. M.
(Wich is Postmaster).

XXXI.

The Amnesty Proclamation. — A Cabinet Consultation over it. — The Safety of the President from Impeachment.

POST OFFIS, CONFEDRIT X ROADS
(Wich is in the Stait uv Kentucky),
September 10, 1867.

I WUZ brot to Washinton by a despatch. His Eggslency hed at last determined to put his foot down — to assert his power, and to take measures sich ez wood bring to the top, where they properly belong, that large class uv the citizens uv the Republic who wuz engaged in the little onpleasantnis, wich the Ablishnists took advantage uv to deprive em uv their rites, and to keep em from exercisin the inflooence in the government they are, and alluz wuz, entitled to. In short, ez Congress wuz adjourned, and coodent, by no means, be got together till November, the President wuz convinced that it wuz his dooty to improve his time, and bu reelly President.

The consultation over the Proclamation wuz long and painful. Binckley, who is now runnin the government mostly, hed written the whereases, wich is the most uv the document. Seward hed taild onto em the Proclamation proper, wich wuz so small ez to give it a tad-pole appearance, and it wuz to be discussed. All uv em wuz in favor uv it but me. Ez anxious ez I wuz for the liberashen uv our friends in the Southern States; ez anxious ez I wuz to give that blessid saint, Deekin Pogram, a chance to wallop a nigger agin afore he died, without bein interfered with by a bloo-coated hirelin, I still hed a dread. "Dare yoo," sed I, "go further in this biznis? isn't impeachment at the end uv it, ef yoo stir up this matter? And with Wade in the Presidenshel chair — my God! Pollock wood hev MY post offis! My liege, I hed a dream last nite. Methawt — "

"Go on with the dream," sed his Eggslency. "Go on, and I will be yoor Joseph to interpret it."

"Kin yoo assoom the caracter uv Joseph and carry it out," sed Randall, "with Mrs. Cobb in Washinton?"

This interupshen preventid me from narratin my dreem, so I resoomed at the pint at wich I wuz interruptid. "And my opinion is the opinion uv all yoor appintees. The offis-holder is naterally a Conservative. Agitashun, my liege, mite shake us out uv our places. On yoo we hang, — yoo are our hope, our anker, and our cheefest trust."

And my remarks, wich I delivered with a tremblin voice, and with teers a rollin down my furrowed cheeks — I felt the solemnity uv the occasion, for wat cood I do ef turned out into the cold world at my age? — wuz receeved with peals uv lafture.

" My deer sir ! " sed A. J.; " yoor innosence surprises me. Impeach me ! Never, so long ez filial and family love is a distinguishin carakteristic uv the leedin minds uv America, — never, so long ez a senator hez a nephew to provide for, or a brother who wants a place. Ah! that love uv blood relashuns! Wat a beautiful thing it is! And how strong is the marriage relation wich prompts a man, when he hez promised to love, cherish, and protect a wife, to go cherishin and protectin all her brothers' and her sisters' children — the love goin frekently, like leprosy, to the third generashun! Thank the Lord for it. It's my only holt! Set yoor mind at eeze by peroozin these," and he tost me a bundle uv letters, neatly done up, and labelled " Letters from Radicle Members uv the House and Senit."

A lite dawned onto me ez I opened the first one.

It wuz from a distinguished Senator, and read, ez near ez I kin remember now, thus: —

"SENIT CHAMBER, March 6, 1867.

"TO THE PRESIDENT: Notwithstandin the slite difference uv opinion that may egzist between us on certin minor questions uv public policy, and despite the unguarded expressions I may hev indulged in in the heet uv debate, I kin trooly say that I hev ever cherished the most endoorin faith in the rectitood uv yoor intenshuns, the honesty uv yoor purpose, and the purity uv yoor motives. I hev a nephew in my State who desires the posishen uv Assessor uv Internal Revenoo. He is capable and honest; and while he hez alluz voted the Republican ticket, he hez dun it so mildly ez not to be objeckshenable to those who differ with him. Indeed, last fall he wuz accoosed, and perhaps justly, uv votin for a candidate for Congress who wuz a supporter uv yoor policy, wich, tho I do not in all respecks accept, hez, I must acknowledge, many pints in it to recommend it to a discriminatin people. I shood esteem his nominashen a persnal favor.

"With sentimence uv the most profound respect and esteem, I remain admirinly, yours,

"———— ————.""

"P. S. It is, I trust, onnecessary for me to state that I regard all projecks of impeechment ez wild, visionary, onnecessary, and dangerous; and no sich projeck kin ever reseeve my support. I forgot to menshen that a brother uv mine, who hez never taken a part in politics, and hez, therfore, his opinyuns to organize, wood gladly accept any posishen under the Government, and a brother-in-law woodent be averse to simlar employment. It's a matter uv no consekence to yoo, uv coorse, but I shel oppose the reassemblin uv Congress till the regler time in December. I am inflexibly opposed to establishin dangerous precedents. Shood yoo make the appintments I desire, I kin git em confirmed by the Senit, ez well ez an ekal number uv yoor own appintments. In matters uv this kind ther must be compromises."

In my surprise I uttered a prolonged whistle. "Them appintments wuz made," sed His Eggslency, with a sardonicle smile. "Them appintments wuz made. Read another — there's a varied and well-selected assortment uv em. The Senit is my fish-pond. I drop my hook therein, baited with a Assessorship, and bless me, how they bite at it! Go on."

"SENIT CHAMBER, March 7, 1867.

"TO THE PRESIDENT: I am, ez yoo are aware, known ez a Radical; but between generous foes there kin be none of that terrible spirit uv blind hate which characterizes some uv my associates, who shel be here nameless. I will say, however, that if the Senators from Massachoosets, and some others I cood menshun, wood resine or die, they wood confer a favor upon the country. I oppose you becoz I differ with yoo, ez does my State; but that opposishen hez never lessened my high admirashen uv your patriotism, yoor even temper, or the many good qualities uv your head and heart, wich shine out so conspickuous. I hale you ez a worthy successor uv the first A. J. I hed not intended to mix things persnel to myself in this friendly triboot, but will do violence to my feelins by observin that the posishun uv Collector at —— is admirably adapted to a cousin uv mine, whose talence ez a lawyer hez never bin appreciated by those who know him best. He agrees with me that impeachment is not to be thot uv, and that sessions uv Congress, other than reglar ones, is uselis. Shood yoo be pleased to make the appintment, I shel be proud to return the favor in any way possible. Ef it woodent be askin too much, a son uv mine wood be glad to serve his country ez a Inspector uv Revenoo. Inheritin from me devoshun to our common country, he burns to devote himself to her service.

"With sentiments uv profound respect,

"I am, yours, as ever,

"———— ————"

"Them appintments wuz made also," sed the great man, "and three or four more throwd in when he found how cheep he cood get em. He visited me after I hed given him all he asked for, and we hed a frendly interchange uv views. He persisted in differin with me; but ez we partid, I askt him ef ther wuzn't jist one more appintment he wanted? Jist one more? Throwin himself on my neck, he exclaimed, 'Not one! Not one! My brothers, my brothers-in-law, my nephews, and the doubtful members uv the Legislacher, wich finally concloodid to vote for me, are all provided for.' Bless the Lord for the appintin power! The biznis uv tradin birth-rites for messes uv pottage, begun with Esaw; but, thank Heven, it didn't end with him."

It wuz unnecessary for me to read more. I hed seen enuff to satisfy me that the integrity uv one third uv the Senit wuz rather honey-combed, and, like a rusty muskit, not strong enuff at the breech to bear a severe trial without danger uv bustin. I saw precisely wat wuz the rock on wich we stood, and what a citadel it wuz. Kin these men, with these letters in the hands uv our respected cheef, and ther relatives all a drawin rashens, turn and rend the hand wich feeds em? Cood I do it?— and ain't they even ez I am?

And so the proclamashen wuz ishood, and I went home a feelin good. We shall yet wallop niggers in Kentucky,; we shel yet redoose em to ther normal speer; our afflicted brethren in Tennessee will yet vote, and them not amnestied will be speshly pardoned ez ther superior merits deserve, and with all ther will be no impeachment. For where the carkis is, ther will be the buzzards also, and we hev the control uv the carkis. Some uv the buzzards are so gorged with carkis that their eyes is shut—enuff uv em to inshoor our posishen till the end uv our term. It is well with us.

PETROLEUM V. NASBY, P. M.
(Wich is Postmaster).

XXXII.

Mr. Nasby details his Adventures in a strong Democratic County in Southern Ohio. — The Suffrage Question in that Part of the Democratic Heritage.

POST OFFIS, CONFEDRIT X ROADS
(Wich is in the Stait uv Kentucky),
September 20, 1867.

LAST week I wuz invited to go into Ohio to assist my brethren uv that State. The Massedonian cry reached me, " Come and help us ! " and ez the cry wuz coupled with the asshoorance that I shood be pervided for, I heeded it. Couple Massedonian cries with whiskey, and I can't resist em. I never try. I knowd there wuzn't much difference atween the Dimocrisy uv Ohio and Kentucky, but I wuz onprepared for the strikin resemblance I found. Twins is not more similar. My 1st appintment wuz in a purely Dimekratic County. It wuz a settlement after my own heart, and the minit my practist eye restid onto it, my sole leaped foi joy. It wuz a town wich hed bin some day the seat uv bizniss, but a ralerode runnin some nine miles to one side uv it hed cut off its trade, and the inhabitants hevin nothin to do, the better part uv em went with the trade. Nacher abhors a vacuum, and there rushed in sich as found it diffikult to live elsewhere. The whole population, hevin much leisure, fell to pitchin coppers, wich, to make the game excitin, they pitched for drinks. Pitchin for drinks soon rendered em incapable uv more violent exercise; and in a year from the time the trade left em, it wus the strongest and most intense Democratic town in the State. Ez they must eat suthin, and ez the groseries coodent run perpetooally without money, they hed occasional spasms uv labor. Then wood their feelins be lasseratid. Then wood they look over to the Kentucky shore, and see thousands uv jest sich men ez theirselves a spendin their lives in one unendin round uv copper-pitchin, hoss-racin, and poker-playin, the nigger meanwhile a sweatin to furnish the means, and they wood break out into murmurin at the crooel fate wich cast their lot where every man wuz forst to sweat for hisself, and the cuss of labor coodent be filled by proxy.

Their proximity to Kentucky tantalized em. They wood hev all gone there cood they hev raised enuff to buy a nigger apeece, but they coodent. There wuz a most deliteful look uv serene repose about the place wich charmed me. Nothin stood uprite. The sign-post uv the tavern hed bin leaned agin so much that it hed contracted the same habit; the hosses, from a too rigid economy in the matter uv oats, wuz leanin agin the side uv the barns; the shutters on the groseries hung cornerin across the winders, in consekence uv the lower hinges bein broke; the clapboards on the houses all hangin by a single nail at one end, presented any but a reglar appearance; and the men were all either sittin on store boxes, or leanin agin watever possessed suffishent strength to keep em up.

I wuz enthoosiastically reseeved. The town wuz excited on two questions. 1. Taxation. 2. Nigger Equality. The Cheerman uv the deputashun wuz the most cheerin style uv Demokrat I hed seen for years. His independent hair hed pushed its way thro the top uv his hat and bristled in all directions, biddin defiance to the world; his toes protroodin from his shoes, and his trowsers hangin lop-sided by one suspender, indicated a sovereign contempt for appearances. He begged me, with tears streemin down his eyes, to rouse the people agin the dangers wich threatem em. "Think," sed he, "uv the hundreds uv thousands uv millions, wich we, the people, are forced to pay in taxes to the General Government, and rouse em to the necessity uv ackshen!"

"I will," sed I, "I will. State to me the amount uv taxes paid the tyranikle government in this Arcajen spot, that I may hev the data from wich to speek."

"Taxes!" returned this patriot, with an amazed look onto his countenance, "taxes! We don't pay any taxes here. The Assessor came here two years ago, and findin nothin to assess, hezn't considered it worth while to come since. But, good Lord, our hearts bleeds for these unfortinit victims uv Ablishn policy wich hev suthin, and is forced to pay onto it! The people is bein ground into dust by taxashen." And the old man wept bitter tears at the miseries uv the sitooashen uv the people. What techin benevolence!

On the question uv nigger ekality, I found em at a most deliteful heat. They hed seen the terrors uv it, and know'd whereof they spoke. Niggers hed come from Kentucky across the river to em, and instid uv acceptin their normal speer, and yieldin

quietly to the irresistible decrees uv Heven, wich
made em the inferiors uv the white, they hed, the
moment they accumulatid suthin to live on, assoomed the airs uv ekality. They refoosed to keep
their places. The Cheerman remarkt, ez showin
the stubborn cussedness uv the race, that one uv em
lived some months next to him. He (the Cheerman) borrored pork on sevral occashens uv him,
twict a bakin uv flour, and, on one occashen, nine
dollars uv the misrable rags wich we are forst, by a
tyranikle Government, to accept ez money. That
nigger hed the soopreme impudence to insist on bein
pade! and even talked uv sooin for it. But, on con-
sultin a lawyer, he didn't, owin to the oncertainty
ez to who wood hev to pay the costs. Another instance. " A nigger, wich wuz neerly white, settled
in the visinity. He hed not only a daughter, but a
farm. My son sores. Labor he despises, as a occu-
pashen only fit for serfs. He proposed to woo this
nigger's daughter. It wuz a struggle with me.
My son marryin a female wich hed the accursed
blood uv Ham in her vanes! But Jimuel, my son,
sir, threw dirt in my eyes. About sixty akers uv
dirt. I thot uv the pleasant time I cood hev a livin
on that farm — uv the days devoid uv labor, and the
evenins filled with ease, and after a severe ethno-

logikle struggle with my feelins, I consented. I wantid to take keer uv that nigger. Pityin him ez an inferior bein, loaded, in his abnormal condishen, with responsibilities wich he cood not be expected to discharge, I would hev taken charge uv his affares. I wood — my son Jimuel and I — hev managed his farm, and his stock, and sich. Alas! Jimuel menshuned the matter to the Ethiopian, sir, and with wat result? He was ignominiously kickt out uv the house, sir. He wuz d—d, sir, for a drunken broot, by a nigger, wich threatened, if he ever showed his pimpled — pimpled wuz the word — face about there agin, he'd break every bone in his body. Sir, this is becomin unsupportable. They must be dragged down to our level. My proud Caucashen blood revolts. There must be a inferior race, and it's us of the nigger. The Injen is out uv the question, ez there ain't any of them here to be inferior. I wouldn't mind the Injen, but there ain't none. It's the nigger or nothin. Give him the ballot, sir, and what'll distinguish us? Speek with a angel's tongue onto this theme, I beg."

The meetin wuz a glorious one, and my speech one uv my most movin efforts. My perorashen moved me to tears. It wuz on nigger suffrage. Depictin its untold horrors, I begged em to organize — to rally wunst more agin this common enemy. " There is," sed I, " seven thousand nigger males in the State uv Ohio. Shel we peril the liberties uv the State by permittin them to approach the ark uv our safety — the ballot-box? Shel we raise em to the pint uv bein our ekals? Shel we marry em and give em in marriage? Shel we contaminate the pure streem uv Anglo-Saxon blood by muddlin it with the turbid streem uv —"

At that pint I stopt. My eyeballs wuz seared. Joe Bigler, wich I sposed wuz a hundred miles away in Kentucky, wuz up in the aujence.

" Agreein," sed he, " with wat the speeker is sayin, I beg to ask a question for enlitenment. I am a Kentuckian."

" Ror for Kentucky!"

Bowin, Bigler perceeded. There wuz a lurkin devil in his eye wich afflicted me.

" Ef I understand the speeker, he holds that the nigger, ef permitted to vote, becomes so much our soshel ekal that we must take him to our buzzums — that we must marry the females, and our gushen daughters forthwith tie themselves to the males uv that accussid race. Is it so?"

" It is!" retorted I.

" My blood biles when I think uv it. Ef I recollect arite, the laws uv Ohio permits all niggers to vote who are only half black. Ez there are a good many mulattos in this region, the produx uv the loose ekality uv the races over the river, there must have bin, ever sence that law passed, much uv that kind uv marryin here. May I be permitted to ask this oppressed people, who hev suffered so from this unnatural state of affairs, how they like it? Is yoor wife a nigger, sir?" sed he, addressin the Sekretary, "and ef so, don't yoo feel the humiliatin posishen yoor in, compelled, ez you wuz, by the force uv Dimokratic circumstances, to marry her, to take her to yoor buzzum, the minit her father got a vote? It's enuff to drive a man into Ablishnism to escape it. My brethren," sed this Bigler, "I'd advise yoo all to abjoor Dimocrisy. Up North, the minit the nigger gits a vote, yoo are forced to legal missegenashun; down South, the affinity Dimocrisy hez for niggers hez bleached out the race to the color uv molasses. There's no hope for yoo, save in Ablishnism, wich hez the happy fakulty uv doin justis to em without marryin em!" And he stalkt out.

It didn't make no difference. They didn't know what he wuz talkin about. The word "missegenashen" struck em with amazement, from wich ther

didn't recover till we left. In speakin to such au-
jences, men must be keerful uv the words they
yoose.

I finisht my speech. The meetin then resolved
they wuz better than niggers; that they never wood
consent to be taxed for the benefit uv purse-proud
aristocrats; that the bonds shood be taken up with
greenbax; that there shood be a return to specie
payment to-wunst; and that they were willin to
give millions, ef need be, to resist usurpashen,
but not one cent in taxes in a unconstitooshnel
manner.

This resolooshn wuz passed, when a colleckshn
wuz taken up to pay for the candles. But, alas!
There wuzn't nary a cent in the house, and I hed
to pay for em myself. Another little insident didn't
please me. The State Central Committee hed furnisht me, ez it does all its speakers, with a twenty
dollar gold piece and a fifty dollar bond, wich I
wuz to exhibit, to show the difference atween Ablishn and Democratic money. I shoved em at the
people, and it excited em to madnis. I laid em on
the table afore me. When the meetin wuz adjourned they wuz gone! Who took em? I know
not, but this I do know, that the Cheerman uv the
meetin hed, next mornin, a new pare of shoes and

a hat, and wuz a talkin doubtfully uv the propriety uv taxin bonds.   I go from here to Pennsylvania, to fill some appintments in that State.

PETROLEUM V. NASBY, P. M.

(Wich is Postmaster).

XXXIII.

The Antietam Dedication. — A Consultation over the Speech of the President, and the Manner in which it was shorn of its fair Proportions.

POST OFFIS, CONFEDRIT X ROADS
(Wich is in the Stait uv Kentucky),
September 30, 1867.

FROM Ohio to Washington! Ther is nary peace for me! The sole uv my foot knows no rest. Wher Democresy is in danger, ther am I. I wuz called to Washinton to consult with the friends uv the President in regard to the Anteetam Dedicashun. The part his Eggslency wuz to take in that affair — wat he wuz to say — what others wuz to say, ez well ez who wuz to say it, wuz a matter wich required not only profound thought, but the most careful considerashun. Hence I wuz called.

I found assembled the entire Cabnet, with the addishen uv Binckley; a gentleman recently arrived from a foreign mission, named McCracken; Gov. Swann uv Maryland, Ex-Gov. Bradford; the poet of the day, Gen. McPounder, late uv Lee's staff, now uv the Maryland Melishy; Kernel Screw, ditto, and twelve or twenty more who hed held posishens uv trust and profit under the Confedracy, and who wuz now holdin correspondin posishens under the Govner uv Maryland, all of wich wuz a discussin the various pints involved in this matter. The President hed prepared a speech wich kivered thirty-eight pages uv legle cap paper, and it was segested that he reed it. In the impressive manner for which he is celebrated he began:—

"Fellow Countrymen—"

"I object to that fraze," said General McPounder. "It's liable to misconstrucshun. Sposin that upon that stand shood be them wich, doorin the fratrisidle struggle wich lost me my niggers, wuz in the Fedral army? I object to bein considerd the fellows uv sich."

The objeckshun wuz finally got over by the President's agreein to turn, ez he uttered the words, to the Maryland delegashun; wich satisfied em, ez the most ultra felt it wuz enuff ef the President shood address himself excloosively to Maryland Dimekrats ez his countrymen. He perceeded:—

"Gathered together onto a field wich the valor uv loyal arms made forever memorable—"

Gov. Swann objected. He wuz for consiliation. How cood our Southern brethren who had taken the oath be consiliated, ef the fact that they wuz walloped wuz bein continually flung at em? Besides, the word "loyal" wuz offensive to the heft uv the Democracy. Mr. Seward thought ef references wuz made to the late onpleasantness they ought to be diluted. I sustained the objeckshun, and it wuz stricken out. The President resoomed:—

"Feelin this day an uncommon solemnity, standin, ez we do, over the mortal remanes uv the thousands wich died in the sacred cause uv Liberty, and in defence uv the flag uv our coun—"

"Hold!" sed the impetuous Maryland General, "I protest. In the name of Maryland I protest. Shel the Conservatives uv that glorious State be insulted by alloosions to liberty uv wich they are deprived, and to the flag wich is the symbol uv oppression, and under wich we didn't fight?"

I sustained the objeckshun, and that wuz struck out. He went on:—

"When I cast my eye over this field, and let it rest for a instant on this spot where the impetuous foemen wuz driven southward by our brave troops—"

Gov. Swann remarked that on sich an occasion it wood be perhaps better not to menshun the partikeler direckshun in wich anybody wuz driven. Let it read, I wood say, thus: "On this spot where the impetuous foeman wuz driven by our brave troops." Left thus it woodent be espeshally offensive to any body. It wood read ez well South ez North, for in that encounter both sides wuz, at times, driven. I sustained the amendment, and the President went on:—

"In fucher years the pilgrim to the shrine uv Liberty will paws a moment on this spot, to drop a tear over the graves uv them who here checked the advance uv the hosts uv rebellion, and—"

Gov. Swann was averse to this. It wuzn't soothin to the party wich wuz checked. It wood be better to reed, "drop a teer over the spot onto wich fraternal blood wuz shed." Seein no objection to the amendment, I hed it done. He went on:—

"The widder in her Northern home may weep, but she may console herself that her husband died for his country. She may—"

Gov. Swann broke in. "Sposn," sed he, "you should say, 'The widder in her Northern or Southern home, ez the case may be, may weep,' &c. Woodn't it be better?" I thot so, and it wuz altered accordinly. The President perceeded:—

" Here, upon this spot, the armed hosts of rebellion were met and hurled back by—"

Gov. Swann sejested that that be omitted. The word " rebellion," when applied to a brave people, who wuz strugglin for wat they deemed their rites wuz, to say the least, too harsh. It wuz struck out, and the President went on : —

" Upon this spot, amid the roar uv cannon, the rattle uv musketry, and the clash uv contendin arms, thousands uv the brave sons uv patriotic sires gave up their lives."

There wuz nothin in this objectionable. It cood apply to either side or to both, but ez everythin before it hed been stricken out, and ez there wuz alloosions follerin it that wood hev to be, it wuz advisable to bust it, and accordinly I drew my pencil over it.

The President then wanted to know wat in thunder he shood say. Feelin that he must say suthin, I prepared for him the follerin remarks : —

" My Fellow-Countrymen : I appear afore you, not for the purpose uv makin any lengthy remarks : I simply desire to express my approbashn uv the ceremonies which hev taken place. My appearance is the speech wich I will make. I cood make a speech wich wood tech yoor feelins, but my thots

is in communion with the dead—uv both sides—
whose deeds we are here to commemorate. I shel
not attempt to give utterance to the feelins and emoshuns inspired by the ceremonies uv the day. Not
any. I shel attempt no sich thing. I am here to
give countenance to the perceedins—to offishally
beam upon em—but I must be permitted to hope
that we may foller the example set us by the illustrious dead—uv both sides—and think uv the
brave men—uv both sides—who fell in the fierce
struggle uv battle, and who sleep silent in their
graves, yes—who sleep in silence and peace after
the conflict hez ceased. Would to God that we uv
the livin cood emulate their example ez they lay
sleepin in the tombs. Wood that we cood live, ez
do the silent dead, in peace and friendship. Yes, in
peace and friendship ez do the silent dead—uv both
sides. You, my fellow-countrymen, hev my earnest
wishes, ez yoo hev hed my efforts in times gone by,
in the most tryin perils, to restore peace and harmony to our distracted and divided country, and
yoo shel hev my last efforts in vindicatin uv the
flag uv the Republic, and the Coustitooshn uv our
Fathers."

I endeavored in this to preserve, ez nearly as possible, the singularly beautiful and loocid style uv the

President, that the assembled thousands who shood hear it mite recognize it to-wunst ez hizzen. The last sentence wuz objected to. The Marylanders didn't know whether they cood sit in silence and hear sich talk about the "Flag uv the Republic" and the "Constitooshun uv our Fathers." But they wuz overruled. It wuz held, and properly, I think, that the Constitooshun uv our Fathers shood be understood ez meanin that instrooment afore the Ablishnists had knocked out uv it all that made it lovely in the eyes of Maryland — the nigger — and the Flag ez it wuz at that period. They wuz finally satisfied with it, and Binckley teched up the speech in some miner pints for delivery.

I didn't stay to the celebrashun, for I hed biznis elsewhere. I writ the President's speech, so I knew that wuz rite; I heard Bradford's orashen read, and wuz pleased with it. It wuz a powerful apology for the Northern soldiers, and must hev had a good effeck onto the Southern mind. Feelin that it wuz all rite, I left agin for my feeld uv labor. Wat the President wood do without me, I don't know.

PETROLEUM V. NASBY, P. M.

(Wich is Postmaster).

XXXIV.

Mr. Nasby assists in the Ohio Election. — The Defeat of the Amendment. — How it was received at the Corners.

POST OFFIS, CONFEDRIT X ROADS
(Wich is in the Stait uv Kentucky),
October 12, 1867.

FEELIN that the time hed arrived which wuz to decide whether 7,000 degradid niggers wuz to grind 500,000 proud Caucashens into the dust, I felt that ef I shood fail in my dooty now, I shood be forever disgraced. Accordingly, I put in on elckshun day at a Dimocratic town in Ohio — the battlefield — the identikle place into wich I made a speech doorin the campane.

I arrived ther on the mornin uv the elekshun, and found that comperhensive arrangements hed bin made for defeatin this most nefarus and dangerous proposishen. Paradin the streets ez early ez 7 A. M. wuz a wagon containin 25 virgins, runnin from 27 to 31, the most uv em ruther wiry in texture, and

FATHERS
SAVE US FROM
NICGER EKALITY!
WHITE HUSBANS OR NUN!

over their heads wuz banners, with the followin
techin inscriptions: "Fathers, save us from Nigger
Ekality!" "White Husbans or nun!" It wood
hev bin better, I thot, hed they bin somewhat
younger. Ther wuz suthin preposterous in the ijea
uv females uv that age callin upon fathers to save
em from anythin, when in the course of nacher their
fathers must hev bin a lyin in the silent tomb for
several consecutive years, onless, indeed, they marrid
young. Ef still livin (I judged from the aged appearance uv the damsels), their parents must be too
far advanced in yeers to take an activ part in biznis.
In anuther wagon wuz a collekshun uv men wich
hed bin hired from the railrode, twelve miles dis-
tant, whose banners read, "Shel ignerent Niggers
vote beside intelligint Wite men?" and the follerin
verse : —

> "Shel niggers black this land possess,
> And rool us whites up here?
> O, no, my friends; we ruther guess
> We'll never stand that ere."

It okkurd to me that it wood hev done better hed
their spellin bin more akkerit; but upon inquiry I
found that it didn't make no diffrence. That wuz
the pervailin way of spellin things in that vicinity.
Hangin over the polls wuz a broad peece uv white

muslin, onto wich was painted, in large letters, " Caucashuns, Respeck yer Noses — the nigger stinks!" Then I knowed it wuz safe. That odor hez never yet bin resisted by the Democrasy, and it hez its inflooence over Republikins.

I never saw sich enthoosiasm, or more cheerin indicasuns uv the pride uv race. Ez evidence uv the deep feeling that pervaded that community, I state that nine paupers in the poor-house demanded to be taken to the polls, that they might enter their protest agin bringin the nigger up to a ekality with em, wich wuz nine gain with no offsets, ez ther wuzn't an Ablishnist in the institooshun. Two men, in the county jale for petty larceny, wuz, at their own rekest, taken out of doorance vile by the Sheriff uv the county, that they mite, by the ballot, protest agin bein degraded by bein compelled, when their time wuz out, to acknowledge the nigger ez their ekal. One enthoosiastic Dimekrat, who cost us $5, hed to be carried to the polls. He hed commenced early at one uv the groseries, and hed succumbd afore votin. We found him sleepin peacefully in a barn. We lifted the patriotic man, and in percession marched to the polls. We stood him on his feet, two men supportin him — one on either side. I put a straight ticket into his fingers, and takin his wrist with one hand, held his fingers together with tother, and guided his hand to the box. Ez it neared the winder, he started ez ef a electric shock hed struck him, and, straightenin up, asked, " Is it the sthrate ticket? Is Constooshnel Amindmint No! onto it?"

Ashoorin him that it wuz all rite, he suffered me to hold his hand out to the Judge uv Eleckshun, who took the ballot and deposited it in the box. "Thank Hivin!" sed he, "the nagur is not yet my ayquil!" and doublin up at the thigh and knee-joints, he sank, limber-like, and gently, onto the ground. Ez he hed discharged the dooty uv an Amerikin freeman, we rolled him out to one side uv the house, wher the drippin uv the rain from the roof wood do suthin toward soberin him off, and left him alone in his glory.

The Amendment got but a very few votes in that locality. The Republikins jined us in repudiatin it, mostly upon ethnologikle grounds. One asserted that he hed bin in favor uv emancipashen in time uv war, becoz the Afrikin cood thereby be indoost to fite agin their Southern masters, and it wood hev the effeck uv makin the drafts come lighter in his township. He wuz a humanitarian likewise. He opposed crooelty toward em. He wept when he heerd uv the massacre at Fort Piller, becoz in the army the nigger wuz ez much a man ez anybody, and sich wholesale slaughters tendid to make calls for "500,000 more" more frekent. But when it come to givin uv em the privilege uv votin beside him, it coodent be thot uv. He cood never consent that a race whose heels wuz longer than hizzen shood rool Ameriky. "My God!" sed this ardent Republikin, "ef you give em the ballot, wat kin prevent em from bein Congrismen, Senators, Vice-Presidents, and even Presidents? I shudder when I think uv it;" and he hurried in his vote.

I didn't quite see the force uv his objecshen, for it never okkurred to me that bein sent to Congris wuz the nateral consekence uv votin. I hev voted for thirty years, at many elections four or five times, but I hev never bin to Congris. Wher is the constitooency wich wood elect me? But it wuzn't my biznis to controvert his posishen. It made no diffrence to me wat his reason wuz for votin ez I desired him to vote.

The nigger-lovers beat up one man to vote for the Amendment, wich, I saw by his dissatisfied look, hed bin over-perswadid. "Sir!" sed I, "do yoo consider a Afrikin suffishently intelligent to be trustid with so potent a weapon ez the ballot?"

Bustin away from them wich hed him in charge, he exclaimed, " No, I don't! I can't vote for it. They ain't intelligent enuff. Sir, scratch off the ' Yes ' from my ballot, and put onto it ' No!' ' "

" Here is a pensil," sed I.

" Do it yerself," sed he; " I can't write."

And I did it. Sich is the effeck uv a word in season. Words fitly spoken is apples uv gold, set in picters uv silver.

One man woodent listen to me, but votid the Amendment. He hed bin a soljer, and for eleven months pertook uv the hospitality uv the Confedrits at Andersonville. Escapin, he wuz helped to the Fedrel lines by a nigger, who wuz flogged almost to death, in his site, for not betrayin wher he wuz hid. I mite ez well hev talked to a lamp-post. Ez he shoved in his ballot, he remarkt suthin about he'd ruther see a nigger vote than a d—d rebel, any time. From the direckshun uv his eye-site, I persoom he referred to me.

I left for home ez soon ez the votes wuz counted, and the result wuz made known, only waitin till the poll-books wuz made out, and the judges uv eleckshun hed got ther names written by the clerks, and hed made their marks to em. On my way home I wuz gratified to see how the nateral antipathy to the nigger hed revived. At Cincinati, the nite uv the eleckshn, they wuz bangin uv em about, the patriotic Democrisy goin for em wherever they cood find em, and the next day, ez I saw em at the ralerode stashens, they hed, generally speekin, ther heds bandaged. It wuz cheerin to me, and I gloated over it.

Full of gladnis, I entered Kentucky, and joyfully I wendid my way to the Corners. I wuz the bearer uv tidins uv great joy, and my feet wuz pleasant onto the mountins. Ez I walked into Bascom's, they all saw in my face suthin uv importance.

"Wat is it?" sed Deekin Pogram. "Is it weal or woe?"

"Is the proud Caucashen still in the ascendant in Ohio, or hez the grovelin Afrikin ground him into the dust?" askt Issaker Gavitt.

"My friend," sed I, takin up the Deekin's whisky, wich, in the eggscitement uv the moment, he didn't observe, "the Constitooshnel Amendment, givin the nigger ekal rites, hez bin voted down by the liberty-lovin freemen uv Ohio. Three cheers for Ohio."

They wuz given with a will. The wildest enthoosiasm wuz awakened. Bascom put a spigot in a fresh barl, and the church bells wuz set a ringin.

The niggers wore a dismayed look, and got out uv the way ez soon ez possible. A meetin wuz to-wunst organized. Deekin Pogram spoke. He felt that this wuz a proud day. Light wuz breakin. The dark clouds uv fanaticism wuz breakin away. We hed now the Afrikin under our feet. We hev got him in his normal posishen in Ohio, and, please God, we will soon hev him likewise in Kentucky. He moved the adopshen uv the follerin resoloo-shens : —

" WAREAS, Noer cust Canan, and condemned him to be a servant unto his brethren, thereby cleerly indikatin the status uv the race for all time to come to be one uv inferiority; and,

" WAREAS, To further show to the eyes uv the most obtoose that a diffrence wuz intended, the Almighty gave the nigger a diffrent anatomicle strucker, for full partikelars uv wich see the speeches uv the Demokratic stumpers doorin the late campaign; and,

" WAREAS, The attempt to place the nigger on an ekality with the white in votin ez well ez taxa-shun, we consider the sappin uv the very founda-shun uv civil liberty, ez well ev uv the Crischen religion; therefore,

" *Resolved,* That the Constooshnel and Biblikle Democracy uv Kentucky send greetin to their brethren uv Ohio, with thanks for their prompt and effectooal squelchin uv the idea uv nigger superiority.

" *Resolved,* That to the Republikins uv Ohio, who, risin above party considerashuns, voted agin suffrage, our thanks is due, and we congratulate em that now they, ez well ez us, are saved from the danger uv marryin niggers; and likewise do we asshoor em, that in a spirit uv mutual forbearance, we care not wat particular creed they perfess, so long ez they vote our principles.

" *Resolved,* That the will uv the people havin bin cleerly indikated, we demand the insershun uv the word ' white ' in the Constitooshun uv the Yoonited States.

" *Resolved,* That we ask the colored voters uv Tennessee, and other States where colored men hev votes, to observe how they are treated in Ohio, where the Ablishnists don't need em. In them States we extend to em a corjel invitashun to act with us.

" *Resolved,* That a copy uv these resolooshens be sent to President Johnson, with an ashoorance uv our unabated confidence in his integrity, patriotism, and modisty."

The meetin broke up with three cheers fur the Dimocracy uv Ohio, nine for the Republikins uv that State, and one for the State at large.

The Fakulty uv the Institoot met next mornin, for the purpus uv revisin the Scripters. It wuz desided that the word " white " should be insertid wherever necessary, and that that edishen only be yoosed by the Dimocracy and Conservativ Republikins. We made progress, the follerin bein a few uv the changes : —

" ' So God creatid a *white* man in his own image.'

" ' Whosoever, therefore, shell confess me before *white* men,' &c.

" ' Suffer little *white* children to come unto me, for uv sich is the kingdom uv Heaven.' "

Wich last is comfortin, ez it shows that the distincshen is kept up through all eternity. I give these merely ez samples. We shel hev it finisht in a few days, and, ef funds kin be raised, shel publish it. Sich a vershun uv the Skripters is needid.

I find the Demekratic mind is exercised over the question uv the succession to Wade. My voice is for Vallandygum. Never wuz there sich a saint, never wuz ther a man so abused by the tyranikel minions of irresponsible power. He hez suffered for us, and now he must hev his reward. It hez bin urged that the ten cent colleckshun in 1863 was suffishent pay for his marterdom. I deny it. I know all about it. He got nothin uv it. Every Demekrat in Ohio who hed taxes to pay, or who wanted a new pare uv pants, or whose boots needed half solin, took up a colleckshun for Vallandygum. I know that's so, for I wuz a Demekrat in Ohio, laborin under pekooniary embarasments in them days myself. Let Vallandygum hev the place he so well earned.

PETROLEUM V. NASBY, P. M.
(Wich is Postmaster).

XXXV.

A Jollification at the Corners, followed by a Dream, which has some Reference to a recent Political Event.

Post Offis, Confedrit X Roads
(Wich is in the Stait uv Kentucky),
October 22, 1867.

WE held, last nite, our formal jollification at the Corners, over the result uv the Ohio and Pennsylvany elecshuns. It wuz a glorious occashen, and one wich wuz calkelated to cheer the long deprest hearts uv the down-trodden Dimocrisy; wich it did. The Church wuz gorgusly illoominatid with candles, hung in festoons in the winders. Deekin Pogram, in honor uv the occashun, loaned us the yoose uv his two keroseen lamps, — the pride uv the Corners, — wich wuz arranged in a tabloo in front uv the pulpit, over wich wuz hung, in peeceful folds, the two Confedrit flags wich Kernel McPelter's regment hed borne in honor over myriads uv ded

Yankees. The survivin heroes uv the Lost Coz in the visinity wuz present, attired in their soiled uniforms, and everythin about the demonstrashen wuz ez inspiritin ez it wuz possible to make it. Short and pertinent addresses wuz made by the offishels uv the church, wich I wuz gratified to observe a pious vane uv thankfulnis run thro em. Deekin Pogram shone with unwonted brilliancy and onparalleled devoutnis. He blessed the Lord for the mercy wich hed bin vouchsafed us. The people uv the North hed vindicated the Skripters, and hed bin weaned from their infidelity. Now he felt he cood wallop a nigger wunst more in safety, and put his foot onto the necks uv the descendants uv Ham, wich wuz ordained from the flood. He felt thankful for wat hed bin done for us by Ohio and Pennsylvany, and he hoped for ez much from Noo York. Shood Noo York complete the work so gloriously commenst by Maine and Californy, and so happily carried forrerd by Ohio and Pennsylvany, then he shood say, " Now let thy servant depart in peese." If he shood survive the joy uv the occashun, he wood to-wunst recapcher his niggers,—sich uv em ez wuz still in the land uv the livin,—and redoose em to their normal condishen. He wood hold em by force, trustin in the result uv the next Presidenshel elecshun to ratify wat he hed done. He shood to-wunst buy up wat he cood uv Confedrit skrip, for, bless the Lord, he felt now that the Lost Coz wazn't ez much lost ez he thot it wuz.

Other speeches wuz made, and the meetin, in a state uv high hilarity, adjourned to Bascom's, wher we made a nite uv it. I survived, probably, the longest uv any uv the square drinkers. There wuz those who held out longer by resortin to sich onmanly subterfuges ez throwin their likker over their sholders and takin lite drinks, but sich ain't for me. It looks, ez it is, like a throwing away uv the good gifts uv nacher; a sacrificin the blessins uv life to a foolish pride, — suthin I never will do.

One by one I saw em droop and roll gently off the benches. Issaker Gavitt first, McPelter next, Bascom next, and finally Deekin Pogram, like a giant oak in a hurricane, tottered, rallied, tottered agin, and finally fell; and I, feelin that my time, too, hed come, went under likewise. I slept, and sleepin, dreamed.

Methawt I wuz in a vast bildin, constructid in the Orientle stile uv arketectoor, to-wit: a roof, supported by pillers. These pillers wuz labelled with the names uv battles fought doorin the Revolushen and the last war with Great Britten, the strongest and newest bein ticketed with the battles fought doorin the late onpleasantnis.

"Wat strukter is this?" askt I uv the janiter uv the institooshn.

"The Temple uv Liberty!" ansered he.

"Wilt show it me?" askt I.

"With pleasure, Sir," sed he. "The present occupant uv the bildin, and he who now hez controle uv it, is in an inner chamber. Woodst see him?"

"I woodst," remarked I, and he showd me in.

It wuz a pekoolyer seen. On the carpet on the floor was stretched the form uv a Giant, hyer in stature, broader across the shoulders, deeper in the chest, and possessin more indicashens uv strength and endoorance than any Giant I hed ever seen. His face wuz ruther young lookin and noble, though onto it there wuz an expression uv wearinis and sadniss. He wuz fast asleep, and sleepin ez a man does after a terrible expenditoor uv physikle and mentle strength.

"Who is this?" askt I uv my guide.

"Republikinism!" sed he.

"Ha! Wat is them wich he holds so lovinly in his arms?" askt I.

"Them is the treasures uv the Temple, uv wich

the okkupant thereof is ex-offisho guardian. He hez
only a part uv em in his arms — ef yoo notis, ther
are ten uv em under his heels."

I looked carefully, and notist that they wuz all
labelled with the names uv the States — those in
his arms wuz those uv the North, and the ten under
his heels wuz them wich hed unfortnitly failed in
their attempt to get out uv the Temple. From the
heft uv his heel onto em, it appeared ez tho they
were under a triflin restraint. Kentucky, Delaware,
and Maryland he hed tightly gripped between his
thumb and finger.

"Why sleeps he?" askd I.

"Exhaustion," sed he. "Sich a fite ez he hez
hed to retane possession uv this place! Four long
yeers hev opposin powers attempted by open hostil-
ities to dispossess him, doorin wich he wuz assaled
at every pint, and for three years hez politikle fite
been made onto him, doorin wich he hez bin betrayed by them he sposed wuz his chosen and
trusted frends. Last year he hed a terrible conflict
with em and wuz victorious, but the strain wuz too
heavy onto him, and he's bin asleep, ever sence,
recooperatin. Besides, some uv his attendin physi-
cians, in whom he hed confidence, proved to be
quacks, and they dosed him with restoratives, wich,

however good they mite be, wuzn't percisely the remedy for the time, and they increesed the stupor under wich he wuz laborin. Besides, he wuz attackt with sore head, and in adishen to all this there wuz barnacles, and vampires, and blood-suckers uv all kinds, wich further weakened him. Listen, how hard he breathes!"

And he wuz a breathin hard.

At this percise minit methawt the guide disappeared, and there wuz a agitashen uv the curtins uv the chamber. Slowly they lifted, and to my surprise I saw feachers wich I recognized. Vallandygum peered in, and seein that the Giant wuz still asleep, come in on tip-toe, beckonin others to follow. They come. There wuz Thurman, uv Ohio; Voorhees, uv Injiany; Florence, Sharswood, and Jerry Black, uv Pennsylvany; Seward, Fernandy Wood, and Morrissey, uv Noo York; and Johnson, Pierce, Bookanan, and the whole glorious company of marters. Cautiously they krept in, and timidly ranged themselves about the sleepin Giant, and communed among themselves.

"That wuz too heavy a load for him to carry at his age," chuckled Ben Wood, pintin to an immense burden strapped to his sholders, on wich was written "Equality before the Law."

"Yes," sed Johnson, "but he wood hev got throo with it, but I tripped him!"

"It wuz I who put the stone down over wich he mostly stumbled," sed Seward in a whisper.

"To biznis!" sed Vallandygum. "Let us git wat we kin afore he awakens;" and he and Thurman slily fingered away Ohio, doin it without disturbin him much. He did groan slitely, and moved uneasily. Sharswood and Jerry Black very adroitly slipped Pennsylvania out from under his arm, and agin he started up restlessly, but sunk back into his slumber agin.

Emboldened by this, Fernando Wood and Seymour attempted to steal away Noo York, wich wuz the piller onto wich his head restid; and while they wuz manooverin it, he made a terrible noise, ez ef he wuz in agony.

"It's the death rattle in his throat!" piped the ten Staits under his heels, strivin to release theirselves.

"It's the death rattle in his throat!" shreeked they all, throwin off all stealth, and each grabbin a Stait.

In an instant the scene changed. They hed overdid it. The Giant awoke, and springin to his feet, glared fiercely onto em.

"The death rattle, is it!" sed he, in a voice uv

thunder. "Ha! ha! you mistake the snorin uv a hard-sleepin Giant for the death rattle! What hev I done? Sleepin so long, and knowin all the time that assassins lurked around me!" Shakin the barnacles off, he laid about him lively. He pitched Fernandy and Seymour out head over heels,—one sweep uv his right arm disposed uv Pierce, Bookannan, and that pack, and then, missin Ohio and Pennsylvany, he observed Vallandygum and Sharswood makin off with them. Utterin a howl uv rage, he sprang after em. Two leeps sufficed, and he wrenched the States from their grasp, but not, however, ontil Vallandygum had bit a thunderin slice out uv Ohio, and Sharswood one nearly ez large out uv Pennsylvany.

At this pint I awoke. The mornin sun wuz a sendin her brilliant beams thro the winders uv Bascom's. Around me lay the prostrate forms uv Deekin Pogram, Bascom, Captain McPelter, Issaker Gavitt, and the others who hed bin with me the nite afore. They wuz a sleepin and a snorin ez peacefly ez men ever did. The doors hed bin left open, and the villagers — the early birds who are alluz around ketchin the worm — hed collected at the door. They did not vencher in, not knowin how sound asleep we wuz, ontil — ez one uv em told me afterward —

he hed seen a hog belongin to Bascom walk in the open door and root about among us, gruntin approvinly, ez tho it reminded him uv his childhood's day, wich indeed it did, ez he hed alluz bin fed at a distillery; and then, satisfied that we wuz trooly asleep, they walked in and helped themselves to refreshments at the bar. Turnin them out quietly, with a stingin rebook for their dishonesty in takin advantage uv one helpless ez Bascom wuz, I emptied the contents uv his drawer, and seekoorin it in my boot, lay down ez tho I wuz asleep, till they shood awake. In an hour he awoke, and diskivered that he hed bin gone thro.

"Who cood hev done it?" sed he.

"My dear friend," sed I, "yoo wuz injudishus enuff to leave your door open. See ther!" and I pinted to the villagers a reelin thro the street. "They're virtuous, but yoo put ther integrity to a test wich it coodent stand. Ther wuz too much pressure to the square inch on ther conshences, and they collapst. Let it be a warnin to yoo. I don't know that *I* cood hev resisted it, hed I awakened first." And I awakened the Deekin, and helped him home, stayin with him, uv course, to breakfas*

Petroleum V. Nasby, P. M.

(Wich is Postmaster)

XXXVI.

A Meeting at the Corners to take into Considera-
tion the best and most feasible Methods of
preserving to the Democracy the States they
won this Fall.

POST OFFIS, CONFEDRIT X ROADS
(Wich is in the Stait uv Kentucky),
October 30, 1867.

I WUZ a sittin in the Post Offis, day before yesterday, a cogitatin over the glorious results uv
the Ohio and Pennsylvany elections, and hopin for
an ekally good report from Noo York, thinkin the
while that perhaps ef my hopes wuz realized, and
sich a Constooshnel Dimokrat ez Pendleton or Seymour shood be elected, I mite, in considerashun uv
my long, and I bleeve valuable services, aspire to
suthin higher, and better, and more profitable than
a Post Offis, sich ez I am at present holdin. I do
not complain, for the posishen hez bin the means
uv establishin a credit upon wich I hev lived thus
far comfortable; but yet I shood prefer a place

where the salary wood be suffishent to give me
enuff so that I cood lay up suthin for old age.
The time is not far off when my individooel exer-
tions will not supply my wants.

I felt good over the victory, and it seemed to me
ez tho we ought to speak, ez Kentuckians, to our
brethren North, instructin uv em how to hold the
Staits wich they hev won for us. When I deside
upon a pint I alluz act, and so it wuz this time.

I give notis, by Issaker Gavitt, that the Corners
wood assemble at the tootin uv the horn, for the
purpose uv sendin forth the voice uv Kentucky to
the Staits North. The evenin come, the horn wuz
tooted from the steps uv the church, and the entire
Corners wuz there. Deekin Pogram wuz in his
regler seat; Issaker Gavitt wuz in his sainted father's
place, wich hez gone hentz. Kernel McPelter wuz
there, and also the others who make up the male
population uv the Corners, and their wives. It wuz
a glorious meetin, and I wuz a rubbin my hands
and feelin good at the prospeck uv an improvin
occashun, when, to my utter disgust, I saw the door
open, and Joe Bigler, who wuz born to be my pest,
come in, with Pollock, and twenty or twenty-five
niggers, old and young, male and female, white,
yaller, and black, and all uv em took seats together

in the corner uv the church. I knowd by the meek look uv the niggers, and the eggstreem quietood uv Bigler hisself, that suthin wuz up, wich would uv course develop itself. Bigler and Pollock generally develop.

I opened the meetin by remarkin that the times wore an auspishus look. The power uv the nigger in Amerikin politics hed bin demonstrated. The nigger hed bin so manipulated in Ohio and Pennsylvany ez to give us these States, which we cood hold ef we choose. But the Dimocrisy uv Ohio and Pennsylvany hed a work to do, wich they cannot neglect with safety. They had declared the nigger inferior to the Caucashen, wich he undeniably is, and they must keep him so. The nigger must be kept jist eggsackly wher he is, to serve ez a irritant to Dimocrisy. Ohio gives the niggers uv that State certain facilities for learnin to reed and write; accomplishments wich no laborin class wich is to be guided, controlled, and worked excloosively by a sooperior class, needs or hez any biznis with. So soon ez a man begins to reed he begins to hev an inquirin mind, and begins to feel a dissatisfaction with his speer. Let Ohio repeel these laws towunst, that the niggers may not —"

"Reverse the arrangement," sed Joe Bigler, risin,

" and git to be the sooperior uv the white. Is that it, Perfesser?"

" Not eggsackly that," returned I, not knowin wat he wuz drivin at, " but ez Hevin ordained the niggers to be inferior to us, and serve us, it looks rather dangerous to — "

" Give him a chance to rise? That's what yoor gettin at, I see. I am, and always wuz a Dimocrat, ez yoo know; but I don't shudder from that cause — not any. I hev faith in the Lord, wich yoo appear to lack, wich is strange, considerin yoor profeshun. Ef my colored friends here wuz ordained by the Almighty to alluz okkepy an inferior position to us, why, they'll do it anyhow, onless, indeed, we degrade ourselves below ther level. Ef I understand yoor idea, it is that the proud Caucashen is the only favored race, wich fixes its own posishen itself, and that all the other races hed places assigned them, wich Godalmity hevin fixed, they can't pass. That bein the case, wat's the yoose, Perfesser, uv our foolin away our time a tryin to strengthen his laws by any act uv ours? Ef the Almighty fixed it so, kin we do it any better than he?"

" But spos'n the nigger, ef we don't keep him down by law, shood rise above us?"

" I shood unanimously conclood that ther hed bin

a mistake in the figgers, and that we wuz, after all, the sons uv Ham and they the sons uv Japheth. How wood yoo like that? But that ain't wat ails us. There, Perfesser, ain't where our danger is. Dimocrisy, like a man with a tape-worm, carries the elements uv its own destruckshen. Missegenashun is wat's sappin the foundashuns uv the party.— Agreein with yoo that the nigger's place is fixed, and that the Dimocrisy coodent git along a minit without the nigger, I here utter my solemn warning agin the continyooal lessenin uv the race, becoz that race is our rock, and onto that we stand. Wat sense is there in wastin our capital, or ruther dilutin it?"

"Wat do yoo mean?" askt I, not gettin at the drift uv wat he wuz drivin at.

"Mean! My meanin is plain. The blacker the nigger is, the further he is below us; the whiter he is, the nearer our ekal he is. In this calculashun we don't take intelligence, or virchoo, or anything of the kind into account, but perceed upon the hypothesis that a devilish mean white man is considerable better than a smart and honest nigger. Therefore, any drop uv white blood in a nigger's veins makes him just one drop less objectionable. Look at the specimens wich I hev brought with me to illustrate my pint. The light-colored niggers will rise."

And every cussed one uv em got up, ez ef by majic, and I saw to-wunst wat he wuz goin for.

" Yoo see, Perfesser, I hev here twenty-two spiled niggers. Every one uv them ought to hev bin the son or daughter uv two pure niggers, but they ain't. This one's mother, for instance," and he laid his hand upon the shoulder uv a likely quadroon uv eighteen years, " wuz wunst the property uv Deekin Pogram, wich circumstance accounts for her hevin the Pogram nose and general cast uv countenance to an alarmin degree, and — "

Ther wuz a piercin shreek heard, and Mrs. Pogram was carried out faintin, and the Deekin turned ez red ez a lobster, while Bigler, ez solemn ez a judge, went on : —

" This girl wuz wunst the property uv Deekin McGrath, who is, I notis, here to-nite. Melissy, stand up," sed he, and a likely mulatto woman ariz. " You will notis," sed he, " that Melissy is rather dark, while her girl, wich yoo see afore yoo, is quite a half lighter. The race bleached out considerable on Deekin McGrath's place. I hev, in my recollection, ten or fifteen more, uv various shades, who hev the McGrath face, but — "

Mrs. Deekin McGrath, utterin a shreek uv rage, swung out of the church, while the Deekin to-wunst assoomed the color uv his fellow Deekin, Pogram.

"I mite go on; but wherefore? Yoo all see the pint. I kin show yoo, in this colleckshun, wich I hev picked up, the pecoolyer feachers uv the Dingeses, the McPelters, the Bascoms, and every family around these parts,— that is, the feechers uv the male members uv em. But sence the emancipashun I hev notist that this thing hez come to a sudden endin. I hev notist that sence the niggers hev owned theirselves, there ain't no more uv this mixter. Yoo purpose, I suppose, agin redoosin uv em to their normal condishun, and makin uv em menservants and maid-servants. Ef this is done, let me entreet yoo, brethren, to stop the bleachin process. Ef yoo hev any regard for the Dimocrisy, don't tolerate it no more. The moment a half-white nigger is born, yoo can't enslave only half uv him; for only half comes under the cuss, and only half under the laws agin niggers. That one half keeps down to the Ham level, but tother half sores to the Japhet place in nacher. Yoo can't whale a mulatto with only half the intensity yoo kin a clear-blooded nigger; and when they keep bleachin out, and out, and out, ontil they are almost white, what then? When a nigger is nine tenths Pogram, and only one tenth nigger, what then? Kin the Deekin be so deaf to the voice uv nacher — so bare uv impulse ez to oppress so much Pogram for the sake uv gettin his foot on so little nigger? I can't beleeve it. Besides, when it's all run out — when the nigger don't show at all — then wat is to prevent em from walkin off alone, and settin up in biznis for themselves ez white men? What will become uv the Dimocrasy then?"

All this time the niggers wuz titterin, and the white women wuz gaspin for breath, and the men wuz turnin red and white by turns. I arose to rebuke him, when Bigler remarkt that he guest enuff hed bin sed, and that probably the meeting hed better be adjourned. And the audacious cuss give us two minutes and a half to get out uv the buildin.

I wood give my next quarter's salary ef the yellow fever wood come to the Corners, pervided I cood be ashoored that Bigler and Pollock wood be victims.

Petroleum V. Nasby, P. M.

(Wich is Postmaster).

XXXVII.

The November Elections. — How the Result affected the Faithful in Kentucky.

POST OFFIS, CONFEDRIT X ROADS
(Wich is in the Stait uv Kentucky),
November 10, 1867.

THE Corners wuz prostrated with joy last nite at the receet uv the news uv the November elecshuns.   Ther wuz nothin demonstrative about our joy ez there hed bin on occasions uv less interest. No! the result wuz too great, too overwhelminly great!   Our nachers wuz filled with joy, and it bubbled up to the eyes, and slopt over in floods uv teers.   Deekin Pogram's dawter Mirandy borrered a tamborine, wich wood answer for a timbrel, and attempted to dance down the street, after the fashion uv Miriam, singin, " Shout the glad tidens," et settry, but we rebookt her.   Sich exultashen seemed to us inadekate.   The Deekin met me, and fallin onto my neck, wept perfoosely down my back, wich I stood ez long ez I cood bear the moistyer.   Gently disengagin him, I led him to Basom's, fearin that so great a waste uv flooids wood cut short the old saint's life, unless that waste cood be repaired. We supplied the deficiency to-wunst. Never saw I sich a picter. The blessid old man sittin onto a bench, a glass uv hot whiskey in his hand; his white hair a fallin scantily about his temples, and tears a running in rapid succession adown his frost-bitten nose, and, glitterin a moment on the tip, droppin, like strings uv pearls, into the space below! It wuz tetchin!

The citizens met that evening, not to rejoice, but to adopt sich measures for turning the victry to account ez the occasion seemed to demand. The Deekin wuz there, and I beleeve every white male citizen uv the Corners wuz in his seet afore the glad peals uv the bell hed ceased pealin. I assoomed the chair, and in a few joodishus remarks stated the objeck uv the meetin. Noo York, I remarkt, hed spoken, and Noo Gersey, the blessed State uv which I hed the honor to be a native, hed returned to her fust love. I wuz not now ashamed to own that I wuz a native of Noo Gersey. I am proud uv it, and were it not for the fact that I owe neerly half uv her citizens, in sums rangin from a half dollar up to eighteen, I wood return there to-wunst. But

I won't. It wood awaken expectations in their buzzums wich wood never be fulfilled, and I'm too tender-hearted, too considrit uv the feelins uv others, to lasserate them feelins. I can't properly express my emoshuns. Thank Heaven the nigger is ourn. The Northern States have spoken, and in thunder tones.   The Ethiopian wunst wuz on the top wave, but wher is he now? Two years ago he wuz needed — but now wher is he? The Ablishnists don't need him no more to fill up ther quotas, they don't need him no more to take ther places in the next draft, and thank the Lord he's the same d—d nigger he alluz wuz! The stink uv the nigger hez overcome ther gratitood to him — ther good feelin hez bin swamped by ther prejoodis. The Dimocrasy uv the two sections uv the Yoonion hez rusht into each other's arms, the nigger wuz between em, and consekently is under our feet. What happinis for Kentucky! The nigger can't go North with the elecshen returns starin him in the face, and ef he stays here he must stay on our terms. Thank the Lord.

Deekin Pogram sed that he hednt felt so good sence his first wife died. He felt too good to speek, and the brethren wood excuse him ef his remarks shood be breef. (We will! We will! with great yoonaniimity.) Four weeks ago, when he heerd from Ohio and Pennsylvany he hed to-wunst drawd up a skedule uv the loss that hed bin inflicted onto him by the tyranical edict uv the Illinoy Goriller, a copy uv wich he wood reed : —

YOONITED STATES UV AMERIKY,
In Account with Gabrel Pogram, Dr.

To 1 nigger, Sam,	26 years old	. . . .	$1,500 00
1 " Pompey, 30	"	. . . .	1,300 00
1 " Scip, 30	"	. . . .	1,400 00
1 " Peter, 40	"	. . . .	1,000 00

To one lot misselaneous niggers, 22 in number, mostly crippled, and not uv much akkount, hevin bin flogd and chawd by dorgs, and injoored by being knockt about the head and back, a dissiplinin uv 'em, at, say, $500 each, 11,000 00
To one nigger gal, Jane, 18 years old, nearly white, with bloo eyes and curly hair, for wich I hed bin offered $2,500 to go to Noo Orleans, 2,500 00
To other wenches, uv all shades and ages, 12 in number, averagin, say, $500, ... 6,000 00

$23,700 00

This bill he hed determined to put in, becoz uv this property he hed bin robbed. Last nite he heerd uv the result uv the Noo York and Noo Jersey elecshuns, and he felt that more yit wuz due him from the unconstooshnel government under wich we are forst to live. He wanted pay, not only for his twenty-four thousand dollars' worth of nigger, but legle interest on the amount, from Emancipashen to date, incloodin wat he paid to hev the calculation made, and the interest figgered onto it, and he wanted it in gold, ez he considered greenbax jist ez unconstooshnel ez emancipashen.

Issaker Gavitt remarkt, that on behalf uv his father's estate he hed a claim on the oppressors. He hed made out no bill ez yit, ez the nigger wich alluz did the figgerin for his father hed got to be impudent, and wooden't do it no more. But he shood get somebody who cood write to copy the Deekin's bill, wich wood answer, ez the two farms workt about the same number uv hands, tho uv fancy stock his father hed alluz kept the most, wich accountid for his bein more bald-headed than the Deekin.

Kernel McPelter wantid no pay. He wantid his niggers. To accept pay wood be to acknollege the right uv a Illinoy goriller to releese em, wich he wood never do. He hed one — he saw her to-day — wich he wood hev back agin. Her and her husband, wich hed bin married sence they wuz torn from him, hed purchist ten akers uv ground up toards Garrettstown, and wuz a livin onto it. Uv course, ez the emancipashun was illegal, the produx uv their labor sence that time wuz hizzen, jest the

same ez though they remained in their normal con
dishen. The ten akers woodent make him good,
but they hed two children born to em sence,
wich, ef niggers brot any price, wood do suthin
toards it.

Bascom perferred to hev Government pay ther
valyoo, and let em stay free. He had arrived at
this conclusbun after givin the subjeck matoor considerashen. They all hed some property now —
leastways they could all do wat they pleased with
their money. Troo, the heft uv the proceeds uv
their labor went to Pollock for dry goods, and groceries, and sich, but he bleeved that they wuz a
imitative race. Ef so, and they followed the eggs-
ample sot em by their white sooperiors, they wood,
in time, leave the heft uv it at his bar. He hed a
few uy em under trainin now, and he notist that
they wuz better customers than the whites, ez they
didn't swaller their rashens and tell him to "jist
chalk it down."

A sense uv the meetin wuz then taken, and a
majority voted to fust try to redoose them to their
normal condishen, and ef that wuz decided to be
impracticable, then we cood, with still better grace,
demand their valyoo uv the Goverment.

"Yes," exclaimed Kernel McPelter, "and for

this great work ther is no better time than now. 'The Yoonyun ez it wuz!' Foller me!"

And forthwith the entire congregashun piled out, rushin toward the nigger settlement on the Garrettstown road.

Arrivin at the settlement, a consultashen wuz held. It wuz desided that I shood advance to the doors uv the houses and demand surrender, but I declined. Kernel McPelter volunteered, and we all awaited the result. He knocked at the door uv the first house.

"Wha' d'ye want?" exclamed a voice.

"I want yoo!" said the Kernel.

"Wa' foah?"

"My friend," sed the Kernel, impressively, "ef I recognize yoor dulcet tone, yoor my nigger. Four years ago yoo wuz set free, you sposed, by Linkin; but we've done away with that. Come forth, and give yoorself up; you shel, ef yoo go peaceably, hev yoor old quarters agin, and be treated ez uv old."

"Go way, white man, and stop yoor foolin. Dis nigga 's in bed!"

"Break down the doors!" yelled the Deekin, "and hev done with it!" and a rush wuz made.

The doors wuz broke down, and in a minit the

nigger and his wife, and two children, wuz out in the street, bound, and the Kernel hed the furnitoor packt, ready to take to his own house. In the mean time assaults hed bin made on two other houses, with ruther different results. Deekin Pogram led one on the house uv a former slave uv hizzen, and wuz disabled by a charge uv shot in his leg, and the infooriated nigger threw open the winder and swore that he'd empty tother barrel into the head uv the first man who came within range. The whole settlement wuz by this time alarmed, and lites sprang up, and we cood hear the click of the cocks uv muskets, and the pilin up uv furnitoor afore the doors. It wuz desided that the attempt to re-enslave em be given over for that nite, and carryin the Deekin, who wuz weak from loss uv blood, we made our way to the Corners agin.

The result demonstrated to me the impossibility uv the two races livin together in harmony. There is a natral antagonism between em wich must result inevitably in a war uv races, onless the status uv the two races is fixed by onalterable law. It can't be denied that, so long ez they are among us, so long shel we be tempted to subdoo em, and so long will sich sole-harrowin scenes ez that uv last nite result. Ez I heer the groans uv that prostrated saint, Deekin Pogram (this is written at his bedside in the intervals uv feedin him likker with a spoon), I feel ez tho I must vindicate my birth by goin out and killin a nigger. Nothin but the oncertainty ez to who wood be killed restrains me. Thank Heaven, next yeer, when Seymore or Pendleton is President, and the unconstitooshnel acts uv a Rump Congress is done away with, all this will be fixt. It is this that soothes the Deekin, and enables him to endoor his sufferins.

PETROLEUM V. NASBY, P. M.
(Wich is Postmaster).

READINGS FOR HOME HALL AND SCHOOL

Prepared by Professor LEWIS B. MONROE
Founder of the Boston School of Oratory

HUMOROUS READINGS In prose and verse For the use of schools reading-clubs public and parlor entertainments $1.50

" The book is readable from the first page to the last, and every article contained in it is worth more than the price of the volume." — *Providence Herald.*

MISCELLANEOUS READINGS In prose and verse $1.50

" We trust this book may find its way into many schools, not to be used as a book for daily drill, but as affording the pupil occasionally an opportunity of leaving the old beaten track." — *Rhode-Island Schoolmaster.*

DIALOGUES AND DRAMAS For the use of dramatic and reading clubs and for public social and school entertainments $1.50

" If the acting of dramas such as are contained in this book, could be introduced into private circles, there would be an inducement for the young to spend their evenings at home, instead of resorting to questionable public places." — *Nashua Gazette.*

YOUNG FOLKS' READINGS For social and public entertainment $1.50

" Professor Monroe is one of the most successful teachers of elocution, as well as a very popular public reader. In this volume he has given an unusually fine selection for home and social reading, as well as for public entertainments." — *Boston Home Journal.*

DIALOGUES FROM DICKENS Arranged for schools and home amusement By W. ELIOT FETTE A.M. First series $1.00

DIALOGUES AND DRAMAS FROM DICKENS Second series Arranged by W. ELIOT FETTE Illustrated $1.00

The dialogues in the above books are selected from the best points of the stories, and can be extended by taking several scenes together.

THE GRAND DICKENS COSMORAMA Comprising several unique entertainments capable of being used separately for school home or hall By G. B. BARTLETT Paper 25 cents

THE READINGS OF DICKENS as condensed by himself for his own use $1.00

LITTLE PIECES FOR LITTLE SPEAKERS The primary-school teacher's assistant. By a practical teacher 16mo. Illustrated Cloth 75 cents Also in boards 50 cents

THE MODEL SUNDAY-SCHOOL SPEAKER Containing selections in prose and verse from the most popular pieces and dialogues for Sunday-school exhibitions Illustrated Cloth 75 cents Boards 50 cents
" A book very much needed."

GEO. M. BAKER'S POPULAR READERS SPEAKERS AND DRAMAS

THE READING CLUB and Handy Speaker Being selections in prose and poetry Serious humorous pathetic patriotic and dramatic In 18 parts of 50 selections each Each part cloth 50 cents paper 15 cents

THE POPULAR SPEAKER Containing the selections published in the Reading Club Nos. 13 14 15 and 16 Cloth $1.00

THE PREMIUM SPEAKER Containing the selections published in the Reading Club Nos. 9 10 11 and 12 Cloth $1.00

THE PRIZE SPEAKER Containing the selections published in the Reading Club Nos. 5 6 7 and 8 Cloth $1.00

THE HANDY SPEAKER Combining the selections published in the Reading Club Nos. 1 2 3 and 4 Cloth Over 400 pages $1.00

BAKER'S HUMOROUS SPEAKER A compilation of popular selections in prose and verse in Irish Dutch Negro and Yankee dialect Uniform with " The Handy Speaker " " The Prize Speaker " " The Popular Speaker " " The Premium Speaker " Cloth $1.00

Baker's Dialect Recitations

YANKEE DIALECT RECITATIONS A humorous collection of the best stories and poems for reading and recitatioos Boards 50 cents Paper 30 cents

MEDLEY DIALECT RECITATIONS A series of the most popular German French and Scotch readings Boards 50 cents Paper 30 cents

IRISH DIALECT RECITATIONS A series of popular readings and recitations in prose and verse Boards 50 cents Paper 30 cents

NEGRO DIALECT RECITATIONS A series of the most popular readings in prose and verse Boards 50 cents Paper 30 cents

THE GRAND ARMY SPEAKER A collection of the best readings and recitations on the Civil War Boards 50 cents Paper 30 cents

Baker's Original Plays and Dialogues

A BAKER'S DOZEN Thirteen Original Humorous Dialogues Cloth 75 cents Boards 50 cents

THE TEMPERANCE DRAMA Eight Original Plays 16mo. Cloth 75 cents Fancy boards 50 cents

THE EXHIBITION DRAMA Original Plays Dramas Comedies Farces Dialogues etc. $1.50

HANDY DRAMAS FOR AMATEUR ACTORS Cloth $1.50

THE DRAWING-ROOM STAGE Dramas Farces and Comedies for the amateur stage home theatricals and school exhibitions Ill. $1.50

THE SOCIAL STAGE Dramas Comedies Farces Dialogues etc. for home and school Illustrated $1.50

THE MIMIC STAGE A new collection of Dramas Farces Comedies and Burlesques for parlor theatricals evening entertainments and school exhibitions Illustrated $1.50

AMATEUR DRAMAS For parlor theatricals evening entertainments and school exhibitions Illustrated $1.50

THE GLOBE DRAMA Original Plays Illustrated $1.50

Sold by all booksellers or sent by mail postpaid on receipt of price

LEE AND SHEPARD Publishers Boston

BOOKS OF PARTICULAR INTEREST • • • •

• • • • • • TO YOUNG MEN AND WOMEN

HENRY WADSWORTH LONGFELLOW

His Life, His Works, His Friendships. By GEORGE LOWELL AUSTIN. Profusely illustrated. Cloth, $2.00. New edition. Formerly published by subscription.

"We have here a clear and popular presentation of the poet's literary life. The details of his personal and private life, or at least so much of it as belongs by right strictly to his family, has been avoided, and that properly. What the public have a right to know is found in this volume, in a style that is easy and pleasing. Here you have Longfellow as a child, as a college student, and as a professor in Bowdoin College; and especially does he appear here as a man of letters. It is a charming volume." — *Christian Standard.*

LIFE AND TIMES OF WENDELL PHILLIPS

By GEORGE LOWELL AUSTIN. With steel portrait and illustrations. Cloth, $1.50. New edition. The only complete Life of the great agitator.

"The life of a man who was so strongly identified with one of the most stirring periods in American history must necessarily be one of much interest, and Mr. Austin has succeeded in presenting its features in a very attractive way. Portions of Mr. Phillips's most important public addresses are given, and there are reminiscences of the man by some of his close friends and associates." — *Philadelphia Record.*

Wendell Phillips's Lectures, Orations, and Letters, to 1861. 563 pages.

Library edition. 8vo	$2 50
Popular edition, with Biographical Sketch, 16mo	1 00
The Scholar in a Republic. Paper, 8vo	25
Eulogy of Garrison. Paper, 8vo	25
Lost Arts. Paper, 8vo	25
Daniel O'Connell. Paper, 8vo	25
Labor Question. Paper, 8vo	25

LIFE AND DEEDS OF GENERAL U. S. GRANT

By Rev. P. C. HEADLEY and GEORGE LOWELL AUSTIN. Profusely illustrated. Cloth, $1.50.

The materials for the early years of the subject of this popular biography were furnished by the immediate friends and relatives of his family. The events bearing upon the war history are based upon the recognized authorities, and will stand the test of military criticism. The work is intensely interesting, and exceedingly popular.

Oliver Optic's OUR STANDARD BEARER

Or the Life of General ULYSSES S. GRANT, his youth, his manhood, his campaign, and his eminent services in the reconstruction of the nation his sword has redeemed, as seen and related by Captain BERNARD GALLYGASKEN, Cosmopolitan, and written out by OLIVER OPTIC. *A new edition*, with supplementary chapters, containing the political life of the general, his travels abroad, his sickness and death. Cloth; illustrated by THOMAS NAST and others, elegantly bound, $1.50.

"It is written in Mr. Adams's happiest vein, and is a most unique and interesting presentation of a subject upon which volumes have been written and read."

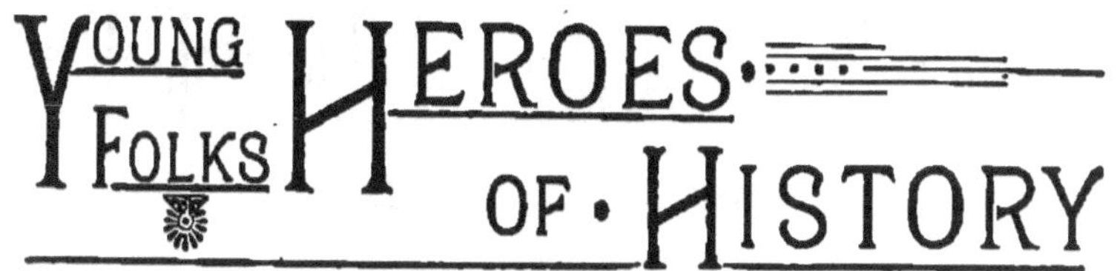

By GEORGE MAKEPEACE TOWLE.

Handsomely Illustrated.   Price per vol., $1.25.   Sets in neat boxes.

VASCO DA GAMA:
HIS VOYAGES AND ADVENTURES.

"Da Gama's history is full of striking adventures, thrilling incidents, and perilous situations; and Mr. Towle, while not sacrificing historical accuracy, has so skilfully used his materials, that we have a charmingly romantic tale."
— *Rural New-Yorker.*

PIZARRO:
HIS ADVENTURES AND CONQUESTS.

"No hero of romance possesses greater power to charm the youthful reader than the conqueror of Peru. Not even King Arthur, or Thaddeus of Warsaw, has the power to captivate the imagination of the growing boy. Mr. Towle has handled his subject in a glowing but truthful manner; and we venture the assertion, that, were our children led to read such books as this, the taste for unwholesome, exciting, wrong-teaching boys' books — dime novels in books' clothing — would be greatly diminished, to the great gain of mental force and moral purpose in the rising generation."—*Chicago Alliance.*

MAGELLAN;
OR, THE FIRST VOYAGE ROUND THE WORLD.

"What more of romantic and spirited adventures any bright boy could want than is to be found in this series of historical biography, it is difficult to imagine. This volume is written in a most sprightly manner; and the life of its hero, Fernan Magellan, with its rapid stride from the softness of a petted youth to the sturdy courage and persevering fortitude of manhood, makes a tale of marvellous fascination." — *Christian Union.*

MARCO POLO:
HIS TRAVELS AND ADVENTURES.

"The story of the adventurous Venetian, who six hundred years ago penetrated into India and Cathay and Thibet and Abyssinia, is pleasantly and clearly told; and nothing better can be put into the hands of the school boy or girl than this series of the records of noted travellers. The heroism displayed by these men was certainly as great as that ever shown by conquering warrior; and it was exercised in a far nobler cause, — the cause of knowledge and discovery, which has made the nineteenth century what it is." —*Graphic.*

RALEGH:
HIS EXPLOITS AND VOYAGES.

"This belongs to the 'Young Folks' Heroes of History' series, and deals with a greater and more interesting man than any of its predecessors. With all the black spots on his fame, there are few more brilliant and striking figures in English history than the soldier, sailor, courtier, author, and explorer, Sir Walter Ralegh. Even at this distance of time, more than two hundred and fifty years after his head fell on the scaffold, we cannot read his story without emotion. It is graphically written, and is pleasant reading, not only for young folks, but for old folks with young hearts." —*Woman's Journal.*

DRAKE:
THE SEA-LION OF DEVON.

Drake was the foremost sea-captain of his age, the first English admiral to send a ship completely round the world, the hero of the magnificent victory which the English won over the Invincible Armada. His career was

Young Folks' Heroes of the Rebellion.

By Rev. P. C. HEADLEY.

SIX VOLUMES. ILLUSTRATED. PER VOL. $1.25.

FIGHT IT OUT ON THIS LINE. The Life and Deeds of General U. S. Grant.

A life of the great Union General from his boyhood, written for boys. Full of anecdotes and illustrations, and including his famous trip around the world.

FACING THE ENEMY. The Life and Military Career of General William Tecumseh Sherman.

The Glorious March to the Sea by the brave Sherman and his boys will never be forgotten. This is a graphic story of his career from boyhood.

FIGHTING PHIL. The Life and Military Career of Lieut-Gen. Philip Henry Sheridan.

The story of the dashing Cavalry General of the army of the United States. — A fighting Irishman. — Full of pluck and patriotism for his adopted country. The book is full of adventure.

OLD SALAMANDER. The Life and Naval Career of Admiral David Glascoe Farragut.

The Naval History of the great civil war is exceedingly interesting, and the life of Admiral Farragut is rich in brave deeds and heroic example.

THE MINER BOY AND HIS MONITOR. The Career and Achievements of John Ericsson, Engineer.

One of the most thrilling incidents of the war was the sudden appearance of the Little Monitor in Hampton Roads to beat back the Merrimac. The life of the inventor is crowded with his wonderful inventions, and the story of his boyhood in the coal mines of Sweden is particularly interesting.

OLD STARS. The Life and Military Career of Major-Gen. Ormsby McKnight Mitchel.

"Old Stars" was the pet name given the brave general by his soldiers, who remembered his career as an astronomer before he became a soldier. His story is full of stirring events and heroic deeds.

☞ Sold by all booksellers, or sent by mail, postpaid, on receipt of price.

LEE AND SHEPARD, Publishers, Boston.

LEE AND SHEPARD'S POPULAR HANDBOOKS

Price, each, in cloth, 50 cents, except when other price is given.

Warrington's Manual. A Manual for the Information of Officers and Members of Legislatures, Conventions, Societies, etc., in the practical governing and membership of all such bodies, according to the Parliamentary Law and Practice in the United States. By W. S. ROBINSON (*Warrington*).

Practical Boat-Sailing. By DOUGLAS FRAZAR. Classic size, $1.00. With numerous diagrams and illustrations.

Handbook of Wood Engraving. With practical instructions in the art, for persons wishing to learn without an instructor. By WILLIAM A. EMERSON. Illustrated. Price $1.00.

Five-Minute Recitations. Selected and arranged by WALTER K. FOBES.

Five-Minute Declamations. Selected and arranged by WALTER K. FOBES.

Five-Minute Readings for Young Ladies. Selected and adapted by WALTER K. FOBES.

Educational Psychology. A Treatise for Parents and Educators. By LOUISE PARSONS HOPKINS, Supervisor in Boston Public Schools.

The Nation in a Nutshell. A Rapid Outline of American History. By GEORGE MAKEPEACE TOWLE.

English Synonymes Discriminated. By RICHARD WHATELY, D.D., Archbishop of Dublin. A new edition.

Hints on Writing and Speech-making. By THOMAS WENTWORTH HIGGINSON.

Arithmetic for Young Children. Being a series of Exercises exemplifying the manner in which Arithmetic should be taught to young children. By HORACE GRANT. American Edition. Edited by WILLARD SMALL.

Bridge Disasters in America. The Cause and the Remedy. By Prof. GEORGE L. VOSE.

A Few Thoughts for a Young Man. By HORACE MANN. A new Edition.

Handbook of Debate. The Character of Julius Cæsar. Adapted from J. SHERIDAN KNOWLES. Arranged for Practice in Speaking, for Debating Clubs, and Classes in Public and Private Schools.

Sold by all booksellers, and sent by mail, postpaid, on receipt of price.

LEE AND SHEPARD Publishers Boston